Gridiron Conspiracy:

Redemption

Book III of the Gridiron Conspiracy Trilogy

By

Christopher R. Paniccia

This is a work of fiction. All the characters and events portrayed in this book are either products of the author's imagination or are used fictitiously.

Gridiron Conspiracy: Part III

To Tee,

The Conspiracy
is everywhere!

Best,

Christopher Gronlund

3

For all those who keep us safe each day,

Those who stand on the wall,

Those who have given everything,

Thank you!

Chapter 1

Explosions rocked the building they were stranded in with no hope of escape. The stench of burning oil permeated the air causing what was left of Steve's entire squad to choke and gag. Smoke filled the air so they could barely see a foot in front of them. Steve could taste the rancid metallic residue of sulfur and the grit of sand in his teeth. Through the intermittent breaks in the smoke with tears in their eyes, Steve and the four remaining members of his squad peered into the crack in the wall, trying to ascertain the gravity of their situation.

Steve saw multiple assailants through the break in the wall. As he turned to speak to his squad, the wall imploded, sending the five soldiers crashing into the far wall with tremendous force. Steve, semi-propped up against the far wall, strained to find his comrades in arms. Next to him was Simmons, a Special Forces Green Beret. Simmons was alive but Steve could see he was in bad shape with a large gash in his left side. A pool of blood formed on the floor next to him. Steve dragged himself over to the hurt soldier, taking out what was left of the gauze in his field pack and stuffing it into Simmons' side.

The soldier looked into his eyes with grim determination, telling Steve without words that he wasn't going to die in this god-forsaken place. Steve frantically looked around to see the status of the remaining soldiers. He could clearly see the slumped forms of two of his remaining squad unmoving in one corner. One of the soldiers sat against the wall with his head bent at a strange angle, telling Steve he'd broken his neck. The other had been next to Steve and it had taken the brunt of the explosion. Steve could see flash burns all over the man's face and hands, and shrapnel wounds riddling the man's body.

Steve just hung his head. This was supposed to be a routine recon mission, one that he'd done a thousand times with many of the people in this room. He was unsure why enemy soldiers weren't streaming into the breach in the wall. By all rights, they should have all been dead by the blast. He searched the rubble for his remaining squad member only to see his lifeless body under a large chunk of the exploded wall on the floor not four feet away.

Knowing that the rest of his team was down, he turned once more to focus on the lone surviving member, Simmons. Steve knelt next to the injured man and could see the gauze now soaked in blood. He knew if he didn't stop the bleeding now that he would lose another team member, and he knew he couldn't let that happen. Reaching to his side, he slid his huge serrated knife out of its sheath. He quickly looked around what was left of the room, quickly locating the flames he needed. Not a foot away from him on the floor, a crashed roof rafter lay engulfed in flames. Steve thrust the foot-long knife into the belly of the flames, heating the knife to the point where the blade glowed. He quickly removed the knife and turned to his downed teammate.

Steve grabbed a piece of cloth from the floor and wadded it up, shoving it into Simmons' mouth. He gave a steel look to Simmons. The Green Beret had been through this before and nodded. The blade found its mark as Simmons' body convulsed as the knife singed the bleeding area. The smell of burning flesh and blood filled the air. Steve was used to this but for some reason this time it bothered him. Simmons gave him a look of thanks and breathed a little

·more regularly. He reached in his pack and took out the last remaining gauze and dressed a wound on Simmons' arm.

Steve felt another explosion from outside the room and heard confused voices shouting at one another. He stretched out on the floor with his automatic assault rifle positioned in front of him, ready to pull the trigger. He gave a quick glance back to Simmons who had his side arm at the ready while still propped up against the wall. He turned his attention once more to the commotion outside the room. Through the smoke and dust, he could see a few military vehicles in his field of view. As he scanned the area, he could see the bodies of the enemy strewn everywhere. It almost made him smile to know that they'd given as good as or better than they'd gotten.

The voices he heard were in the distance and he couldn't see any living enemy before him. Explosions still rang in the air and the sound of gunfire echoed off the walls of the remaining buildings. He gave a quick glance to Simmons, trying to measure his chances of escape with the wounded man. Simmons, without a word, flipped his hand, telling the big man to get going. Steve gave him an unsure look but knew they had no supplies and couldn't hold out here. Their only chance he knew was to find another squad to help him with his wounded comrade.

Steve reached over and grabbed the man's hand.

"I won't leave you behind!"

The man nodded and Steve grabbed a few more guns from the ground and ran into the smoke. Once outside, the sun glare blinded him for a moment. He sometimes forgot how strong the sun was here. The heat also raised by a factor of ten as he now was unprotected from the scorch that was the sun in this sand trap that was the place he now found himself. Gaining his bearings, he remembered from his briefings that a few clicks away to the north was a rendezvous point.

Looking to the north, he could see the road strewn with the devastation of a battle. Burned-out military vehicles still on fire with smoke billowing into the air. He gave a quick look to his left where the oil fields were still alight with fire plumes shooting into the air. One of their objectives was to see if any of the wells had survived the carnage, but they'd been too late. The Iraqi Republican Guard had blown everyone, creating a fire ball of oil flowing into the open air. Looking at the blow torch that stood before him made him even more upset, if that were possible at this moment in time.

He'd become an Army Ranger to protect others and his way of life. He'd been on many missions that made him feel proud to be of service. This mission however had made little sense because the overall Iraqi Army had given up without a fight. The fighting was all but over but his commander had insisted they check on the wells. As any good soldier following orders, he'd complied and his squad went to recon the situation. Even before they'd gotten close, they could already see the black smoke filling the air. As they entered the field, the heat from the oil wells now ablaze was stifling, as if the desert heat wasn't enough already. They'd already received the news of the unconditional surrender and had expected much more of a fight than they'd been in.

The leader of the Iraqi Army had told the world that this would be the mother of all battles. The Iraqi forces had offered little resistance and had surrendered in many cases without a single shot fired. This may have given his squad a sense of not much danger awaiting them, which cost them dearly. Steve and Simmons were close friends and had served together on many occasions; they knew from experience not to take anything for granted. Their commanding officer had other plans however. A butter bar, fresh from officer training, he was a cocky little jerk that had already had his squad ready to kick his ass.

Steve's squad for this mission had been chosen as a small attachment because of the thought by the higher ups that the danger was minimal. At first, that logic seemed sound until the squad made its way to the small village on the other side of the oil field. Someone had forgotten to tell the Iraqi soldiers in the town that the surrender had gone through. So when Steve's squad entered the town, they were immediately fired upon and found themselves fighting for their lives.

The fire fight had been intense and Steve's squad made quick work of the Iraqi regulars. They made their way to the interior of the village and found a small garrison of the Iraqi Army in their midst. Not wanting to engage a superior force without the proper support, Steve and Simmons had recommended to their commanding officer that they find cover and call in an air strike. The lieutenant disregarded their advice and ordered an incursion. The rest of the squad prepared to take the garrison, leaving Steve and Simmons furious. They both knew this was foolish that they were recon and weren't equipped for an assault on an unknown target.

Steve, knowing what was at stake, took charge and set a plan before his squad, which pissed off his officer. Too bad. Steve wasn't about to lose a whole squad to stupidity. Steve sent one of the squad members that was of Middle-Eastern descent to peek. The hope was to get a little intel without calling attention to themselves. The squad member returned with a great deal of information. The garrison wasn't manned with a huge contingent of men. Steve went back over his plan with everyone. He sent half of his squad to the front and the other half to the back to assault the garrison on two fronts. The plan worked to perfection and they took the garrison with little fanfare.

Steve and company grabbed as much intel as they could and got out of there quick. They felt good and made their way to the outskirts of town when they were attacked. RPGs rained from the rooftops, smashing into their squad, scattering them quickly. What had seemed as a terrific victory had turned quickly into a nightmare. In initial onslaught, his commanding officer had been blown to bits, leaving Steve as the ranking man in charge. He gathered the rest of his men and ran for cover. They made their way through the maze of streets, fighting from house to house, trying not to get blown up from IEDs left about the roads.

Steve and his squad, which now numbered five including himself, found a strong-looking house to regroup and take refuge. Once inside, they tried to determine their next move when they were once again attacked. They returned fire and held their own, but were quickly running low on ammo. Steve had told them that they couldn't stay here. He told them they should break through the mud wall and slip out the back. They made a small hole in the wall to see if the coast was clear. That was when the explosions rocked the area.

Chapter 2

Steve awoke with a start and scanned the room to try to gain his bearings. He could still taste the sulfur and the sand in his mouth. His mind coming back to where he was as he'd been dreaming on his incursion into enemy territory in the Persian Gulf War. He'd left his friend Simmons in the house as he made his way through the streets of the village as he saw jet fighters overhead. His boys had arrived and were making a path. He made his way to the edge of town, meeting up with another squad of men making their way toward the village. Together, they went back, clearing the last of the resistance and took the town. Steve returned for Simmons and took him back to base. Simmons survived but due to the nature of his many wounds, his career was over.

Steve had decided that a career in the Army for him was no longer what he wanted and he was ready for something else. When he'd returned home, he had a difficult time finding a position that he could use his special military skills. He was about to give up when he got a call from Mr. William Peters, the owner of the Massachusetts Bay Marauders professional football team, inquiring if he wanted to become his head of security. It was a dream come true and to Steve, it saved his life; he was lost at that point as to what to do with his life.

Thinking of Mr. P. shook him back to reality as he came out of the dream once more to take in the room he now found himself in. As he strained to look where he was, he felt the tug of restraints on his arms and feet. He lifted his head as much as he could to peer around to see his surroundings. Steve almost laughed at the situation he now found himself in, considering part of his job for the Marauders had been detaining various people and clones, much the way he was now.

As head of security for the Marauders, Steve had found himself stuck in the middle of what could only be described as a science fiction movie. The owner of the team, Mr. P. and the head doctor, Dr. Henry Chase had been secretly working on a program to replace his human players in their games with cloned replicas. This program had been very successful and had been in place for years until a young draftee named Chris Strong joined the team. Chris had awoken during the sleep phase of the program, during which the original players went into an oxygen chamber only to be put asleep during the game. Their cloned counterparts would take their place during the game and then they'd be awoken after the game with a memory implant of the game, as if they'd actually played the game.

Chris had brought the whole program down by awakening in the middle of the whole process. This had never happened before and caused a ripple effect that brought the whole program to its knees. The public was made aware of the situation and Mr. P. was brought to trial for his crimes. Steve joined Chris and his small group of heroes during this time as he realized he had been played the whole time he'd worked for Mr. P.

Steve and his companions had gone on to find out that they'd not fully put the program to rest. They soon were faced with an even more dangerous challenge and found a mysterious figure chasing them. As they closed in on their shadowy figure, they found more than they'd bargained for as the shadowy figure turned out to be an old friend. In the process of figuring out what the entity was now up to, they all found a military base attached to the stadium in which they'd all worked in for years.

The companions had gone to the military installation to confront their shadow once and for all during which time Steve and Chris came face to face with their nemesis. They dispatched the shadow only to find that other things were at work and the shadow itself had been but a puppet of the evil that was behind these diabolical programs. Instead of clones, this time Chris and company had come face to face with something altogether new, Artificial Intelligence. The shadow had planned to use these A.I. players to now take the place of the original football players, in the hopes to fool the viewing public.

In the process, Steve and Chris were forced to flee with the rest of their companions through the underground labyrinth of tunnels that made up the military installation. Their shadow had one final parting shot in the form of a self-destruct sequence in which the whole bunker would come down upon them. They'd managed to get everyone to safety, but just as they were about to leave, Steve heard another voice. It turned out that the clone version of their shadow, Mr. P. had escaped. Steve being an Army Ranger and never leaving a fallen man behind went back to retrieve the clone.

Steve and Mr. P. were about to escape the bunker when the roof collapsed upon them, trapping them inside while their friends watched. Chris and company tried tirelessly to break through the rubble and rescue their friends. When they could finally get through the debris, Steve and Mr. P. were nowhere to found. They were then taken into custody by the military and could no longer look for their friends. Chris had escaped the soldiers only to come back to the stadium to gather help to find Steve, and confronted a terrible horror. The woman of his dreams, April Jones, Dr. Chase's daughter was held captive by none other than her father who seemed to be at the center of this whole conspiracy once more.

Chapter 3

Gus sped down the highway, slamming his hands down onto the driver's wheel. Gus Malzone, a reporter of many years' experience, rarely was caught off guard or unaware, but this whole cloning A.I. situation had him perplexed. He'd always considered himself like a Monty, always getting his man, but in this case, he seemed to be chasing his tail. He still had the crumpled sticky note with the coordinates in his hand to remind him where he was going. Not that he needed the coordinates, he knew where he was going. The better question was what would he find there when he arrived. He knew the military base and had been there many years ago, looking into a story involving the military.

Back then, Gus had been asked by the government to squash the story to protect the American public. Gus had chosen to do just that but it had always bothered him. Not that he wanted to ever do anything to bring danger to others and his country, but he was the consummate bloodhound and wanted every story. During his long and distinguished career, he'd only squashed this one story. It left a taste of unfinished business in his mouth. That feeling had never sat well with him and now as he drove toward the site of that anguish, his stomach was in knots.

Hands gripped the wheel to the point his knuckles turned white, Gus stared at the oncoming road, struggling with his decision to come at all. He knew he'd agreed to squash this story as well but he had to know. Whether he printed the story, well, that was another matter altogether. He would still investigate thoroughly and find out exactly what his friends were up against. If nothing else, he could help them and arm them with information to help their cause.

He thought about Chris; the boy had just begun his career and now stood amid a conspiracy that could unravel everything he'd ever worked for in his life. Gus, being on the back end of his career, had great perspective as to what it was like to build a career. Everyone assumed once one made the big time that was it, but Gus knew better. Just reaching one's goal was never enough; one had to continue to push to become something more. Right now, Gus feared that Chris would be swallowed up by this situation, causing him to never reach his potential. Gus had known the kid for a long time and knew the depths of his resolve, but he knew family was first to Chris. If ever it came to it, Chris would choose family and walk away without another thought.

The thought of Chris not playing out his career pained Gus greatly. He'd watched this scrawny kid make his high school team and build himself into a force on the field. He watched as he matured physically and mentally into one of the best all-around football players he'd seen in a long while. Chris had surprised everyone with his talent, but better yet, his leadership on and off the field. People gravitated to this kid and people looked to him. This was never more evident than during this continuing saga they now all faced. Chris and company faced the challenge head on, never once running anywhere except headlong into the fray.

Gus had been on many field assignments that saw people running from danger, but here was Chris and friends who were there helping others while moving toward danger. During their latest harrowing experience, Gus watched a mountain blowing up around them and Chris running back in to help survivors. He'd written stories about the human spirit his entire career and here it was on display right next to him. Watching Chris in action, it became easy to understand why others followed him. Gus himself found it hard not to be pulled in Chris' direction.

Gus, watching the road speed by, thought just that. How had he been sucked into this situation again? He should have known, after dealing with the clone situation, that he needed to take a long vacation. Whether it was his unrelenting thirst for the story or his genuine affection for Chris and his friends, he found himself once more up to his eyeballs in the story. As the car approached the military base, he could feel that energy return. He would always get an extra boost of energy when beginning a new story. Just the unknown to him added that little extra that caused him to get giddy like a school child being let out for recess.

Pulling along the access road leading to the base, he noticed differences before even getting to the gate. The road had cameras everywhere and the fences all had coiled barbed wire at the top, preventing access. The road itself was highly lit. He remembered the last time he came here, there was barely any light and he'd nearly missed the road altogether. This time, everyone on the base would see him coming. There was no sneaking up on these people. Gus sat up a little straighter in his seat, straining to take in the scene around him. He tried to look through the fence, but the lights were so pronounced that it made it difficult to look beyond.

Gus slowed the car as he approached the gate. Gone was the small guard shack that he remembered. In its place was a modern structure that looked impenetrable. The solid structure didn't look inviting but said to intruders, "Don't try it!" With so many powerful lights everywhere, to Gus it looked like day rather than night. Twenty feet before the entrance, Gus was forced to stop for fear of running into the large circular metal structures sticking straight out of the road. Gus had seen these before on many stories in front of buildings and other places where people didn't want suicide bombers to get too close. These metal barriers were quite ominous and Gus swallowed a couple of times as if trying to rethink this decision.

Gus just remembered this base being a small remnant left over from World War II, where they'd housed a few planes and military equipment. His brow furrowed and he looked out his windshield to see that his car was now surrounded by armed guards. One especially bulky young man wrapped on his window with the butt of his weapon. Gus quickly opened the window, not knowing what to say but offered up his media credentials, which in most cases had been enough to gain entrance to almost anywhere. The soldier stood waiting for something more and for some dumb reason, he handed the soldier the crumpled sticky note. The man took the note, looking at it suspiciously and then noticed the coordinates. He stood firm and asked, "Where did you get these coordinates? Most people think this base closed years ago!"

Gus gave a helpless look to the young man. "I'm on assignment. My editor sent me out here to investigate that very thing. It seems that your activity out here has brought on many questions lately."

The soldier didn't look the least bit surprised by this response. "Yes, this base has seen quite a rebirth in recent years. Most of what goes on here now is computer tech work. Sure, we still have a contingent of fighters that we train with, but for the most part it's just technology."

Gus was astounded that this soldier even divulged this small bit of information, but he'd obviously been coached to make things sound very normal. On the surface, it would seem normal because many bases had done just that and had become havens for computer technology.

The soldier looked once more at the reporter. "I have to say though, Mr. Malzone, that I'm surprised by the late hour of your visit." Gus hadn't even thought of this when he made his decision to come straight out here. The ride had taken several hours and he'd left late to begin with.

He looked at his watch and then meekly at the soldier. "You know, I didn't even realize the time. I'm working on several stories right now and I just wanted to get moving on this one. I kind of expected what you're saying in relation to what's going on here now. I know they wouldn't keep it open if it weren't necessary."

The soldier then did something Gus didn't expect and reached for the microphone on his shoulder. "Sir, Mr. Malzone has arrived." Gus sat bewildered. They knew he was coming. Panic rose in him and he quickly looked in his rearview mirror to plan his exit strategy. Fright built as he now saw that a military vehicle blocked his path. He was now surrounded and noticed that weapons were pointed at him in all directions. Afraid to take his hands from the wheel, he just looked helplessly at the young man.

The soldier smiled smugly. "Yes, Mr. Malzone, we knew you were coming." A coded response came on the radio and the soldier once again spoke into the microphone, "Yes, sir. We'll keep him here." He then pointed his weapon directly at Gus without another word.

Gus couldn't help himself. "Hey, I wouldn't by chance get a phone call?"

The soldier just sneered at him and gave him a weapon butt to the head. The pain shot through his head and caused him to instinctively press the gas, shooting the car forward. The car lurched forward, striking the metal barrier, crushing the front of the car and leaving Gus pinned behind the airbag.

With his head cloudy, he looked around him to see if anything was injured. His head hurt but he seemed to be intact. As he looked out the side of the car, he heard shouting. Then he saw soldiers racing toward his car with panicked looks on their faces as well as another more reserved figure behind them. As the figure approached, Gus could make out a more polished uniform of a high-ranking officer. The officer came to Gus' window, asking him if he was all right. Gus, through hazy eyes, peered at the man with recognition.

The officer smiled. "Yes, Gus, it's me. Why didn't you listen to me? I told you I'd come get you when I needed you. Now you've put me in a tough position. I've no choice but to place you in custody."

Gus, for the first time, felt a wave of nausea flow over him and with his head already cloudy, he felt as if he were about to get sick. The once-clear figure of the officer became fuzzy around the edges. He blinked his eyes in the hopes of clearing his vision, to no avail. He shook his head, which was a huge mistake, and brought on a new wave of pain shooting down his neck. His head now pounding, he felt faint. His vision continuing to become more unclear, he could feel himself fainting. His last thought was of the officer before him and sudden realization set in, the man had been the officer that had come to his office. Gus had one last thought. What the hell was he doing here?

Chapter 4

Chris lined up the running back and shot forward, launching himself into the back's mid-section with devastating results. The back was stuffed behind the line of scrimmage for a huge loss. Chris was on a mission today during practice. He'd promised the coach that he wouldn't let what was going on affect him on the field. The defense was pumped up and everyone came over and slammed him on the back, praising his hit. Chris wiped the sweat out of his eyes, making the next call. He called a blitz and wasn't going to let the offensive have anything today. He took his position in the middle of the defense and noticed one of the linemen shading over to one side with his hand turned in slightly. This telltale sign told the defender where the play was going.

Chris read the quarterback's eyes as he scanned the defense and Chris already knew the play call. Chris shouted out an audible to his defense and they all shifted to line up with his play call. The quarterback countered with a change in cadence to catch the defense offside. It didn't work and the quarterback hiked the ball. Chris immediately shot the gap left by pulling the lineman and flew toward the quarterback for a free shot. Chris' anger at this point was at a flashpoint and he gritted his teeth as he neared the quarterback.

He felt nothing but rage at this point for everything he and his friends had been through and he let that rage take over in that moment. The rage was so powerful it exploded into the quarterback as Chris struck him in the chest and wrapped his arms around him. He was supposed to peel off as this was practice, but the rage took over and Chris drove the quarterback into the ground with all the terrific force his six-foot-four-inch, two-hundred-sixty-pound frame could muster. As he rolled off the quarterback, he could tell that something was seriously wrong.

Joe Morton, the quarterback of the Massachusetts Bay Marauders lay on the field lifeless. Chris stood unaware of what had happened as Christopher came flying up to him. "Dude, what the hell was that? You just killed our quarterback!"

Chris immediately came to his senses and saw Joe down on the field for the first time. "What have I done?" He immediately went to Joe's side yelling how sorry he was. The training staff pushed their way in and Chris backed up slightly. His eyes found Christopher's and without a word, told his twin what had happened.

He turned once more to check on Joe, only to come face to face with his seething coach, Ray Ridel. Coach Ridel grabbed his face mask and almost tore his head off. "Chris, what the hell did you just do? That is our season lying on that field right now! You're the quarterback on defense but we can't win the game without a quarterback on offense! You're suspended! Get off my field! Get off my field!" Chris tried to say something but no words came out. The coach shouted to the security officers, "Escort him off the property! He's suspended until further notice!"

Chris could feel the rage return and turned to face the security forces as though they were the enemies. After everything he'd been through, how could the coach take away the one thing that was still normal in his life. The security officers didn't stand a chance. There were only two at that point and Chris was, being the imposing figure that he was, more than a match for two security officers. Still wearing his uniform covered in dirt, sweat, blood, and grime, he looked more like something one might see in a horror movie. The first officer tried to grab his arm and paid for it with a clothes line to the neck, flipping the man over, sending him crashing to the ground. Next came the larger of the two officers. This one was closer to Chris' size and he had a nasty look on his face until Chris stood to his full height before him and snarled at him.

The security officer knew he was in trouble but attacked anyway. He rushed at Chris and to him, it was like a red cape being waved in front of him. He planted his foot in the turf and exploded into the officer, bringing him to the ground much the way he'd just planted Joe. He straddled the helpless man and rained down punches. His rage unquenched, he hit the unmoving man until he felt huge hands grab him and pull him off the security officer. Chris rolled off the ground and went to face his next attacker, only to come face to face with his own eyes.

Christopher stood before him, grabbing his shoulders. "It's all right! Chris, it's me! It's all right!" Chris stood dazed for a moment as if coming back from a dream. He looked around for a moment at the carnage before him and the weight of everything came crashing down upon him. Everything washed over him—the clone program, the A.I. program, the loss of April, and the seeming destruction of his career hit him all at once. He just stood there in the middle of the football field and let out a blood-curdling scream. The primal scream felt good, as if it vanquished demons from his soul. When the power of the scream subsided, he felt weak and let his body go limp. He fell to the ground on his knees weeping.

Once again, he looked up to see his coach's eyes looking at him. This time the look was of extreme pity. The coach knelt by him. "Chris, it's okay! Listen, I don't know what's going on, but you need to come with me right now! Joe is all right; you just knocked him out cold, but otherwise unharmed. We'll go to my office and talk." Through blurry watery eyes, he could see the concern in his coach's eyes. He immediately felt embarrassed and jumped up and got into step with his coach, following him off the practice field. He didn't even bother to ask the coach who would finish practice.

Chapter 5

Chris became aware of someone else on his elbow and turned to see Christopher on his right-hand side, walking in step with his twin. The coach just peered over his shoulder and shook his head while continuing forward without a word. The trio walked right into the practice bubble and headed for the coach's office. Once inside, the coach shut the door and motioned for the two players to take a seat.

Chris felt as though he was once again in the principal's office and sat awaiting his punishment. For what seemed an eternity, no one spoke as the coach contemplated his next move. With surprising humility, the coach began, "Chris, I cannot begin to understand everything you've been through, but please understand I have a team to run. I understand your life is extremely important and I can sympathize, I can. However, I must worry about everyone's life on this team. You're more than just a player to me." He paused and looked as if he couldn't believe he said this aloud.

The coach looked at Chris with genuine care. "I've watched you for years and taken an interest in your development and your growth. I'm enamored with your resolve and your drive. Your heart is amazing and I wish I could bottle it up and give it to each of my players. What most amazes me however is your willingness to do whatever is necessary to improve the team even at your own hindrance. That is why for the good of the team and as I look at you right now for your own benefit, I'm putting you on the Injured Reserve with the opportunity to return when you're ready."

Chris felt as if he'd just received a punch to the gut. The person he respected the most in the world beyond his family had just told him he could no longer play for him. He felt the rage grow in him once more and felt his face turn red. The coach caught sight of this and put his hand up. "Now wait a minute! I'm not abandoning you, but we need to make things right with you before you can get back out on that field." Chris stood and was ready to just walk out. He turned only to meet Christopher's hand on his shoulder, stopping him. One look from Christopher told him he had to sit down and talk to the coach.

He began, "Coach, as you know, I've wished my whole life to play for you and this team, and just as my dream seems to be coming true, events have ripped it away from me again and again." His eyes involuntarily watered. "Coach, what if I never make it back? What if all this has caused permanent damage that's beyond repair? Coach, I almost killed our quarterback today. What if I lose it on the field and someone pays for it with a serious injury? I don't know if I could handle that on top of everything else."

The coach sat stone faced, staring through Chris. "Chris, I know this. You were playing out there like a crazed dog today! Not that I mind reckless abandon and people willing to sacrifice everything out there, but you were on another whole level today. Scary actually! I've had my share of players that have played on the edge during my career, but they knew when to pull back. You weren't going to pull back today and that's why this decision pains me beyond everything to tell you this. As a football coach, I want that fire on my club but as you know, to me football acumen is as important. Those who play for me must be able to use their brain out there and not cost the team in critical situations. What I saw out there today was someone who couldn't rein it in and could cause major damage during a real game. Until I feel you're up to the task, you will be on IR for your own good."

Coach Ridel then did something very out of character for him. He walked around his desk and embraced his player. He then backed up. "Sorry, it just seemed appropriate." Chris practically melted and fell into his seat as if the coach had just fired him. His one thing, the thing that defined him his entire life, had just been ripped once more from him. Rather than rage at that moment, he felt his defenses vanish and there before the coach was the little boy that had played outside in the sandlot with every older boy in the neighborhood, in the hopes of learning how to play with the big boys.

He now sat before the coach broken. He had nothing left. The one thing that had held him together was now gone and along with April, his life crumbled before his eyes. Chris sat slumped in the chair and could feel Christopher's hand on his shoulder. After a few minutes of silence, he straightened himself in the chair and faced his coach. He tried to begin but his mouth seemed so dry and parched that his words croaked out, "Coach, Dr. Chase has taken April prisoner and we cannot find them."

It was the coach's turn to be enraged. "What? What's that idiot up to now? Taking his own daughter, are you sure?"

Chris recalled the whole episode to the coach, not leaving out any details. He went on to lay out how Gus had good intelligence about what was going on. Chris described for the coach how Mr. P., along with the doctor, had disappeared. He further explained that they were led to the military installation that turned out to be the lair for the shadow that seemed to be the cause of everything that had happened to them in recent years. He told the coach about their encounter with the real Mr. P. and their escape only to lose Steve and the clone Mr. P.

The coach seemed unreadable at this point and just sat listening. Chris continued and told the coach about how they'd come to him and tried to not let anything get in the way of football. He explained to the coach that April had gone with her father to a lab in the bowels of the stadium and Chris figured out what was going on. At this point, Chris could hardly speak as he went on to describe losing April in the tube and breaking into the room too late. Exhausted by his tale, Chris just let his head lay on the coach's desk.

When he'd enough energy to lift his head, he realized that he had a terrific headache. The coach had yet to say a word. He just looked at Chris several times as if he wanted to say something, but Christopher piped in, "Coach, that's our thoughts exactly. We still cannot believe the events that have swirled around our lives. Honestly, I don't have the human experience that you all have, being new at this, but my heart is broken for my brother here. You were his last refuge and you just destroyed him!"

The coach winced slightly at the tongue lashing. "Christopher, it may seem like that but believe me, the last thing I want to see is my defensive captain sitting on the sidelines. As a coach, I have to make the most difficult decisions even when they're not popular."

Christopher just took a seat next to his twin and put his head in his hands as if all out of thoughts. Chris just looked lost as he sought guidance from his coach. This wasn't lost on the coach and he responded in kind, "Chris, you will always have me. That much is certain. I cannot foretell what will happen with your career, but I'll do whatever I can to ensure that you have a long fruitful one!" Chris seemed energized by this statement and looked at his coach with gratitude. It was the coach's turn to look exhausted, as he leaned back in his chair looking up at the ceiling.

All three sat in the coach's office for several minutes, not wanting to say anything. Then as if shot with a bullet, the coach stood straight up. "A military base attached to the stadium! A city under us! This is crazy! I'm a football coach. How the hell am I supposed to coach if I don't know what the hell is going on? Of course, I can completely understand why you didn't tell me, but I don't know whether to be mad at you because you didn't tell me. Listen, you two. That doctor has always been a pain in my backside. I never know what he's doing and he's never there when I need him. This does not surprise me one bit. I always knew in a million small ways that the doctor was working on something else besides my players."

The coach sat down once more and looked straight at his players. "Since I've been left out of the loop in terms of what the doctor has been doing, I can't help you much. What I can do I will, but that's all I can contribute. Honestly, I pay little attention to the doctor except to yell at him to fix my players." His face turned red. "I just got used to the idea that I had clone players on my team and now this! What next, aliens? This is ridiculous! Whatever happened to the days where I'd have to worry about a player doing too many drugs? Now I don't even know if my players are real or not!"

Coach Ridel sat stewing and slammed his hands on his desk. "This really pisses me off! How the hell am I supposed to coach a team now?" He swung to Christopher. "How many more of you are on my team?"

Christopher looked embarrassed. "Coach, as far as I know, I'm the only one. Chris wouldn't let them take me."

The coach returned a sympathetic look. "Yes, of course. Sorry, this is a lot to take. No wonder you freaked out. I'm just on the outside looking in and I'm freaking out. Chris, I'm so sorry this has happened to you! What do you need me to do?"

Chris looked at a loss for words. "Coach, I'm not sure you can do anything. I think the thing you could do, you just did and gave me some perspective. I have to focus on my life right now and football as much as it means to me, has to wait." He stood with renewed vigor and looked at his coach as if he were cleansed, sending his hand toward the coach across the desk. The coach rose with conviction and took his player's hand warmly.

"Just make sure you keep me in the loop this time. Coach and player should have an open dialogue. I'll be here when you need me. Be sure to punch that idiot doctor in the head for me!"

Chris smiled. "Coach, something tells me more than that's going to happen to the doctor when we catch up to him. Thank you for your understanding and compassion. I'll be sure never to mention a word of it to anyone."

It was the coach's turn to smile. "You just make sure you get back here as fast as possible!" The coach already had begun to look at all the notes on his desk, getting back to work. As Chris and Christopher left, they heard the coach say, "Good luck, gentlemen!" The two looked confidently at each other as though they now had permission to kick the doctor's ass for real.

Chapter 6

Jessica looked up from her tear-soaked tissue and looked at the clock. It was well after two thirty in the morning. She'd had a great deal of trouble sleeping since losing Steve in the tunnels of the bunker. Her grief was unquenchable and the fact that April was now gone had made things worse. The two women had developed a very strong bond forged in the crucible of tragedy and had become more than friends. Losing two of her dear friends in the same day was too much to bear and no one could console her.

Christopher had come to see her almost every day and he was extremely sweet. He wanted to help, but had no reference point from lack of life experience. Being a clone, he was in many ways a newborn just learning how to live in the harsh real world. She glanced over at the large vase of fresh flowers he'd brought over in the hopes of making her feel better. For a moment, she smiled, thinking of the kind gesture and then thinking of what Chris was now going through. He too had lost his love to this horrid situation and was just as much a mess as she at this point.

She stood uneasy from her perch on the couch and stayed in place, waiting for something to come to her. The silence of her house was deafening. She looked around to the dark corners, expecting to see military personnel coming out after her. That had become her frequent nightmare. She'd just had the dream again, that of everyone about to escape once more and then the tunnel collapsing around them with the soldiers coming to take them all away. In her dream, she could see the soldiers dragging the lifeless body of Steve away, shaking their heads as if to say he didn't make it.

Just standing there, she shook as if coming awake from the nightmare once more with the room spinning. She threw herself down on the couch and cried once more. She curled up into a ball, holding a throw pillow close to her, and cried some more. When there were no more tears, she sat in the dark silence, viewing the void of her hallway, hoping beyond hope that Steve would come walking through the door to make everything whole once more.

Jessica Reali, the pit-bull lawyer of the clone trial, had been reduced to a puddle of tears. This was the woman who had stared down the government and now here she was on the couch in pieces. After what seemed to be hours, she could no longer cry and rose, finding her way to her office. She plopped herself in her chair, slouching slightly. If anyone could see her now, the woman with not one hair out of place was a disheveled mess. She poured over the files on her desk, hoping once again that work would fill the void.

Her hand came to rest on a file Gus gave her. The file folder was extremely well worn and looked quite old. She'd just placed it with all the other work she had and Gus told her it was probably nothing, but he would try to follow up on an old lead. She hadn't thought anymore of it and just tossed it with all the others. For the first time, she opened the folder and her eyes immediately almost popped out of her head. According to the articles and the notes in Gus' hand, Gus had been investigating the possibility of a clone program years before what they'd just faced. This program was much different because it tried to create super soldiers to strengthen their military might beyond compare.

Jessica sat straight up, holding the file in her hand, contemplating what this could mean. Gus had gone to investigate a lead from a cold case from years ago. Jessica knew quite clearly that meant Gus knew something. She couldn't help but think why Gus hadn't told them about this information from the very beginning. She placed the file back down on her desk and once more opened the file, looking at the first hand-scribbled note on the top of the pile. Jessica could clearly make out Gus' scrawl across the paper, but she couldn't tell what the set of numbers meant.

She sat far into the morning, pouring over the papers in the file folder, trying to grasp what it was exactly that Gus had been on to. Gus had done his due diligence and had amassed a large amount of information on the project. The one thing that was missing in all the research before her were the key players. Everything in front of her implicated the military, but there wasn't one specific name that always popped up during the investigation. Jessica thought this very strange due to Gus' nature as a bloodhound. There was no way Gus didn't know who the power players were, yet here there was nothing.

Jessica kept coming back to the many references to a Massachusetts base near Cape Cod and was surprised to see that the base wasn't mentioned by name. She knew of one base but knew that couldn't be what Gus had been talking about. The base she knew was a National Guard base and was used all the time for exercises with quite a public profile. Jessica shook her head as she knew that a secret clone program wouldn't be developed on a base with so much traffic. She sat and thought a moment. That meant that there was another base that no one knew about.

She jumped up. Gus had found it and was going out to investigate. Where, she pondered, where would the base be located? Looking up quickly at the clock, it finally hit her that she'd been up all night reviewing the file. This was normal behavior for the seasoned attorney, but this morning she was very weary. She reached for her phone, contacting another attorney that had collaborated on other cases in the past. This attorney had a wealth of experience with military cases and had consulted on JAG cases. She nodded as he gave her the information she'd requested.

Jessica had described the numbers on the paper to him and sent him a picture of the paper on her cell phone. The man had responded quickly, telling her that the numbers were GPS coordinates. He told her how to put them in her phone and she did as she was instructed. Looking at the small map on her phone, she could see where the base was located. Glancing quickly at the location, she tried to estimate her travel time in her head. The distance wasn't overly concerning, but the route that she would have to take was notorious for having big time traffic delays. An hour and a half trip could take four hours without an eye blink. Jessica held the phone to her hip and looked at the clock to see if the trip was doable at that time. She ran to the bathroom to get ready.

With a towel wrapped around her head and one around her waist, she ran to the phone, looking quickly at the screen to see who it was. She smiled widely and answered sarcastically, yelling at Agent John Bradley, "Agent Bradley, what took you so long? I had time to straighten my hair while you were taking your time getting back to me."

Agent Bradley retorted, "Jessica, are you kidding me? You just called me ten minutes ago! I have the time you called right here on my phone. Also, something tells me that you're standing talking to me fresh out of the shower. You forget I know you and how long it takes you to put yourself together. Remember?"

Jessica couldn't help but laugh. "John, I need your help!"

Agent Bradley laughed. "Jessica, I'll always help you. It seems my lot in life to help beautiful women without the chance of one of you falling for me."

Jessica snapped at him, "John, that isn't fair. You know as well as I do, you don't have time for women."

Agent Bradley responded, "Jessica, if you remember correctly, you didn't have time for men before Steve and you fell for him like a ton of bricks." The phone went silent while Jessica tried not to lose it on the phone. Agent Bradley could sense it and continued, "I'd be happy to help. What can I help you with? A murder case, a high-profile robbery, a missing persons case, what?"

Jessica regained her composure. "John, Gus was working on finding some leads that relate to what we're already involved in. He'd worked on a case years ago that involved the military creating cloned super soldiers. What's interesting is that I cannot find one name associated with this program. No names at all and no photographs, just information."

Agent Bradley said, "That is quite unlike Gus. You know as well as I that Gus never misses anything. No, the information was taken out or not included on purpose. The only thing I can think is that someone got to Gus awhile back and asked him to squash the story. That is the only plausible explanation. That is very concerning if you think about it for a moment. Gus would have had to have a great reason for not pursuing the story. If the military is involved, they probably threatened him or his family."

Jessica took a moment before responding. "That is all well and good, but I tried to call Gus and his number says it's no longer in service. There is no way Gus wouldn't be without a phone. That phone is his life line and he would never change his number."

"He hasn't checked in with you? When was the last time you heard from him?"

Jessica thought. "It has been several days. He gave me the file and practically ran out of my office saying he was hot on a lead."

Agent Bradley came back, "We have to stop letting people go off to places on their own. We need to stick together! All right, get dressed. I'm coming over right now. Then we're going to pick up those two lugs from practice and we're going to get Gus."

As Jessica was about to hang up, she heard, "Jessica, we'll find out what happened to Steve and April. You know I won't rest until we have answers."

Jessica welled up, "John, I know you're an amazing friend and an even better man. Trust me when I say this, when the right woman comes along, you will fall like a ton of bricks."

Agent Bradley wanted to say something, but got choked up. "Thank you, Jessica!"

Chapter 7

Dr. Chase had worked his whole life to save lives but lately, it just seemed as though he put them all in danger. All his plans were in jeopardy. Why couldn't his friends just return to their everyday lives like anyone else? No, these people just kept coming; they were like a bad nightmare. He just wanted to see his plan come to fruition and then things would be the way he hoped. With April on ice literally, that took one distraction out of the equation but Chris and Christopher were another matter entirely. He genuinely liked those boys. but they were becoming a serious problem and would have to be dealt with now.

The doctor looked at his computer, checking his daughter's vital signs and when he was satisfied she was stable, he returned to the screen to his right. On the screen was a high-definition picture of an interrogation room. The room was the typical square-shaped room with a table and chair in the middle. In the chair, the doctor could see the injured reporter barely awake. It was clear he was concussed but he needed information and once he had it, he might see to the reporter's needs.

He watched as Gus peered around the room, smiling to himself. Where did this old man think he was going? He couldn't escape. The doctor couldn't help but give the man a fright and spoke into the microphone in front of him.

"Gus, welcome to my stronghold! You're quite the pain in the ass, I must tell you. I thought you were smarter than this. Some years ago, we came to you and asked you to leave this one alone. Back then, you were smart enough to back off. What changed? Did you think you were old now and that you had nothing to lose?"

Gus awakened but his head remained cloudy and he had a massive headache. He felt the pain around his nose and tried to move his hands to feel for damage, only to realize his hands were shackled to a table. He regained some faculties and took in the room. The funny thing was, he'd been in these rooms many times on the other side, trying to get information about a case from a perpetrator. He almost laughed but thought better of it with his damaged face. He thought back to the soldier striking him in the face with his weapon and the pain that ensued. What perplexed him was that they just could have told him to go home. They were waiting for him but what good could did it do to keep him prisoner. His knowledge of anything having to do with them had to be quite minimal.

When the voice came over the speaker, he almost jumped as the crackling voice broke the silence, pulling him back to reality. His situation was grim and this mysterious voice now added a new twist. He listened to the voice and couldn't help but think he recognized it, but couldn't place it at this point. Gus was livid. Hadn't they just gotten rid of this idiot? Then it hit him. Someone else was always pulling the strings. He more than anyone knew that this case went to its highest reaches. To Gus, each time he thought he had a grasp on what was going on, he was sent back to the very beginning once more.

Gus smirked and looked at the camera in the corner.

"Come in here and take these cuffs off, and we'll see whose old. As for squashing the story, you told me this was national security. From where I'm sitting, it's about money and how much money the NAFL made because of this program. I also am sure with the unlimited applications of this technology, you're making money hand over fist in other areas as well. Hah, so much for national security! Why does everything always come back to money? You asked me to think of others and I have! What have you thought of but yourselves?"

The speaker remained silent and Gus laughed. "Just what I thought. You bully people into doing what you want and you operate without impunity! Don't try to give me that crap that people don't need to know everything either. I've spent my life trying to give people the information they need to protect themselves. I still can't believe I let you jerks sway me back then and almost once again this time. I can tell you this, it won't happen again! I'm bringing every one of you sons of bitches down!"

Gus hoped for a response to that last statement and he didn't have to wait long. "That, my friend, is why you're sitting there right now. You have caused enough problems for us. You will be put out of commission and it will be one less thing I must worry about. Who knows? If you behave yourself, maybe, I mean maybe I'll give you the exclusive of what's going on here. For now, though you will be my guest where I can keep an eye on you and you can't do any more damage. My plans have almost come full circle and I won't let some old fart reporter screw it up!"

The reporter sat up. "What exclusive? What the hell are you talking about? The exclusive is right here in this installation. The clone program, the A.I. program. Take your pick. You have your super soldier program. Now what? Have you found a way to harness a person's spirit? Where does it stop? Someday you're going to reach too far and annihilate us all! I don't know about you; despite all humanity's problems, we're a pretty cool species. You cannot be happy with just saving a human life; you want to control every aspect of it like a video game!"

Gus caught himself and stopped immediately. He'd let these creeps get under his skin, which was also something that never happened. Gus had always been the stoic one, the one people couldn't read and here he was spilling his guts to a camera. He sat once more unspeaking, just waiting for the next exchange with his invisible captor. The exchange didn't come and everything went radio silent. The room once more became a hollow shell with brick walls that felt as though they were closing in on Gus.

After a few minutes of nothing but his own thoughts, he heard the click of the lock and looked to the door to see the soldier enter. Gus felt a wave of panic flow through him as the soldier came into the view of the light. In the dim light, he saw that the soldier was none other than his friend with the weapon butt. He cringed as the man reached for his shackles and this didn't go unnoticed by the soldier. He unlocked the shackles, telling the reporter to stand. Gus did as he was instructed as the nausea took him again and he felt as if he would faint once more. The soldier steadied him.

"I'm sorry, Mr. Malzone! I get a little over-zealous sometimes. I'll take you so you can get some treatment." Gus tried once more and with the soldier's help, stumbled to the door. He leaned heavily against the wall as the soldier opened the door. Once open, Gus thought of escape but quickly changed his mind as he could hardly stand. Escape would have to wait. What he could do however, was a little reconnaissance and find out all he could.

With his head clearing, he decided his best bet was to pay close attention to his surroundings and keep his ear to the ground. As the soldier propped him up, he could feel his legs shaking beneath him. This prompted the soldier to lift Gus' left arm and slide his shoulder under Gus' to give extra support. Gus felt a huge difference, much more stable this way. The soldier looked in his eyes but said nothing and continued walking down the hallway.

The hallway resembled many other military installations he'd visited over the years. It was made for functionality and not for aesthetics. Gus looked down the plain hallway, looking for any distinguishing features but could only see a long white stripe from ceiling to halfway down the wall with the rest painted a dull gray. Gus couldn't help but smile as he realized how much the military enjoyed the use of gray in everything they did. His favorite memories of this military grey brought him back to his childhood when his dad had taken him to visit his battleship.

Gus thought of his father for a moment, a lifer in the military and an extremely hard man. He rode Gus very hard as a young man and expected his son to follow him into the military. It became such a bone of contention within his family that Mom had threatened to walk out if it didn't stop. Gus remembered the day he came home with the great news that he'd been hired on at the local newspaper. His father practically tore the door off its hinges leaving the house.

Gus later found out that his father's loathing for the media came from the way they handled the Vietnam War. His father felt the soldiers had given enough in service for their country and should not have to come back and fight their own countrymen. Gus' father blamed the media directly for this treatment of returning servicemen. Gus grew up in that era but thought the public should know what was happening to their troops. His father argued that armed with this new easily accessible intelligence, the enemy had a big advantage over our boys. He told his son that a great many lives were lost because embedded reporters all but led the enemy to our troops.

Gus, over the years, learned not to speak to his father about his assignments, which was a great strategy. Years after, it was apparent that his son was a professional and quite serious about his profession. Gus' father relented, telling his son how proud he was. He told Gus his pride was such because his son relentlessly pursued the truth, but he'd never seen his son put others in danger. As an adult, Gus could now see his father's perspective about protecting those that protected our freedoms. This thought process was the reason Gus had agreed to squash his story years before.

These emotions came flooding back when the officer recently asked him to continue to squash the story all these years later. Going back and forth caused a great deal on anxiety for Gus and in the end, he decided he needed to do more research. He found himself in a difficult position once more and wished at this point that some other young colleague would take over for him. Since none of the young guns had his love for the truth, it was hard to pass anything on. All the young reporters just wanted the sexy stories, the stories that would get them on TV.

Gus was a dinosaur; he knew the truth and that was all he ever wanted out of a story. Over the years, there were plenty of opportunities to advance with more sexy stories but Gus preferred chasing the obscure stories. Although this was Gus' niche, his friends kept dragging him into these high-profile cases. Gus thought the clone case was enough for anyone's career, yet the A.I. program blew everything out of the water. These stories propelled Gus to a stardom most only dreamed of but it only pissed Gus off as he wanted to be left alone to work on the next story.

He was the talk of the office these days and many of those so-called young guns noticed him following him around like a dog in heat. At first, Gus tried to help as many as he could but it ended up that all they were after was exposure, just trying to attach themselves to Gus' newly found fame. Gus quickly got tired of this returning to his lone wolf tactics. It was only when he got back to his older cases did he find the folder with the coordinates for the location that he now found himself. The folder he'd given to Jessica.

At that thought, he almost shot straight up. The soldier peered at him. "Are you okay? Can you keep going? It's only a little further. I'm sorry there are no wheelchairs on this side of the base as the infirmary is on the other side. Just a few more doorways."

Gus croaked, "No, I'm okay, just thinking of how old I am and how this is a young man's game." It was the soldier's turn to look surprised.

"Gus, are you kidding me? I read your stories all the time! No young man includes the details to the stories that you do. You always uncover more than is needed. Honestly, I think that's why we were asked to detain you, simply to keep some details from leaking out."

Gus looked perplexed. "I've squashed this story for many years in the hopes that many of your comrades wouldn't lose their lives. The fact of the matter is I'm here because I don't want to see servicemen and women mistreated. That is exactly what's going to happen with this program. If this program can continue, wars may be fought by Artificial Intelligence armies bearing our orders, but did you

.ever give credence to the fact that these soldiers have their own consciousness? Orders coming from what they may see as an inferior race would only fall on deaf ears. How long before they take over for themselves? How long before they decide the humans are no longer needed? How long before this planet is overrun with machines?"

He'd regained more strength and pushed himself unaided. Standing straight up, he turned to the soldier and poked him square in the chest. "Don't you get it? They're going to replace you! Us! How the hell does anyone not see this? I may be an old man and my time has come and gone, but I'll be damned if I don't leave this place better than I found it!" The soldier stopped dead in his tracks. "A.I., what are you talking about? Our program is a continuation of the clone program. Oh, crap! I shouldn't have said anything! Let's just get you fixed up. Come on in here!"

The soldier swiped a card on a reader on the wall and a door slid silently open to reveal a computer lab which, to Gus, resembled the same set up at the stadium. Looking around, he had a sick feeling. The place looked exactly like the labs at Marauder Stadium, right down to the same card readers. Gus felt hot and sweat beaded on his forehead. They'd put an end to the clone program and the A.I. program sat under thousands of tons of collapsed tunnels.

Gus saw a chair nearby and leaned himself into it softly. The soldier said nothing as he could see Gus could go no further. He instead left Gus in the chair and made for the other side of the room. Gus could clearly see him meeting with the officer that had come to Gus' office. He leaned down saying something in the officer's ear. The officer seemed startled and then got an upset look on his face. He quickly looked at the soldier and waved him off. The officer then turned an upset face toward Gus.

Gus, expecting the worst, braced for another blow that never came. The officer rolled over another chair and sat across from him. He looked at Gus with a red splotchy face. "Gus, this has become a real mess! I cannot get into anything in detail with you right now. I know you don't believe this but we're the good guys. As a matter of fact, we're trying to end the A.I. program. Believe me, the last thing we want is for another organism to take over the planet. The problem is many of our soldiers really don't know fully what's going on."

Gus let this wash over him for a minute. "You mean these soldiers have no idea they're about to be replaced? How could you do that to them? They have the right to fight for their own survival. They have to be told before it's too late!"

The officer stood, flourishing his arms outward. "Gus, it's not that simple! Most of them, thanks to you, just found out they are clones. They're having a hard-enough time with that little nugget without worrying about being taken over by another race of beings."

The reporter looked the officer square in the eye. "How is this possible? You're responsible for both programs? Look at this place! It's exactly like the labs at the stadium. Exactly! Exactly like the labs under the stadium! You're a liar!" Gus was furious but his energy already ebbed again and he slouched back into the chair. He looked once more at the officer, shaking his head before holding his head up with his hand. The headache was coming back with a vengeance and the nausea returning.

The officer, exasperated, looked at Gus. "I've no idea what you're talking about. Our program has always been the clone program. We've been working on this for years. I mean years! You know that? Whoever is responsible for the A.I. program must just use much of the same equipment. There is no way it's exactly like our program." He paused. "Unless it's another military program. That's it! The military is always working on multiple projects! No! They've spent too much time and effort on this program and have seen it become highly successful. No! They wouldn't risk humanity like this. Not in a million years! I refuse to believe that!"

It was the soldier's turn to look exhausted. He joined Gus and leaned back in his chair. "Gus, this isn't good. We're in a lot of trouble if this program is at the stage you profess! Let's get you patched up. I have some phone calls to make. This is crazy!" He stood and waved Gus to follow. Gus, with unsure arms, pressed himself to a standing position, taking a moment to steady himself. The officer waited for him to show he was ready. Gus took a few steps to test himself and feel his legs underneath him, following the officer across the lab.

The reporter found himself in another small room with an examination table and a desk in the corner. It looked as though they'd tried to turn it into a room for small treatments. Gus couldn't think of what small treatments lab technicians might need, but then he remembered where he was and that this was a clone lab. He recalled Dr. Chase telling him about the memory implants the clones had. At this, he panicked until a lovely young nurse came into the room with instruments to take his vitals. She was very striking and pleasant with a good demeanor. She finished quickly and then flashed a light in his eyes that made him almost pass out.

She looked at the officer worriedly. The officer just nodded and she told him to lay back for a little while; she was going to run a series of tests. She told the officer to not let him fall asleep and then left the room. Gus propped himself up. "Being concussed isn't fun. Now I know what those young men go through on the football field." He laughed as he'd seen Chris and his teammates try to decapitate one another on many occasions. He thought about his deep affection for the young man and all he'd been through. He had to deal with much in his young life.

Chapter 8

Mr. P. walked into the palatial office that once belonged to him and looked at the empty room. Finding out that he'd been a clone had been devastating to him. Even more disturbing was finding out that the real Mr. P. survived and pulled the strings of these secret programs like a puppet master. He couldn't help but feel dirty inside. The kind of feeling a person who was used by others felt inside. At that moment, he thought back to Chris and company with their only wish to return to normalcy. Normalcy, Mr. P. tried to put an image of what a normal life would look like.

In that instant, he felt a surge of energy rolling through his body. His body shook as if someone receiving a chill up their spine. He looked down at his arm only to see it covered in goose bumps. With an odd feeling he was being watched, he whipped around to see who had invaded his solitude. Surprised to see nothing but the empty room, he shook his head, trying to clear the cobwebs.

Peering around the room once more, he decided nothing was here and turned to leave. As he strode toward the elevator, another jolt of energy struck him, causing him to stop mid-stride. The pain this time caused him to put both hands on his head as if somehow this would cease the pain. This was when he noticed that some unknown force controlled him as he walked back toward the back wall. He felt himself being led as if on a leash and found himself standing in front of the secret trophy case.

Mr. P. felt his hand raise and he watched as it pressed just to the right of the key card reader. When his hand touched the polished smooth surface of the wall, it immediately lit up with a soft glow below the surface. With a small click, the trophy case opened to reveal an empty case. He wasn't surprised; after the trial, everything was confiscated. Looking at the emptiness of the case, he thought of the emptiness that was now his life. Feeling tired and worn down, his head slunk toward his chest.

He couldn't move even though he told his body to leave. His eyes still looked at the floor when he thought he heard a voice speaking to him. With all the odd things that he found happening in his life, he just chalked the voice up to his own thoughts. When he looked up once more, the trophy case was gone and in its place, was a large flat screen TV. Mr. P. blinked his eyes rapidly, trying to adjust to what he saw before him.

On the screen, larger than life peering back at him was himself. Mr. P. was once again face to face with himself. The clear high-definition image of himself sneered back at him and spoke, "Well, you idiot. It took you long enough!"

Mr. P. responded to the image, "You're dead! I know that for sure this time. Are you another clone?"

The image smiled. "No, I'm something altogether better. I now am part of the internet. One of my parting shots to those of you who thought you were so smart." Mr. P. didn't know how to respond to this taunt and looked at the screen in disbelief. The computer image laughed once more. "You were always slow to catch on! I've put what would amount to my soul, my very essence, into the computer. Everything I was except my physical body now resides in the internet. I found a way to save myself where others failed to keep me alive. They all think I'm long gone but can you imagine the look on their faces when they find out I'm alive and well?"

The confused clone stood staring at the screen. "You're not alive! You're a bunch of numbers coded together in an electric box. You call that alive?"

The image on the screen smirked. "Haven't we pushed the very boundaries of life and death? You yourself are living proof of those boundaries. The Artificial Intelligence program is another example of the blurred lines between life and death. You whine about me being dead but many have pondered through history as to what happens when we die. I'm here to tell you that the energy that was once another person is something that never goes away. We know that energy does take different forms and my energy now takes this form."

On the screen, the image now grew serious. "Now listen to me. I need you to do a few things for me. I need you to get back to running this team! This is my team and I won't let anyone take it from me!"

Now worried, the clone spoke, "How am I supposed to do that? The team was just sold to a group of investors."

The image nodded. "That's right. Where do you think a bulk of the money came from? Don't forget, I'm now part of the internet and I moved a lot of my former money back into position to buy the team once more. Now I know that you cannot run the team directly so you're going to have to run it from the shadows."

This was too much for the clone Mr. P. and he staggered forward leaning on the wall. The image on the screen continued, "Oh, knock it off, will you? I'm not asking you to do anything bad. It's my team and no one else should have this team. One of the things that I learned during this whole ordeal was that I left no legacy but that of destruction. I cannot let my team pay for my sins."

This brought a confused look from the clone Mr. P. "What do you need me to do?"

The image smiled genuinely. "Why the change of heart?"

He looked at the image. "Maybe this will be a way for both of us to make things right! We've caused so much pain that I don't know if we can change things around, but I'm willing to try."

On the screen, the image now looked concerned. "Yes, we've made a mess of things, but you're right. This is a chance to right many wrongs. I know we'll make a great many changes in lives to come."

He looked back up at the screen. "How did you get me to come here?"

The image's facial expression now possessed confidence. "Now that's something altogether spectacular! Well, compliments of Dr. Chase, you have a special chip inside your brain and I've taken it upon myself to make use of it."

The clone's face twisted with rage. "What are you talking about? Do you mean to tell me you can control me?"

On the screen, the digital Mr. P. shrugged. "If you want to look at it that way. I prefer to view it as being your coach. Let's face it, you have zero life experience and I bring a wealth of it to both of us. Together, there is nothing we cannot accomplish. Just think for a moment. We can help put the Marauders back on top where they belong!"

Mr. P. shook his head. "No! I can't believe I'm even listening to this. You're nothing but a devious master of manipulation. I won't work with you or for you ever again!"

It was the image on the screen's turn to get angry and it lit into the clone. "You ingrate! You're there only because I had the foresight to pass on what I knew, in the hopes of keeping the team in the family. Are you that selfish to not understand that I only had you made to have my will done? You also have a short memory because as I recall, you did exactly what was asked of you when you led my team into oblivion!"

Contemplating what the image asked him, he again forcefully looked at the screen. "No more! No more will I help you! No more will I be led like a dog on a leash! No more will you determine the fate of others!" Without looking at the screen, the clone Mr. P. ran over to an outlet on the other side of the room. All the while, the screen kept badgering him.

"What are you doing? Get over here! I'm not finished with you! I have many plans for you. When I'm done with you and only then, maybe I'll give you back your life."

The image couldn't exactly see what the clone was doing, but could tell that his pleading wasn't working the way he expected it to. The clone knelt, looking at the outlet as he remembered Dr. Chase once telling him about the chip in his brain. He also remembered the doctor telling him to be careful around electricity because he could fry the chip as well as his entire brain. The doctor developed this as a fail-safe in case something went wrong. He'd explained to Mr. P. that he took the chips out of most of the clones but with Mr. P., his chip was almost hardwired to his brain.

Without another thought, he reached into his pocket for his keys. As he was about to shove the key into the outlet, he felt a shooting pain in his head. The pain caused him to fall to the floor, convulsing on his side. Tears formed in his eyes and he searched once more for the outlet. Through watery eyes, he pulled himself to his knees attempting to make his way back to the outlet. The pain was unrelenting and he put his head to the floor, leaning on his elbows. He could feel himself being overwhelmed and didn't know how much longer he would last.

He bent his neck upward as snot and tears flowed. The outlet stood less than two feet from him at this moment. Mr. P. gritted his teeth to dull the pain and dug his feet into the floor. With strength he didn't know he had, he launched himself at the outlet. His outstretched arm held the key outward in the hopes of hitting its mark. With one final gasp, he reached out, putting the key into the outlet. The pain that had been in his head stopped only to be taken over by electricity running through him, causing his whole body to seize. Unable to move, he smelled something burning before everything turned black.

Chapter 9

Chris and Christopher spent the morning searching the lab where they lost April. After speaking with the coach, they decided that would be the best place to start. At first, Chris was taken in by the devastation around him. In the throes of trying to rescue April, he not only destroyed his hands but most of the lab as well. The scene was shocking. Blood sprayed on the walls along with smeared blood all over the white floor. Chris couldn't help but gulp when he saw the blood. It wasn't the blood that bothered him; it was the fact that he couldn't save April.

Deep in his thoughts, Chris didn't even feel the hand on his shoulder. Christopher stood next to him, apprising the situation. He turned to Chris. "You sure make a mess!"

Chris turned to his newly found brother. "Well, I did have a little help. Where do you think he took her?"

Christopher gave some thought to this question. "Something tells me they're still here."

At this, Chris perked up. "Christopher, you might be on to something there. We certainly know that this place has an entire city beneath us. Who knows how big this place actually is! We also know the good old doctor has been holding out on us and working in the shadows.

"We have to get in touch with Gus and have him really dig to find out how far this whole bunker/city goes underneath us. What I couldn't understand was that Dr. Chase seemed to genuinely love April. Why would he do this to her? They both finally had found the family they so

55

desperately sought. April was in her glory. I've never seen someone so fulfilled as when she spent time with her father. Christopher, I could see the betrayal in her eyes as she went under that floor."

Christopher searched his twin's eyes. "Chris, I hear you loud and clear! Something else must be going on here but what? You're right; the two of them were like peas in a pod. There is something we're missing. What we have to do is figure out how to get below where we are right now." Chris nodded and looked to the floor where April went down in the tube. This issue remained that in his rage, Chris had destroyed all the computers in the room. He sat trying to figure out how else he could open the tube and get below to follow the doctor.

He kept running his fingers over the seam in the floor where the tube had been, hoping to touch some magic latch to open the tube. Christopher searched the lab for anything that might give them a clue as to how to find their friend. He picked up one of the monitors that still sat on the floor and to his surprise, it was still on. He set the monitor on one of the tables that still stood and looked at the image. The picture was grainy and dark, but he could make out what looked to be another lab. This lab looked to be quite large and he could see dark images moving around.

Christopher watched the images on the screen and almost jumped out of his skin as Chris came up next to him. Chris nudged him. "Dude, what did you find?" He looked at the screen and squinted to see the small dark figures. One figure came across the screen, bringing a quick response from Chris. "That is Dr. Chase right there! I know that's him! What the hell is he doing? Wait till I get my hands on him!" The two young men continued to watch the screen, hoping for more insight into what the doctor might be up to. Then one image made them both perk up straight. They looked at one another and Chris remarked, "That certainly looks like some kind of military person. Look at how he's standing, talking to the doctor. That is no enlisted person; he definitely has the air of someone important."

Christopher responded, "We just have to find out where that is and how to get there. Chris, this is crazy. Just when you think you have a grasp on things, everything gets turned upside down."

Chris punched his twin playfully in the shoulder. "Don't worry, man. I'm right here with you. We'll figure it out together and get her back. I can't wait to see the look on the doctor's face when we come storming through the door. I guarantee his face won't be so smug this time, as I'm pounding him into oblivion. He has a lot to pay for and I plan on collecting the bill!"

Christopher smiled. "Something tells me that he's going to have to contend with both of us!" The two behemoths turned and high-fived each other.

The two men stood looking at one another, trying to decide their next move when Chris' phone rang. They just looked at each other for a moment and then Chris scrambled to get the phone from his pocket. He answered it quickly and listened intently to the person on the other end. He said little but kept nodding and looking at Christopher with a smile on his face. Christopher wanted to interrupt but kept quiet until Chris hung up the phone. He looked at Chris with impatient eyes and then finally spewed out, "Tell me! What's going on?"

Chris eyed his double quickly. "That was Agent Bradley. He and Jessica are on their way to pick us up. They may have found something. Let's get out of here. We must meet them in the player's lot in fifteen minutes and I want to stop by the kitchen and grab a quick bite to eat. I'm starving and I don't know when we'll eat again." Christopher said not a word, but fell into place next to him as they both headed out the door.

Chapter 10

Steve almost laughed as he looked down at his restraints, thinking of how many times he'd placed others in the same predicament. His eyes naturally scanned the room to work out an escape plan. Whoever it was that restrained him chose not to secure his head. This was a great relief to Steve as it allowed him to look freely at his current prison. To Steve, the room looked like any doctor's office with its white walls and sterile environment. Steve thought back to when he'd placed Chris in a chair exactly like this one at the behest of Dr. Chase. Chris' only crime was that he woke up in the middle of the slumber portion of the clone program.

As a man of honor, Steve couldn't help but think about some of the many things he did in the past that would be considered not honorable. The prospect of losing integrity made him upset and ultimately, it made his decision to work with Chris and company to right the wrongs done to them. Thinking of his friends at this moment brought a pang of regret to his stomach. He especially missed Jessica and felt the anger boil up within his huge frame. If anything happened to Jessica, he would destroy them with his bare hands.

He imagined Jessica's soft face with her stunning eyes. Her eyes could reach into a man's soul and see his worth. Steve still couldn't understand how Jessica would even give him the time of day. He could recall the first time he saw her in her power suit preparing to take on Mr. P. in the clone case. His heart skipped several beats looking at this amazing beauty before him. He'd dated a few very pretty women in his time but Jessica seemed miles out of his league. As he got to know her and found out how down to earth she was outside the courtroom, he became immediately smitten.

Steve looked down once more at his hands, flexing them, testing if he could work his way out. He had to get back to Jessica. His heart ached for all he was worth at the prospect of spending any more away time from the love of his life. Again, his mind was brought back to Chris and his fight to keep his career as well as the love of his life. Steve thought back to his military days and how he could have used a good man like Chris. Early on in their relationship, they'd been on opposite sides and squared off many times. Steve slyly smiled as he thought about how much of a worthy adversary Chris proved to be. As far as he could recall, Chris was the only opponent that had bested him in combat. Sure, Chris told Steve it was because Christopher backed him up but Steve knew better.

The door opening brought him back to reality. Steve's veins popped out all over his neck with the strain from him yanking the restraints as he saw the person stroll into the room. Steve's eyes followed the man with surgical precision as he strode to within a foot of Steve. The man's face revealed a smug grin as he appraised Steve's current situation. Steve could feel his blood boiling as he beheld the sheer arrogance that stood before him. Despite the tension, neither man was willing to speak.

The man finally broke the silence. "Well, this is an interesting turn of events! There was a time not that long ago that you would be the one taunting a prisoner." Steve stood fast and it took all his military bearing not to come back with an offhand remark. The man laughed aloud. "Tell me, Steve, how does it feel to be in that chair in which you've placed so many times over the years? I doubt it's comfortable, but you should not have to be there too long if you're a good boy."

This was too much for Steve and he rasped, "What is it you want? Out with it or do you plan to bore me to death?"

At this, the figure before him just shook his head and sat down on the chair next to the examination table. He looked straight into the big man's eyes. "I wouldn't be so quick to dismiss me. I've some news for you that you may not want to hear." Steve didn't take the bait and maintained his silence. The figure reached out and patted Steve's arm. "Did you know that you're dead?" This brought an eyebrow raise from Steve. This pleased the man. "I see you're interested. Yes, you're dead, at least that's what all your friends think. Trust me, I was there. It didn't look promising and when they finally cleared enough debris to get to you, all they found was blood."

Steve hadn't thought about any of this as he'd been so worried about Jessica. Again, the thought of Jessica brought more panic to an already dismal situation. He glared at his captor and spoke, "If I'm already dead, then I'm no use to you. So why am I here?"

This statement took the man by surprise. "You're here, Steve, for my pleasure. I watched for years as you tortured prisoners and football players alike. No, Steve, this is purely for my entertainment. I want you to squirm for a while and then we'll see what else I can do with you."

Steve was now in a full rage. "You truly are a scumbag! I've known it for years but you fooled everyone, didn't you? Even your daughter." The person in the chair quickly lifted his hand and punched Steve square in the face, snapping his head back. Steve brought his head back to its normal position and spat the blood out of his mouth that he could feel building. He then responded, "Well, that's something I never expected from you. You're always so willing to let others do your dirty work. Wow, getting your hands dirty, now that's impressive."

The man stood up quickly, causing the chair to fall back on the floor and hastily spun back toward Steve, threatening to strike him again. The blow never fell as the man composed himself. "None of you idiots have any idea what I've done for my daughter! You have no clue what kind of danger she's now in because of Chris and his little temper tantrum. There are a lot of evil forces at work here and she's in now in mortal danger thanks to you! I've had to take matters into my own hands to ensure her safety. Mark my words, Steve. I'd do anything for her as you would for Jessica."

At the mention of Jessica's name, Steve once again felt rage rise in him and again he railed against his restraints. To his surprise, one of the leather straps that held the restraint in place snapped. He felt a rise of hope and reached over and yanked at the other restraint, snapping it off the exam table. The figure looked at Steve panicked, and scanned the room frantically for something. Steve was one step ahead of him; he'd noticed the needle on the table next to him some time ago. With both arms now free, he easily leaned over and grabbed the needle, waving his captor to come closer.

He barked, "One thing you should never do is underestimate your prisoner. Something I learned from Chris. That guy turned out to be quite the pain in the butt for both of us but he certainly grows on you."

He then reached down, keeping his eyes on the frightened man the whole time. The man that was the captor now was paralyzed with fear as he watched Steve undo the foot restraints. When Steve stood to face his captor, he dwarfed the small feeble man. The man then spun to reach for the door, but Steve lunged for him first and caught the man in the shoulders. Both men went sprawling on the floor with Steve bouncing up quickly and, with cat-like reflexes, spun his leg around, connecting with the man's face. The look on the man's face when Steve's huge foot struck his face was priceless. People always underestimated how quick and nimble he was to their own detriment.

Steve reached down and pulled the man up by the scruff of his neck, raising him off the floor until he was face to face with Steve. The man squirmed but Steve held fast and the man had no chance of escape. He felt himself thrown through the air onto the exam table. The force with which he struck the metal table was shocking. The helpless man slumped in pain on the table waiting for the inevitable punishment to begin. Steve had other ideas and glared at the man.

"You're going to get me out of here!" He walked over and yanked the small man up once more, pushing him toward the door. As a precaution, he held the needle close to the man's throat.

He whispered in his ear, "One wrong move and this goes right into your jugular. Got it?" The frightened man said nothing, which told Steve all he needed to know about what was in the needle. He pushed the man in the back at the door. "Open it and no funny business!" The man with shaking hands reached in the front pocket of his lab coat, retrieving a card key. He proceeded to open the door and they moved into the hallway.

Steve was very surprised to see the corridor empty and asked, "All right, get me out of here, will you?" The man just walked cautiously toward the end of the hallway. They quickly approached an elevator and the man swiped his card once more, revealing a plain inner elevator. They both moved into the elevator and still the little man said nothing. When the door opened, Steve pushed them both forward out into another hallway. He was glad to see a shorter hallway with a doorway at the end with a window in it. His heart rose as he saw the sunlight peering through that door and pushed his captive toward the luminous light. Steve stopped quickly at the door, spinning around to make sure they'd not been followed. The hallway remained empty and he grabbed the man roughly once more, bringing him within inches of his face.

He growled, "Dr. Chase, this is where we part company. If I ever see you again, I'll kill you!" With that, he struck the feeble doctor in the head and dropped him like a sack. He opened the door and rushed into the sunlit unknown.

Chapter 11

The colonel sat listening to his superiors on the conference call with an exasperated look on his face. He couldn't understand what they were talking about regarding the Artificial Intelligence Program he was investigating. According to the people most in the know, the ones currently on the phone, the A.I. program was still in its infancy. His puzzled look turned to one of anger as he didn't like being taken advantage of. He clearly felt that he wasn't being told everything when it came to this program.

The most confusing part for him though turned out to be that he'd worked with the people on the phone for many years. In most cases, he considered these people his friends and wouldn't expect them to lie to him. For the military officer, this only meant one of two things—one that the A.I. program was a black-government program which they weren't privy to, or that it was a completely independent program. He thought for a moment about each prospect and each to him wasn't a very comforting situation.

He shook his head and dismissed the clandestine government program, leaving the only other alternative, an independent contractor. The colonel had worked with uncountable numbers of scientists over the years and searched his memory banks to think of any capable such a program. Pondering the list in his head, he kept coming back to two names, Dr. Emile Schwartz and Dr. Henry Chase. He walked over to the computer on the table and leaned over, banging quickly on the keys.

What stared back at him on the screen before him was surprising. He almost laughed at the screen but then turned back toward the phone on the table. It almost seemed as if the voices droning on about the current clone program and the government's involvement in this program mattered at that moment. The colonel sat back down and rubbed his eyes to make sure he'd viewed the screen properly. He even proceeded to punch in the search again, only to come up with the same results. Head in hands, he looked down at the surface of the stainless-steel table in disbelief. The name staring back at the screen was highly disturbing.

Without hesitation, he strode over to the large phone sitting in the middle of the small round table off to his right. The officer reached forward, pressing a button, and announced into the speaker, "Ladies and Gentlemen, please excuse this interruption but new information has just come to my attention! We need to discuss this matter quickly and I understand this is a secure line but this may need a face-to-face meeting. I believe I've discovered the head of this independent Artificial Intelligence program."

On the other end, the voices all came over the phone as one with different versions of, "Are you certain? Who is it?"

The colonel composed himself and responded, "I really feel that at this time we should meet in a more neutral location before I reveal my information. If I let this information over this channel, I feel it will be compromised." His listeners took a moment to digest this information and then one by one, they agreed to meet two days hence at secure location Alpha. The colonel knew exactly what that meant and said that he would be there and looked forward to sharing what he'd discovered.

After hanging up the phone, he plopped back down on the chair and immediately cancelled out of what was on the computer. To cover his tracks, he deleted his entire search history and the backup history. The last thing he wanted now was the wrong person coming across this accidentally or otherwise. Nervously, he even went so far as to wipe down everything and gave serious thought about going to the security office to erase the footage of the room.

Feeling more secure, he decided to leave the facility immediately and as quietly as possible. He walked briskly to the door, waving his security card and whisking out into the lengthy hallway. With each step, he felt his pace quicken and reached his office with little fanfare. Scanning the room, he found the file he was looking for and grabbed it on his way out. Armed with the information he needed, he turned to exit the building.

Halfway down the hall, he experienced an uncomfortable feeling and leaned his head slightly forward looking backwards. He noticed someone behind him. As he lifted his head once more he slammed into the chest of a huge Military Police Officer. Rubbing his nose, he proceeded to look up into the eyes of one of the biggest men he'd ever seen. The MP took him by the arm roughly and escorted him back down the hallway. He resisted, saying, "What the hell do you think you're doing? I'm a colonel! You get your meat hooks off me right now!" His pleas fell on deaf ears and the man clamped down on his arm even harder, as if a vice were gripping his arm.

At this point, the MP was practically picking him up as he forced him down the hall. They came to another office and the man shoved him inside, standing guard outside. Once inside, he rubbed his arm furiously to put blood back into it and stood before a man at a desk. The man didn't look up from what he was reading, but spoke to the officer, "So Colonel, I hope you're having a productive day. You couldn't leave well enough alone, could you? You just had to dig. Being too smart for your own good has become your downfall."

The colonel looked at the small man in the lab coat sitting before him and almost launched himself across the desk. "You have got a hell of a nerve to speak to me and treat me this way! I'm your superior! I demand to know by what right you think you can handle me in this way!"

The man at the desk finally raised his head, looking square into the colonel's eyes. "That, Colonel, is an interesting concept, you being my superior. No, I believe it to be the other way around. Now sit down and shut up! You're not going anywhere and I'm certainly not letting you out of my sight with your newly acquired information."

The colonel decided to play along. "Okay and just what is it that you think I know and why is it so important to you?"

This brought a cackle from the seated man. "Oh Colonel, you must think me quite incompetent if you don't think I know everything that happens in this facility. I've been a part of all your conference calls."

A panicked look came across the officer's face. "So you heard that I'm going to look for Dr. Schwartz. So what, what does that have to do with you?"

The man behind the desk now rose and placed both hands on the desk, leaning forward. "Colonel, Dr. Schwartz is dead. You know that."

The officer, with face twisted, responded, "What are you talking about? If you know what I was researching, then you know I've found out that Dr. Schwartz is the head of the independent Artificial Intelligence program. I must put a stop to that program. If that program is allowed to continue, all our very lives are in danger. Why would you stop me when I know you want that to happen as well?"

The man in the lab coat nodded. "Yes, sir. You are right about that. I want to put an end to the A.I. program but you're incorrect about one thing. Dr. Schwartz isn't the head of the program. I can assure you he's dead." The colonel now had a dumbfounded look on his face. The man behind the desk continued, "You haven't figured it out yet, have you? Who the head of the program is. Well, I'll tell you. It's the man standing before you."

Once again, the officer shook his head and said, "You! Are you insane? I know you're the expert on cloning but what would you ever get involved with an A.I. program for?"

Flipping his lab coat around, the man moved from behind the desk to stand in front of the colonel. He looked at the colonel. "That, sir, I cannot tell you. I'll say this though. It is to protect everyone. I'd love to explain it to you, but right now I must prepare for a massive confrontation with my future son-in-law. Goodbye, Colonel. Thank you for your service!" With that, the colonel felt a pinch in the back of his neck and immediately a warming sensation coursed into his neck. Within a few seconds, everything went black.

Chapter 12

The occupants of the car maintained their silent vigil as they neared the coordinates on the GPS. Each person scanned the area, searching for recognizable landmarks of which they found none. This lack of familiarity made each rider very anxious, causing a mounting tension inside the vehicle. Agent Bradley broke the silence, "From what I can see on my phone, it looks as though we're very close. According to this, we're three minutes away from our destination."

Jessica turned to the federal agent. "John, we've no idea what we're walking into. Just look around here. There is nothing for miles."

As if appearing just over the horizon, they all made out their target. Driving ever closer to uncertainty, they all squinted to get a better look ahead of their position. Agent Bradley slowed the car slightly. "This isn't what I expected at all. That looks like another military base. Jessica, I think you're right. We would have been better served coming at night. Right now, we're sitting ducks. There is no chance they haven't seen us coming."

At this comment, Chris shot forward, "John, should we back off for now and regroup to figure out our strategy?"

Agent Bradley peered into the rearview mirror at his good friend with concern in his eyes. "Chris, you may be right. A frontal assault in the middle of the day on a military base by four civilians isn't what I call a sound strategy. The only reason right now I'd even consider such insanity is because we've no idea what they may be doing to Gus. That is if Gus is still alive."

Jessica chimed in, "I've no doubt seeing this place that this is where Gus is and it's up to us to get him back."

Christopher reached over the backseat and gently touched her shoulder. "Jessica, there is no way we're going to leave him in there, but John is correct. What chance do the four of us stand in the daylight? We definitely don't have the element of surprise."

Jessica's face saddened. "Guys, we have to do something. We can't just leave him to his fate."

Agent Bradley interjected, "All right, listen. I have an idea but we need to get out of here right now." He quickly spun the wheel, squealing the tires and spraying dirt in the air as the car skidded sideways, almost ending up on two tires. They swerved back onto the road as Agent Bradley fought the wheel to straighten the car out. With the car solidly back on the road and heading away from the base once again, everyone became silent, waiting for the agent to share his plan.

The federal agent looked back at his friends. "We're going to need some help for this one and we're going to call in some reinforcements."

Chris spurted out, "Reinforcements! John, look at us; our group has continued to get smaller, not larger. Who do you plan to get us to help with such a mission?"

Agent Bradley laughed. "Chris, you just answered your own question, my friend. You're exactly right; this is a mission and what we need is a military presence." At this, there was a collective gasp by the parties in the speeding car.

Jessica spoke first, "John, how do you propose to do that? Did you not just see that we're once again coming from a military installation? Our luck with the military hasn't been the best, if you haven't noticed."

Agent Bradley just spoke over his shoulder, "Jessica, to pull this off, we're going to need trained personnel. Chris and Christopher are terrific in a battle. You have proven able to handle yourself and I'm handy in a fight, but this is altogether different. Like I said, I have an idea. On our way up here, I saw what looked to be an abandoned barn. I'm going to make for that point and we'll use that as our base of operations. If memory serves me correctly, it was about five miles away. When we get there, I'm going to contact a friend of mine. He should be able to help us."

Chris grabbed the agent's shoulder. "John, you're not going to get the FBI involved, are you? With all due respect, another federal agency isn't going to assist us and most likely is partnered up with whatever is going on at that base."

The agent contemplated this statement. "Chris, I understand your concern but what I have in mind is going to blow your mind. I just can't explain it right now. We have company!" The passengers could feel the car surge forward as the agent pressed the gas further toward the floor. They immediately searched the area around them to look for their pursuers with no luck.

Jessica spoke, "John, what are you talking about? There is no one for miles."

As the agent was about to respond, they felt the car being struck viciously from above. They all looked to the ceiling of the vehicle, only to see it had caved in slightly. Again, they felt the car shudder as something struck them from above. This time Agent Bradley stopped the car, swiftly skidding off to one side of the road. This allowed the passengers a full view of the helicopter as it sped by their vehicle. It was a small helicopter dressed out in all camouflage with fumes pouring out the back of the engine as it shot back up into the air.

The federal agent once again gunned the gas and the car shot off in a forward direction. Jessica and company, with windows open, scanned the sky to give Agent Bradley updates on the location of the helicopter. They could clearly make out the aircraft as it turned back toward them and made a downward run straight at them. The agent kept the car firmly planted on the road, in great concentration on the road ahead of him.

Jessica screamed, "John, they're coming straight for us!"

The agent responded, "Good! Let's see how these idiots are at chicken!"

Chris spoke, "Ah John, are you nuts? Playing chicken on bicycles is one thing; this is an aircraft."

The car sped down the road toward its target. Agent Bradley didn't slow down but rather increased his speed. As the helicopter came closer to the car, they could clearly see two military personnel. One pilot and one navigator manning the helicopter. It was difficult to see their expressions through their goggles and helmets. Both vehicles were now on a direct collision course and no one seemed ready to back off. The passengers of the car put their arms straight out, bracing for impact, and closed their eyes.

Impact didn't come as the helicopter broke to the right at the last minute, avoiding the car. Agent Bradley refused to stop and continued down the road at full speed.

Jessica called out, "John, what do we do now?"

He responded, "There is no way they're going to risk a million-dollar piece of equipment or themselves for that matter. They're trying to scare us and get us to stop; that way their buddies can pick us up."

As he finished his statement, the ground to their right exploded into a cloud of rock and dust spewing into the air. The concussion could be felt in the car and the agent spoke, "Now that's interesting."

Christopher, who hadn't said much the entire time, chimed in, "John, what's so interesting about having rockets shot at us?"

The agent looked back. "Christopher, trust me. If they wanted to take us out, we would already be dust. No, these idiots are just having fun."

Jessica squeaked, "This isn't fun, John."

Again, they saw the helicopter come screaming overhead, just missing them. They all looked up to see the aircraft take a sharp turn back toward them. Agent Bradley kept his eyes on the road ahead of him, unfazed by the excitement. They couldn't see the helicopter now and waited for the next missile to strike. The strike never came as they could no longer even hear the helicopter.

Chris shouted, "Did they go back to the base?"

Their car turned a slow curve only to have Chris' question answered in front of them. Directly in front of them on the road itself stood the helicopter, blocking their exit. Agent Bradley quickly looked to both sides of the road, but soon felt panic as both sides went up into hills too steep for him to veer around the helicopter.

Jessica screamed, "John, we can't get by them!"

Agent Bradley shouted back, "I'm tired of these guys! Watch this!" He immediately spun the wheel sharply to one side and brought the car to a sideways position within fifty yards of the whirling blades. Agent Bradley skidded the car to a halt and in one motion, whipped out his sidearm straight out his window, aiming directly at the helicopter. The stunned passengers watched as Agent Bradley, with both hands firmly holding his weapon, squeezed off several rounds at the helicopter. The agent's aim was true and the windshield of the helicopter easily shown off a few fresh bullet holes. They could see the pilot shouting something to his navigator. The federal agent shot at the helicopter as it made its way slowly off the ground.

Smoke could be seen coming out of the side of the engine as the agent reloaded his weapon. He fired once more, clearly aiming for the engine and again the aircraft sustained damage to its most important component. Black smoke now billowed out of the side of the helicopter as it raised into the air. Agent Bradley was now out of the car and fired at the wounded aircraft. The passengers watched as the agent fired upon the helicopter, not knowing what to do. They could see now the engine was a mixture of smoke and flames shooting out into the air.

As they all watched the agent fire once more, they felt a huge concussion as the helicopter blew into a million pieces. Out of instinct, they all covered their eyes. They could hear pieces of the helicopter hitting the ground nearby.

Shocked, they all scrambled out of the car, running to Agent Bradley. He spun toward them and waved them back.

"Get back in the car, you fools. There will be more and I'm out of bullets!" He sped past them and jumped back into the car. They all followed suit and ran back to the car.

With the car speeding once more in the opposite direction, the agent could feel a hand on his arm. He peered at Jessica as she spoke, "John, should we go see if anyone survived?"

He turned and gave her a look of pity. "Jessica, I'm sorry but with an explosion like that and with those small pieces crashing to the ground like that, there is little chance anyone survived. I'd have preferred they'd just given up but they just kept coming. Their mistake was putting that bird on the ground." They all gave him a questioning look. He peered at them. "Their advantage had always been in the air. There is a reason tactically armies always search for high ground but what they did was give up their advantage. Once on the ground, their maneuverability no longer was to their advantage but ours. They were sitting ducks. I'm not sure they expected return fire. I feel terrible that it had to happen this way, but it was them or us. We must get off this road soon because they'll be back in full force next time. The good news is that we're very close to that barn I was telling you about."

The inside of the car returned to silence as the only sound that could be heard was the agent's labored breathing from his running back to the car. As his breathing became more regular, the shock of the events they just witnessed became less harsh. They all looked forward to getting to the barn to regroup and hear the agent's plan to get them out of this predicament. He turned the car onto a small dirt road and headed straight for the barn rising before them. He didn't even stop to check the area but rather pulled the car directly into the barn.

He jumped out of the car and told them all to follow him. They watched as he grabbed a branch from the ground and made for the road. He instructed them to follow him. The agent told them all to brush away their tracks all the way to the main road. Without another sound, they all rushed to grab their own branch and cover their tracks. When they were satisfied that no one would see their tracks, they rushed back into the barn.

Agent Bradley was a little nervous about all the dust he could see going into the air from their brushing away the tracks. He hoped the pursuers would be focused on the wreck of the helicopter and not them. The members of the group sat with their arms wrapped around their legs, thinking of what just transpired. Each member was covered with the brown dust from the dirt road. The agent opened the trunk and pulled out water bottles for each person. They all gladly guzzled it down.

Feeling more refreshed and calm, Jessica once again spoke, "All right, John, you got us here. I don't know how but you did it. Now what? What's your plan?" The two twins stood up looking at the agent and nodded.

The agent stood and paced for a moment before turning toward his friends. He gathered himself. "Well, the answer to that's simple." He smiled and continued, "We call in the cavalry!" Everyone looked at him as if he were insane. He went on, "Trust me. I've been working on this for months and have been waiting for this moment. We're about to put an end to this whole thing once and for all. When I'm done with these guys, all the head honchos will be doing life in prison."

They all gawked at him, waiting for details of his plan but remained disappointed as the agent went to the wall of the barn. He peered outside, scoping out the surrounding area. When he was satisfied, he took out his phone and placed a call. No one could tell to whom the agent was speaking, but the conversation was quick and he hung up just as quick. Everyone just stared at him, waiting for him to speak. He looked at his friends. "What?"

Chris punched him in the shoulder. "Out with it! What's going on?" The massive man threatened to put the man in a head lock.

Agent Bradley just ducked under the attempt and stood his ground. "Listen, guys, you have to trust me! I don't want to tell you too much right now because I'm afraid if I do, you will all want to kill me." He shrugged his shoulders. "Just let me take care of this and then I'll explain later, okay?"

Christopher moved toward the agent with an angry look on his face. "John, we've been in the dark too much during this whole ordeal. We have a right to anything at this point."

The agent looked as if he may break, but then straightened as if he heard something. The agent raced to the wall once more, looking through the crack in the wall. He called back to them, "They're looking for us. I see two choppers circling the area. I can also still see the billowing smoke in the distance from the wreck. Hopefully, that will keep them busy and give my friends some time to get here." He continued to look out the hole. "All I can see is the choppers but we'll have to set a watch in case we have to move. You guys rest. I'll take first watch."

No one argued with the agent's suggestion and each found a comfortable piece of dirt to rest. Chris, not knowing what to do or say, just sat staring at the wall. He felt lost without April near him and more than once, instinctively reached for her over the last few minutes, only to grab air. As he leaned his head back to picture April's beautiful captivating eyes, he caught sight of Jessica. She was such a beautiful woman and Chris' heart hurt to know her loss of Steve weighed on her.

Jessica sat with her head forward and arms wrapped around her legs. She stretched her arms up and Chris could clearly see tears streaming down her cheeks. He was about to bounce up and comfort her when he saw Christopher move over to her. Christopher sat next to her and said a few short soft words. She gave way and laid her head in his lap. He took her hand in his and just held fast to it. Chris couldn't move as he watched these two friends cling to one another in support. Christopher always had a connection to Jessica and the two were great friends. Seeing the two comfort one another made Chris' heart soar, but at the same time yearn more for April. He once more leaned his head against the wall, looking up at the crumbling ceiling. He wondered where April was at this moment. He thought about what he would do to the doctor next time he saw him.

Catching sight of the insects flying and swirling around the ceiling, he became mesmerized by their freedom. He wished so much to be free once more. The freedom he so cherished was constantly being tested and taken away from him. He could feel his eyelids growing heavy as he watched the flight of these free creatures. Once again, April's face came into his thoughts as he could feel himself drifting off in the stale warm air of the empty barn. His last thoughts were of April once again in his arms.

Chapter 13

Steve wiped his brow of the sweat that beaded on his forehead. The sun was high in the afternoon sky and beat down on him with unforgiving rays. He glanced down at his sleeve and saw the wetness sticking to his arm. A bead of sweat worked its way down into his left eye, causing him to blink. The security officer needed to find shelter as he felt too exposed. He couldn't remember his last drink and he knew he would have to rest soon. After his encounter at the lab and subsequent escape, Steve made his way swiftly into the wilderness. He was reminded of his many military operations having endured lack of water much too often for his liking.

For the first time since he decided to make for the hills, he was now seeing vegetation. He hoped this would bring some of the precious water his body so craved at this moment. Steve walked toward the line of trees that he could now see and noticed a sound in the distance. Not wanting to be seen, he quickly made his way to the cover of the trees. Once under the trees, he noticed quite a change in temperature and sat under a large tree to recover his strength.

In the shade of the tree, his body temperature came back down to a more comfortable level. This made him think more of the lack of water and he smacked his parched lips. He ran his tongue over the dry cracking skin, tasting the blood from the newly developed cracks. As he sat with his back against the tree, he once again heard a sound coming from the air. The sound now much closer, Steve listened intently. He crept to the edge of the shadow of the tree, looking up into the sky. As the helicopter made its way overhead, Steve scrambled once more under the cover of the tree.

He leaned back against the tree once more, wondering if the aircraft was searching for him. The security officer brushed that off quickly, pronouncing himself not important enough to require this type of search. This did however intrigue him as to who would be important enough that someone would send a helicopter after them in this isolated area. He listened as the helicopter made several more passes over the general area. He noticed that each time the craft made its way further from Steve's position.

It was at this time that he noticed the small sound of water trickling nearby. He thought he was hearing things, but sure enough as he walked closer to the sound, he could see a small brook running along the tree line. Nearly diving on the bank, he thrusted his face into the icy water. The coolness immediately made him feel better. He lifted his head out of the water to stop for a moment. Unsure if the water was safe to drink, he looked cautiously at the water. To Steve, the water looked crystal clear with no mud in it. He decided that it was worth the risk and once again pushed his head in the water, opening his mouth wide to let it flow in unencumbered.

With his thirst finally quenched, he rose back to his feet only to feel the water slushing in his stomach. He smiled as he thought how all he needed right now was a good burger. Feeling more energetic now, he chose to make it to high ground so he could see the lay of the land. The terrain of trees gave way to a more rocky and slippery steep passage. When finally at the top of the hill, he scanned the wide area before him. At first, his eyes only noticed a wide-open expanse with little to catch his eyes, but then off to his right, he caught sight of a small dust cloud rising. He kept his eyes peeled on the area to see any little detail that might appear. The dust cloud split in half as a helicopter came spurting through the dust, shooting back into the air.

Steve was intrigued as the bird rose higher in the sky and cut sharply, turning around to face its target. He clearly could see the vapor left in the air as the helicopter released a missile. As the missile worked its way downward, Steve couldn't take his eyes off the deadly instrument of war. The missile struck the ground, exploding in a cloud of rock and dust shooting high in the air. For the first time, Steve noticed the target. A small vehicle swerved to avoid being struck.

As the helicopter worked its way back toward the vehicle, Steve thought the car was in dire peril. The pilot brought the helicopter once more in line with the car, preparing for attack. After one more run by the car, the pilot must have chosen a different tactic as he rose in the air in the other direction. Steve watched as the helicopter landed directly on the road. He couldn't help but think what a mistake this was tactically.

He thought of how he would have handled the piloting of the craft when he noticed the car speeding straight toward the helicopter. Steve was riveted as if he were watching the ultimate action movie and couldn't take his eyes away from the scene. The car swerved sharply within fifty feet of the aircraft and Steve could see flashes of light coming from the car. He watched with growing interest as the helicopter began to smoke. Aware of the meaning of smoke, he thought once again of the mistake of landing the craft. To Steve, the hunter was now the hunted.

After several more flashes, now he could hear the pop of gunfire. He watched as the engine of the helicopter caught fire. The pilot then made a deadly mistake and chose to take the bird back into the air. Steve saw a passenger from the car scramble out with his arms raised toward the aircraft. Once again, the pop of gunfire rang in the air as the man emptied his clip into the rising helicopter. Just as the craft came out of gun range, it exploded into a fire ball of glowing metal and parts flying into the air.

The remaining shell of the helicopter was now engulfed in flames and Steve watched the fireball crash into the ground with terrific impact. He couldn't help but feel for the crew of the craft as he'd seen these scenes many times in his own military career. The wreckage still spewing smoke and fire, he knew the fate of the crew was nothing short of disaster. He once again turned to see the car speeding away of into the distance. Steve gave a quick thought to going to assist the crew of the craft, but looking at the fire raging, he gave up on this quickly. Realizing he could be spotted from his spot on the hill, he moved quickly back down. Once at the bottom, he struggled with which direction he should travel. While he was on top of the hill, he was sure he saw some type of building off in the distance. Since it was in the same direction the car just traveled, Steve easily made up his mind to follow the lead of the vehicle and travel this way. Feeling confident about his decision, he threw himself down at the edge of the brook. He shoved his face into the brook, drinking his fill of the chilled water. Refreshed once more, he rose to his feet. Regaining his bearings, he moved off in the direction the car traveled.

Several hours later, Steve noticed the terrain begin to change from a rocky dusty landscape to one of a more hospitable terrain. The dust gave way to thick grasses and trees rather than bushes. Being smart enough to follow the road, travelling had been slow but constant with little to slow his trek beside his own exhaustion. It was at this time that he saw to his left the building he hoped to find an hour ago. From his vantage point on the hill, it was very difficult to tell what type of building it was but the dilapidated barn was a welcome sight.

He was about to walk to the barn when voices broke the air. Steve quickly darted behind a tree, trying to listen intently to what was being said. He could make out a few voices, but the gist of the conversation was difficult to gather from this distance. Steve saw a small shed at the corner of the barn and stealthily wormed his way to the shed. The door was latched with a small lever and he lifted it softly, opening the door. Inside the shed were different tools of all makes and styles. Steve viewed many of these as weapons if needed and slid into the shed, closing the door fast behind him.

Listening with his head against the back wall of the shed, he could more clearly make out the conversation taking place inside the barn. He shot straight up when he heard the woman's voice ring out and almost fell over. Slipping slightly, he broke his fall with his arms out. He pushed into a pile of rakes leaning against the wall of the shed. The pile fell over, crashing into a large metal tool box on the floor. The racket caused by the noise of the falling tools gave away his position and he cringed at his carelessness.

Regaining his balance, he ran to the door to exit the shed quickly to escape without any further distractions. He grabbed at the door, yanking it open, hoping to run back into the trees before anyone spotted him. As he stepped out of the shed, back into the fading sunlight, he was met with a wooden beam across the knees. He heard the crack of wood and felt the piece of wood snap on his shins. A sharp pain in both legs caused him to lose his balance and fall forward, crashing to the ground. Steve threw his arms out to break his fall but went skidding face first into gravely mix of grass and rock. His hands took the brunt of the damage, but he managed to get back to his feet quickly to face his attacker.

With a combination of dirt and grass in his mouth, which he spat into the air promptly, he stalked his attacker. He brought himself to his full height and expected to dwarf his opponent, but instead he came face to face with a seething man equal in his dimensions to Steve. The two men viewed each other for a moment, not ready to make the next move. Steve knew he must look a disaster after his ordeal and could excuse the man before him for his lack of recognition.

The man across from him raised what was left of the beam to strike again when Steve shouted at the man. "Chris, stop! It's me, man! It's Steve!" In that instant, he thought the man would still swing the wooden beam his way but at the last instant, he tossed the piece of wood to the ground. He stared at Steve, trying to decide if this man before him was indeed his long-lost friend.

As he felt himself begin to relax, he saw Chris jump at him with his hands up, yelling, "No, Christopher! No, it's Steve!" The plea came too late as the security officer felt something strike the back of his head. The last thing he could recall before blackness was seeing a woman running in his direction.

Chapter 14

Dr. Chase came to as he felt himself being lifted off the floor. He shook his head trying to clear his blurry vision. At first, his legs felt like lead and were very unsteady, causing him to nearly fall back to the ground. The doctor heard a voice telling him he was okay, but had sustained quite the hit to the head. With assistance, he stood to full height and took in his surroundings, hoping for an explanation to events surrounding his time on the floor. His head still fuzzy, he leaned heavily on the person assisting him and turned to see his attendant. He took in the military attire and thought back to what transpired with Steve.

A wave of recognition flew through his mind as the events leading up to this flooded back to him. In a panicked moment, he almost fell out of his attendant's arms. He turned quickly to the soldier. "Steve has escaped! We must send someone to track him down. I can't have him running around. He could ruin everything! They all think he's dead. If they find out he's alive, it would be like giving them another battle cry."

The soldier nodded. "Easy, Dr. Chase. We will get a squad out there right away. He couldn't have gotten too far on foot. We will capture him once more and I promise I'll personally throw him in the brig. It would be my distinct pleasure."

The doctor nodded in agreement. "Yes, I'm sure you will. Now please help me back to my office. I have a few calls to make and time is running out. My plans are finally taking shape and I can't allow them to be thwarted by anyone."

Slowly, with great assistance, the doctor made it back to his office and sat at his desk for a moment to clear his head. Everything was finally falling into place and once again, someone threatened to derail all his plans. Thinking of his plans brought him back to his beloved daughter and what he felt he was forced to do to her to protect her interests. He thought back to the last time he'd seen Chris destroying the lab to get to April. The doctor shuddered at the thought of what Chris would do to him the next time the two came face to face. Knowing Chris' passion for his daughter almost made him smile as he could picture them two years down the road protecting one another.

Dr. Chase spent much of his adult life taking care of others' interests but now it was his own that were in grave danger. The worst part of his little plan was that he could tell no one even his daughter. Especially his daughter; she could easily say her knowledge of events that would transpire was little to none and keep a straight face. The doctor decided that even that wasn't enough and sidelined her as to not involve her any longer. This was a harsh reality but when everything was over and explanations were given. He hoped everyone would understand his rationale.

On his desk in front of him among the countless clutter of files and paperwork stood a photograph of April in a beautiful wood frame. He reached over the desk carefully and gently lifted the picture to within a foot of his face. The figure on the photograph teemed with life. April, always the bubbly one, didn't even want to go on the camping trip where the photo was taken. She was a great sport about the whole thing and they'd spent a remarkable time together. The doctor looked fondly down at the photograph. "April, when this is over, we'll go on many more of these trips. We have so much catching up to do."

He gingerly replaced the photograph, keeping his hand on the frame as if he didn't want to let go. With a remorseful look on his face, his hand brushed by April's face on the photo before returning to the pile of papers on the desk before him. The doctor rifled through the papers until his hand grasped what he was looking for and lifted the cell phone from the desk. Scrolling through his contacts, he stopped at the one he was looking for and pressed send. While waiting for the party on the other line to pick up, he looked through the top file trying to find an important piece of information.

When the person on the other end picked up, the doctor spoke swiftly, "We have a big problem! Steve has escaped and I've no idea where he is. Gus is under wraps but we lost Chris and company. These people never quit! They really are a bunch of pains in the asses!"

A voice came over the other end. "We can't worry about that right now! Is everything set for Project Wipe Clean?"

Dr. Chase smiled. "We're a go! I just would feel much better if Steve were still here. I don't want anything to get in the way of my retribution. These scumbags are going to pay for all the pain they have caused me and my family."

The voice on the phone continued, "Doctor, calm down and stay the course. You have spent years putting this into place and now it's a reality. Your revenge will be complete and you will have the last laugh."

The doctor spoke, "When are you going to be here? I not going to throw the switch without you being present."

The voice spoke up, "I'm on my way! We will do this together and put our lives back together. As long as you're ready, then we'll get on with it and watch them all scramble like ants coming out of a broken mound. This is going to be a day for the ages! What we do today will change the face of humanity!"

The doctor thought for a moment before continuing, "Yes, this time there will be no one to stop destiny. We will finally be able to walk in public once again without looking over our shoulders. April will have the life she deserves! I think I'm looking forward to that the most. She has been caught up in this even though I did what I could to keep her in the shadows. My greatest hope is for her to live a life I could only dream of."

On the other end, he could hear breathing. "Doctor, one step at a time! Just make sure everything is ready. We're not out of the woods yet. Not by a longshot. When it's done, we'll celebrate and not until. Make sure the base is set and that nothing gets through. The last thing we need is some last-minute screw up. Everything must go off without a hitch. As soon as I arrive, you will have the last of the code to institute your revenge."

Dr. Chase hung up the phone and threw it back on the desk. He looked quickly around his office for a moment as if contemplating what his next move would be. With hands on his hips, he decided to give his troops their final instructions before moving on to Steve. He didn't care what the voice said, Steve was dangerous and could screw up everything. The doctor reached down and pressed the button on his desk phone.

A voice came over the speaker, "Yes, sir!"

The doctor spoke, "Is everything ready?"

The voice crackled, "Yes, everything is in place. We're just awaiting final instructions and the installation will be locked down. Should I assemble the men?"

The doctor looked at the phone for a second. "Yes, have the men ready in fifteen minutes! I'll give you all final instructions and we'll set the final act in motion. There will be no one to stop us now. They'll never know what hit them. It'll be the equivalent of sending them back to the Stone Age. I can't wait to see all their pompous faces when they realize what has been done to their precious program!"

The voice called once more over the speaker, "We will be ready, sir! I'll see you when you arrive."

He was about to hang up but pushed the button once more. "Captain! We will be having a special visitor. Please alert the gate that he will be here any moment and let him through without delay."

The captain spoke, "Sir, it will be my distinct pleasure. Are there any other special instructions at this time?"

The doctor responded, "No, Captain, that will be all." He released the button, not waiting for another response. Turning back to the mess that was his desk, he grabbed the file and walked straight out into the hall. As he made his way through the corridor, he couldn't help but feel a strange calm come over him. His life's work would now be complete and his revenge would be swift.

Chapter 15

Chris, as if waking from a dream, could hear a woman screaming. He looked down at his feet only to see a slumped figure. Jessica, still yelling hysterically, told them to help her. As she raised the man's head, Chris could clearly see it was Steve. Jessica cradled the man's head gently in her hands with tears streaming down her face. She looked up at Chris, pleading for help. Immediately, Chris and Christopher moved to help their distraught friend. Chris carefully bent down to put his hands under Steve's shoulders as Christopher reached down to grab Steve's legs. At once, they lifted the hulking man from the ground and brought him into the barn, afraid to be seen by watching eyes.

Once inside, they carefully placed their friend on a bed of straw while Jessica rolled up an old horse blanket to put under Steve's head. Jessica, with her hands on her knees, sat beside Steve, pleading for him to wake up. Her tear-stained face shone in the sunlit rays coming through the cracks in the barn walls. She turned to Christopher with rage in her eyes. "Why did you have to hit him?"

Christopher looked pathetic and had no answer. Chris came to his rescue. "Jessica, we had no idea who it was. We thought it was someone coming after us. If we had any idea it was Steve, we never would have hit him. You have to believe us!"

Jessica didn't respond but turned back to stand vigil over her fallen loved one. She reached down, caressing Steve's face. "Where have you been? How are you here? We thought you were dead! Oh, Steve, what's going on?" She was joined by the two mirror images as each sat on their knees, peering at their unmoving friend.

Chris reached over to Jessica. "Jessica, he will wake in a few minutes and then we can find out what happened. Right now, we still should keep watch. If Steve is here, you can be sure someone is looking for him."

At this comment, Agent Bradley, who hadn't said much the whole time, chimed in, "Chris is right. We're going to have to pay attention now. They'll definitely send someone out to search for Steve."

Anyone viewing the scene from outside the barn peering in would have seen a group of worshipers on their knees, holding some kind of healing. The sun rays along with the dust made for a mystical picture and the friends with their heads down surrounding their fallen friend made for a powerful religious feel. As if the prayerful looks at their friend worked, Steve stirred. The friends all at once fell forward to come to his aid. Jessica held his head once more.

"Steve, it's Jessica! You're all right. You're safe with friends."

Steve blinked his eyes, trying to clear his aching head, and looked at his friends' relieved looks. It almost made him laugh that Chris and Christopher were there with looks of caring on their faces. He tried to lift himself but Jessica asked him to stay down for a minute until they could make sure he was okay. Steve relinquished his care to this beautiful creature and smiled, reaching out to cup her face with his hands. He remained in a lying position but looked right at Chris. "Dude, what the hell was that?"

Chris winced, "Sorry, man! We thought you were one of those military thugs coming for us."

Steve turned to his side with his hand holding up his head. "Tell me, quickly! Tell me what happened!" Chris didn't hesitate and told his friend how they'd found the coordinates and made their way here in the hopes to find Gus. He went on to describe their run in with the military helicopter and subsequent escape to their current location. Steve nodded a few times but didn't interrupt and when Chris was done, he made his way to his feet. Jessica tried to stop him, but he took her hands in his and looked at her, telling her he was all right.

The massive man put his hands on his two counterparts' shoulders, almost as if in a football huddle on the field. He began, "Listen, we have to get out of here. These idiots will be coming after all of us. I saw your encounter and these people won't be happy about you taking down one of their birds. No, they'll come for vengeance!" He looked around and spotted the car. "Is that your transportation? Is it sound?"

Agent Bradley stepped in. "It can get us out of here but before we decide that, I've another plan."

Steve looked at him, confused. "John, we have to get out of here. We can't wait! We have no help coming! It's just us!"

The federal agent smugly laughed. "Oh, yes we do!"

Steve looked perplexed. "Go on, please do explain!"

The agent smiled. "I have a secret army!" Everyone at once jumped in with responses of what are you talking about. The agent calmly raised his hands. "I told you before; when they get here, you will know everything! It's a surprise!"

94

Jessica scowled at him. "John, this is no time for surprises. As a matter of fact, I've had enough surprises to last me a lifetime!"

John raised his hand to reassure her. "Jessica, I feel your pain. Honestly at this point, I feel like you and I'm ready to live a nice simple life away from all this. I really can't explain everything until you see for yourself." Agent Bradley's phone rang and he went to the side to answer it.

They all stood staring toward the agent with anxious eyes, waiting for the agent to speak when he returned. The agent, with an air of confidence, gazed at each one of his friends and then spoke, "The advance team will be here within minutes. The remainder of the force will be coming under the cover of darkness."

Steve's eye nearly shot out of his head. "Advance team! Where did you get that? With all due respect, John, but we need a real military force, not just a few federal agents."

Agent Bradley turned to Steve. "Like I've been saying all along, it's very difficult to explain. They'll be here momentarily. Just be patient."

All the confused people staring back at the agent felt their patience was all but used up at this point. They badgered the agent about what was coming until his phone rang once more. He held up his hand to silence his friends and ran to the barn door. Agent Bradley turned quickly and waved his friends to join him. That was when they heard the whirl of helicopter blades breaking the silence. At first, they thought of running but looked at the agent's smiling face and went to look for themselves. Each person crept around to the edge of the opening, looking out the barn door to see two helicopters landing next to the barn.

Agent Bradley left the security of the barn door and walked briskly to the first helicopter to meet the men jumping from the craft. Steve ran after the agent, along with Chris and Christopher following behind. They weren't about to leave their friend's side and not have his back. The agent didn't falter in his steps toward the helicopter and extended his hand out to the meet the first of the soldiers emerging from the aircraft. The man lifted the visor on his helmet, smiled brightly, and grasped Agent Bradley's hand warmly. The two men clasped hands as old friends might after not seeing one another for quite some time.

Chris, much too impatient to wait for introductions, ran past Steve and Christopher, catching up quickly to Agent Bradley. He was about to thrust himself in the middle of the agent and the soldier when he looked closely at the soldier's face. Chris stopped dead in his tracks and stood staring at the soldier. Steve and Christopher bumped into him as he stopped right in front of them. This jostled Chris back to the moment and he went in for a closer look.

His comrades quickly joined the soldier, surrounding Chris and company. Steve immediately went into defensive mode, watching cautiously the moves of each soldier. Chris and Christopher followed Steve's lead and looked ready to plow into an offensive lineman. Agent Bradley, seeing this, stepped up to Chris, placing a hand on his chest to diffuse the situation. Chris just swiped his hand away and looked at the agent with anger building.

"John, how could you? These soldiers aren't here to help you; they're here for us!"

The federal agent remained calm and stood between the two groups, hoping to avoid confrontation. Tension grew as the soldiers clearly gleaned the gist of their opponent's intentions. There were five members of the squad from the first chopper now circling the three massive men before them. Chris, Steve, and Christopher stood back to back, waiting for the first attacker to make a more. They just looked at each other, knowing this was what they did know. They took care of each other and covered each other's back.

Jessica ran in and was the voice of reason. As if negotiating a settlement in a highly contended case, she once again was marvelous. Immediately, all parties stopped their approach and looked at the stunning beauty before them. Despite her current state, Jessica was the complete vision of beauty. Her hair shone brightly in the fading sun and her eyes sparkled like diamonds of a million facets. Her now-ruined clothing didn't hide the assets underneath. The men were enthralled when she broke the silence.

"Why is it that men always have to solve everything with destruction?" The question hung in the air and no one accepted the challenge to answer. Jessica seemed amused by this lack of response. "Well, boys, I'm sorry to inform you that there will be no fighting right now. Now if you would be so kind as to get your asses into the barn so we can discuss our plans before the real enemy shows up."

She made that last statement with such conviction that every man stood at attention and immediately followed Jessica into the barn with just two words said, "Yes, ma'am!"

Once back inside the barn, Jessica turned to Agent Bradley and smacked him upside the head. He looked so surprised that he had no words to respond. Jessica, her face turning red, screamed, "Are you out of your mind? You told me this program was disavowed and every soldier released back into civilian life!"

The agent shrank like a student being reprimanded by his teacher. "Jessica, does it look like we've much of a choice? Steve is right. As talented as my FBI brothers and sisters are, they're not a military unit. These men are military through and through. Ask Steve, he will tell you. Once in the military always in the military!"

Jessica glanced back at Steve where she saw him nod his head, telling her the agent was correct in his assessment. She glared back at Agent Bradley. "So this is your brilliant idea, to use their own soldiers against them? You're nuts! You know Dr. Chase put chips in each of their brains to control them. He's probably listening to us right now, you moron!"

It was Steve's turn to try to bring things back. "Jessica, honey, we need some help and right now I'd take anything I could get. Let's just listen and then we can kick his butt after if you still don't like what he has to say. Trust me, honey, I'll be right there with you to crush his little butt!"

She looked at her love and then her face softened. "Steve, you're right! I'm sorry! I'm just so tired of not knowing what the hell is going on and having someone else determining my fate. Just for once I'd like to make someone else sweat a little."

Agent Bradley jumped right in. "Jessica, that's what these guys are for and you've nothing to worry about. You're right. These soldiers are no longer officially soldiers, but they have unfinished business with Dr. Chase as you have. Each of these young men have had their lives destroyed as you have and now it's payback time. Jessica, the bill has come due and these men are here to collect.

"As for the chip in their heads, you're right. I cannot take it out but I've bypassed it for now and Dr. Chase cannot use it. Jessica, think about it for a minute. What better justice than having his own creations destroy him. These men sought me out because they have been struggling so mightily with integrating themselves into society. They're lost! All they know is military life. They were bred for that purpose alone and now we want them to be civilians. In some ways, we may have been worse than Dr. Chase. Think about it. 'Hi, guys. You are free! Now get a job and make some money. By the way, you can't be in the military anymore.'"

Jessica's face reddened with embarrassment. "John, you're right. I'm sorry. These men have been through hell and back along with the rest of us! We need as much help as we can get and these men have every right to fight for their way of life." She turned to the soldiers. "Gentlemen, please accept my apologies!"

The leader approached Jessica and took off his helmet, standing before her. With his helmet now off, Chris and company finally got a good look at the soldier's face. Everyone but Chris gasped at the sight of Zack Johnson, middle linebacker for the Massachusetts Bay Marauders.

Everyone knew that this wasn't the original Zack, but each time they ran into a clone, they knew it still surprised them. At this time, each of the men took off their helmets, revealing various members of Chris and Christopher's football team. Realization set in as Chris and company stood looking at the stern faces of the soldiers. They all now knew that Agent Bradley was correct that these men could help them. The friends all looked at the agent, waiting for him to outline his plan.

Agent Bradley stood before them and explained what would happen when the rest of his team arrived. He went on to explain his plans for an all-out assault on the military installation. Jessica stopped him here. "John, how are we supposed to assault a military installation? Don't you think that will bring down the entire might of the United States Military down on our heads?"

Agent Bradley calmly stated, "No, according to my research, Dr. Chase is on his own. As a matter of fact, I have a man on the inside that says Dr. Chase is starting to lose it, along with any support he once had from the government. No, Jessica, he's completely isolated in this and this is our perfect opportunity to take the head off the snake."

The federal agent outlined his plan for the assault and went into detail as to where specific targets were located. One target brought raised eyebrows as the agent told them where Gus was being held. As he wrapped up their exit strategy, they all couldn't help but be impressed with Agent Bradley's attention to detail. It was quite clear that he'd spent a great deal of time putting this operation together. It was also very apparent that he'd kept a great deal from them, which didn't make them feel secure in their own part in this mission.

As Agent Bradley concluded his briefing, they all heard many vehicles making their way to the barn. Everyone ran to the door to make sure they weren't being ambushed. Much to their delight, they were joined by the rest of Agent Bradley's team. Steve viewed the manpower in the last light of dusk. "Now that, my friends, is a welcome sight! Ever since this whole thing began, I've felt woefully outgunned. For the first time, I feel as though we're on even footing with this madman. Honestly guys, John's strategy is sound and with this firepower, we'll have the upper hand. I know this will be an offensive and we'll be going up against a force that's defending a position but we'll have the element of surprise."

Agent Bradley responded, "Steve, that's my thought exactly. With the cover of night, we'll strike and put an end to this menace once and for all. I can't wait until I see that arrogant doctor's face when we capture him. He has a lot to pay for!" He looked right at Chris, who had stood silent during this exchange.

Chris looked at everyone. "You know me, I'm with you all to the end! Feel free to do what you want but the doctor is mine. After I have April safe, you have my permission to level that place to the ground and turn it into crater."

Christopher stood beside his twin and nodded, saying he agreed with Chris. The clone had said little during this time and now he turned to his friends. "It's my honor to serve with you against this evil and I'll see it done. He needs to know our lives matter and we won't stand by and let others determine our lives for us." They all came up to Christopher and patted him on the back as they knew what this meant to him. The soldiers came up to Christopher and shook his hand with a look of understanding.

At this time, it was decided that they needed to make final preparations for the assault. Agent Bradley grabbed Steve and walked over to Zack to go over strategy while the others prepared themselves. Each member was given full military attire as well as a side arm along with a small assault rifle. They were all fitted with a backpack with rations and first aid equipment. Chris, Steve, and Christopher all looked the part of a soldier, but Jessica looked very much out of place. Jessica, who was used to being dressed in a power suit, looked awkward in her camo outfit until she checked her sidearm, snapping a round out of the top of her gun. This didn't go unnoticed by the rest of the soldiers nearby who nodded with pride at their newest member.

With the team briefed and outfitted, all there was left to do was wait for the right moment to strike. Agent Bradley brought everyone together for a time check and synchronized watches with team leaders. He gave them final instructions and told them to return to their vehicles and prepare to leave at midnight. This gave them a few hours to rest. They all returned to their men, awaiting go time. When alone, Chris and company sat themselves on some overturned boxes and looked at one another. They all thought the same thing. How could a bunch of normal everyday people once again end up in the middle of a play to save the world?

Each member of the group entered their own thoughts. Chris felt as though he were preparing for a big game as he swayed back and forth, trying to visualize what would happen during the assault. Christopher, perhaps the most nervous, searched his thoughts for courage, not knowing what to expect during this mission. Steve, having been through these missions numerous times, had a nervous excitement building in him about getting back into the fray. Jessica kept thinking of Steve and how she'd out of nowhere had him returned to her. She still didn't know the details of Steve's escape and how he was returned to her.

As if on cue, they each drifted off to sleep thinking of what would happen once their lives were returned to them. They all wanted so much to live normal lives like their boring neighbors. Just going to a backyard barbeque would seem like a ball to them at this point. So much of their life recently was one of escape. Escape from evil, escape from tragedy, and escape from their current life. In a few hours, their lives would be changed forever.

Chapter 16

Gus, resting comfortably on the exam table, reviewed his last set of notes. Over the years, he developed a keen sense for small details most people would easily miss. He poured over his scrawl and looked at what amounted to his own made up language. Anyone else viewing the writing on these pages would have no idea what Gus meant. The thought of no one having the ability to decipher his notes comforted him greatly. As a news man, his stories were constantly among the most informative and concise. His peers marveled at how Gus could present a story that railed against the subject, but still left it in a positive light.

Gus smirked as he gave thought to how he would package this story once he wrote it. He couldn't help but think about the reams of material he could write with what his firsthand knowledge of events could offer him. To him, the thought of his participation in this earth-shattering conspiracy was almost too much to bare. The sheer weight of the amount of intimate details of the key events and key players was enough to crush him as he stood.

One bit of information kept creeping up on him as he looked at the pages again—the words, "Head of the snake," on the page. These words popped right off the page and caused him much confusion. During the clone trial, blame was easily dropped at the feet of Mr. P. Only to find out that they were all still being pursued by an evil shadowy entity. Of course, it shocked everyone to learn their nemesis was none other than the original Mr. P., long thought dead. Mr. P. was subsequently dispatched for good, leaving what they all thought was a clear path to getting their lives back. Still Gus, with his eyebrows scrunched up, couldn't figure out for the life of him how they all still found themselves caught in the eye of the storm once more.

To find the head of the snake, Gus knew his hands would get dirty once more, but he never thought he would find himself a captive. With his head clearing and his thought process returning, he looked around for an escape route. As his eyes took in the room, he didn't see anything that would keep him from leaving. The door wasn't even completely shut. The nurse that spent time tending to him left him comfortably alone. Gus' antennae went up naturally, thinking setup. He thought better of escape. He posed a scenario to himself as one of an imbedded reporter in a warzone.

Gus felt that he was behind enemy lines here and he knew running interference for his friends would be the least he could do. With a plan secure in his mind, he lifted himself from the examination table and walked carefully to the door. Slowly opening the door, he peered out into the hallway, allowing his head to just barely stick out. What he saw caught him off guard as the hall was abuzz with activity. With the hustle and bustle of an emergency room, people whisked around the room, barely slowing down to hand files to one another. No one even looked up to see that the old media man stood in their midst in awe. Gus spotted the nurse that so wonderfully cared for him and made straight for her station. As if alarms went off, she looked into Gus' eyes with a panicked look on her face. She dropped the file on the table and flew over to Gus' side.

"Gus, is everything okay? I'm not sure you should be up. Are you feeling sick to your stomach or do you have a headache?"

Gus raised his hands, responding, "No, everything is fine. I just had to get up and move around a bit. I looked for someone but I got tired of waiting and in old reporter fashion, went searching."

This remark brought a smile to the young lady's face as she said, "I'm glad! I was very upset to learn how you were treated. I'm a very outspoken individual and trust me, I let my displeasure known." Gus raised one eyebrow while looking at the face of the young lady before him. Her stern look and pursed lips told the entire story that this was someone he didn't want to mess with. He just bobbed his head up and down, letting her know he appreciated her sacrifice.

The nurse put her arm under his and walked with him for a moment toward a door at the back of the room. Gus allowed himself to be led, but was quite curious as to the nature of this excursion. He said not a word, but rather used the time to take in the details of his surroundings as he entered the next room. Looking like a major control room, it was set up in a huge semi-circle with gigantic screens lining the twenty-foot-high walls. As if it were possible after what he witnessed in the last room, here was more action and people stuffed everywhere. It was apparent to Gus that something big was about to happen.

He turned to the nurse with a questioning look on his face. The nurse beat him to it. "Dr. Chase wanted you to be here to see this."

Gus' jaw almost hit the floor as he stammered, "Dr. Chase? Isn't this a military installation?"

She stared back at him with her own questioning glance. "Yes, Dr. Chase has been planning this for a long time.

He's on the verge of an unbelievable discovery and wants to share it with the world."

Gus almost shouted out, but restrained himself. "You mean the Artificial Intelligence he has created? He's insane! You can't be serious that he thinks he should share this with the world."

For the first time, he saw uncertainty in the young lady's eyes. She shook slightly as she responded, "Gus, what are you talking about? Dr. Chase is about to reveal he has successfully regenerated damaged brain tissue. He's about to revolutionize brain surgery. No longer will people have to worry about losing a loved one to brain death. Gus, this is amazing! What Artificial Intelligence are you talking about?"

Gus refused to explain and could see by the look on her face that she wouldn't have understood anyway. He turned to her and said, "Brain regeneration! I remember Dr. Chase telling me about this research. He once told me that was what he originally hoped to secure before finding himself in the middle of the clone program. But you're going to have to tell me more about Dr. Chase and his affiliation with the military."

The woman grew nervous as she spoke, "Gus, he does not have a military affiliation. As far as I know, he's funded by his original government contracts but this place was all but abandoned when he refitted it for his usage. I've been here since he opened the facility and most of the military personnel you see here were assigned here as protection only. After the whole clone fiasco, he felt the need for a much more secure location. The idiot that struck you is a real hothead and needs to be brought down a peg or two. Most of the military folks here just focus on their job, but for some reason, that guy has an inflated sense of his overall worth around here."

The reporter stood listening as this nice young lady kept spewing out more and more information. He loved this, as it made his job that much easier and he took mental notes of everything that was said. Subjects that clammed up or those that thought they were smart and tried to make things up upset Gus. He knew that if he were patient enough, someone would always divulge information they never intended to reveal. This young lady was very cooperative. A little too cooperative, thought the media man but he would listen for all he was worth in the hopes to catch something that would help him down the road.

He looked around the control room now and scanned the screens quickly to see if anything stuck out as important to him. Much of what he saw on the screens looked to be code based on the doctor's brain research, but the screen dead in the center of them all looked to be a radar screen of sorts. This screen intrigued Gus and he turned, walking in its direction. The nurse followed him, but remained silent. Gus stood in front of the screen and for the first time, noticed that the radar was securing this location. The screen flickered with a yellow greenish tinge to it as the blips on the screen became more pronounced.

It was at this moment that the technician sitting in front of the station grabbed the phone, calling for Dr. Chase. He frantically told the person on the other end of the line that a large group of aircraft just entered their airspace. He explained in which direction they were coming from and said he would alert everyone. The man hung up the phone and returned his focus back to the screen for a moment before pressing a button on his panel. As he held the button, his voice rang aloud around everyone, "All military personnel to their respective assignments! This is now a live mission. It's go time! We have contact five miles out and closing! Listen to your squad leaders for additional instructions." With that, he released the button and went back to his screen.

Gus couldn't help but wonder what might be going on here. He blurted, "What's that all about? Are we expecting visitors?"

The young nurse looked anxiously at the reporter. "We have to find a safer place!" Gus refused to move and kept a vigilant watch on the screen as the blips became more pronounced and frequent. She pleaded with him, "Gus, please, we're going to be in the way here!"

He put his hand softly on her hand. "My dear, if you feel unsafe here, then please find a haven for yourself. As for me, I'm always in the action. Trust me, I've been in much more dangerous situations than this."

The nurse struggled, searching for safety and not wanting to leave her patient unattended. Gus made it easy on her. "Please, it's okay. I'll be quite all right! I'm feeling much better. Honestly, this place is my speed and I can learn a lot by being here right now. Go on to your designated area and I'm sure we'll see each other some other time."

She grasped his hand firmly with relief. "You're sure you're okay?" He nodded and rubbed her hand, reassuring her that it was safe for her to leave. She released his hand and turned to walk away. A few steps from Gus, she turned and looked back but he waved her on, turning back to look at the screens.

His full attention turned to the radar screen once more, he could clearly see that whatever was coming their way was now almost directly on top of them. He could hear people talking into microphones from their stations, barking orders when the first blast hit. The entire room shook as pieces of the ceiling cracked and fell to the floor. Several computer stations were smashed with a shower of sparks shooting into the air. Gus could see one man clinging to a damaged shoulder with blood soaking his shirt. As he turned to examine the overall scene before him, another blast struck the facility.

The impact from this latest strike was much closer and more damaging than the last. Gus found himself thrown to the ground and just moved to the side as a large chuck of concrete ceiling crashed down just to his right. Pulling himself to his feet, his head hurt once more. As he scanned the room, it was in shambles and a heavy dust cloud now permeated the air, making it extremely difficult to see. Through the chaos, he saw that three of the large screens on the wall were either down or destroyed. He looked around at the computer stations only to see devastation.

He could see people attending to the injured as others made their way to the exit. Some steadfast folks maintained their stations as only a few computers worked at this point. The one area that seemed intact was the radar station. The man attending the station didn't look fazed by all the commotion around him and kept his eyes peeled to the screen. Gus made his way to the man's right shoulder. Glancing over his shoulder. He could clearly see whatever was here was a good size force but what caught his eye was another set of blips entering the screen from another direction.

The radar technician tried to radio his superiors, telling them that he tracked another set of advancing vehicles. He tried to raise someone several times, only to hear dead silence on the other end. The tech unraveled with a panicked look on his face. Gus could see the man's dilemma and swooped in to assist. He reached out and touched the man's shoulder. The man almost jumped out of his skin.

"Who are you?"

Gus put his hands up and responded, "Does it really matter at this point?" The tech just nodded. Gus asked, "What's the protocol for this situation when communications are down?"

The tech shrugged. "To this point, it was never an issue. We were just trained how to use the equipment. I'm former military but we always had a backup system in place. Here this is the extent of the equipment."

Gus looked down at the monitor once more and asked, "Is that what I think it is?"

The tech looked at the new set of blips on the screen that Gus pointed at. "Yes, it certainly is. Whoever coordinated this attack is approaching us on two fronts!"

Gus looked once more at the screen and responded, "I'm not sure. That second force seems to be quite a bit larger and from what I can see, I make out many more vehicles than the previous attack. How much time do we have until they get here?"

The young technician didn't take his eyes off the screen as he blurted out, "We have a matter of minutes! We have to get out of here and find our way down to the bunker."

The reporter didn't want to leave this place of information but looking around at the damage before him, it became apparent that this site wouldn't withstand another attack. He added, "You're right, of course. We should go right now! Lead the way!"

The two men walked through the fallen debris and heavy dust still hanging in the air. Both men could just barely see in front of them, stumbling over items strewn all over the damaged floor. The technician led him to another door toward the back of the room. He waved his key card in front of the reader, waiting for the door to respond. Nothing happened and the man tried several more times with no luck. Gus stepped in front of him and using his sleeve, he wiped the card reader clean of the dust that now clung to the box. The man tried once more and the door came to life, opening wide in front of them.

As both men were ready to walk through the doorway, another blast rocked the installation, causing both men to be thrown into the wall. Gus felt his shoulder snap as the full weight of his body struck the wall. He was slumped against the wall and looked for the technician, only to see him trapped beneath a large piece of the ceiling. Gus staggered to the fallen man with his stomach churning and tried in vain to lift the piece of concrete from the pinned man. His head was pounding now and his own wounded shoulder was useless. He leaned heavily against the wall and slid down to the floor. He reached over to feel for the man's pulse and was relieved to feel a heartbeat. Gus leaned his head back, only to see one of the ceiling lights falling right on top of him.

Chapter 17

Coach Ridel squinted into the early morning sunshine, feeling the brilliant rays beating on his taut face. These mornings always fascinated the coach as he watched his team continue to grow and come together before him. The coach knew that a team was only as strong as its weakest link. This was always the toughest struggle for the coach, making the call to end one of his player's career. Sending one of the assistant coaches to ask for one's playbook was the worst job in coaching. All coaches hoped the cut player would catch on somewhere else but most would never see the field again.

With the reputation as the most ruthless coach in the league, he felt for these kids but had to do what was best for his club. This year was particularly difficult as he could keep on several more players because of Chris and Christopher taking what amounted to a medical leave of absence. Also, only talking about those players present on the field this year was much more difficult to deal with. Coach Ridel felt as though his defense was finally ready to take off this year with Chris leading the charge.

As he watched his team go through tackling drills, he couldn't help but think of the first day he saw Chris join the team during the same drills. It almost made the coach laugh. He recalled seeing Chris get pancaked several times being so amped up to impress the coaches, he forgot almost everything he'd learned about leverage. The one thing that surprised the coach most was the spirit the kid showed as he refused to back down and kept coming. The coach knew from that moment on that Chris was a player.

Coach watched as a few of the practice squad players were manhandled in the drills and tried, but didn't have the same heart. He watched as the assistant coaches moved the players into position drills. His line-backing corps were very thin and he called up a street free agent to build some depth but knew it wasn't a great solution. The coach watched as a few of the young linebackers failed to shed blockers and kept getting cut. This was a great source of frustration for the coach as he knew that Chris and Christopher were excellent at not being blocked. He watched for a few more plays before turning his attention to the offensive side of the ball.

Coach Ridel strode over to the other practice field to get a look at a fresh crop of young offensive linemen. He watched as the young men dug their hands into the turf and launched themselves into the sleds with dust and sweat flying into the air. The sound of thud of pads hitting the sled made the coach feel right. This was what the game was all about, one man lining up against another, fighting for domination. The greatness came however when the coaches could get them to block and work as a unit. When the offensive line blocked correctly, it was extremely difficult for any defense to dictate game tempo. Offensive tempo was one thing the coach prided himself and was highly successful most years. This year would be a struggle as he lost three members of last year's starting line to free agency. The loss of these key members of the line was always difficult to absorb, but losing three in one year was cause for alarm.

Over the years, Coach Ridel learned that he must do what was necessary for his club, whether it was popular or not. The proof was in the pudding as his model over the last twenty years proved to be the most sound and lasting. His run of division titles, playoff appearances, and titles was unheard of in this era of parity in this league. Of course, this created many jealous critics along the way, hoping for the coach and his system to fall from grace. Though there were some bumps in the road, the coach remained steadfast in his beliefs and system.

He spent a few more minutes watching the linemen pound on the sled before making his way over to the backs. The coach was still a dinosaur using a gauntlet drill, causing the backs to hold onto the ball with two hands. One thing the coach couldn't stand was someone who fumbled. He didn't have a spot on this team for anyone who couldn't hang onto the rock. A few veteran backs made it through the drill with little difficulty but the rookies looked like fish out of water. The coach smirked to himself as he knew they did none of these drills in college any longer. He almost burst out laughing as one young man went into the gauntlet only to be bounced right back out onto his backside. The furious young man looked at the apparatus with disbelief and got back in line.

Coach had seen enough and walked over to his quarterbacks. The media was all in an uproar because the coach had taken a quarterback in the second round, hoping to create a quarterback controversy. Joe Morton, the Marauders current quarterback, was aging and still playing at a high level, but the coach saw this kid sitting there on draft day and couldn't pass it up. The other thing on the coach's mind was the two-quarterback system their division rival now ran. The coach always looking to be an innovator wanted to create his own system and this kid could pass from the pocket or slide outside to run from trouble. Of course, the coach would not divulge anything to the media and therefore according to them, he must be fading out Joe.

The media, that band of vipers that would do anything for a story, had little use for the coach as he wasn't forthcoming with any information whatsoever about his team. Inside, he laughed because what did any of these people know about running a football team? They just hid behind a microphone or their credentials and never put their money where their mouth was. He just watched as all these young coaches came out in a press conference and laid open their souls, only to have the media chew them up and spit them out. The coach didn't have time for games as he had games to win and a team to build.

What to do with Chris and Christopher. The coach spent quite a bit of time contemplating whether to just cut bait with these kids. In years past, he wouldn't have even bat an eyelash before just releasing them both, but these two were special and he found himself feeling for the young men. Rather than cut them, the coach gave them what amounted to medical leave, but still he sat stewing on the field that morning because these two weren't on the field. After what he just witnessed on the field, he thought about reevaluating his decision but thought better of it.

Coach Ridel, having coached many players in his career and seen them come and go, was at a loss over Chris. This young man was a special talent and not so much for what he could do on the field. The coach witnessed firsthand the meddle of this young man in the face of unbearable adversity. He watched as Chris fought for others and saved not only himself but in turn made a difference in the lives of many others. The coach couldn't help but be impressed by the character that Chris demonstrated and he knew this wouldn't be someone he would ever have to worry about off the field. This was the bane of the coach's existence as he spent so much time over the years cleaning up after players who couldn't take care of their lives off the field.

Not only did Chris handle his business off the field, he did so with dignity and class. Usually Coach didn't spend too much time getting to know what a player did in his off time if he was a quiet person, but Chris was front and center, thanks to the clone trial. Even the coach was enthralled by the trial and watched as Chris and company fought tooth and nail to make things right. For the first time, the coach found himself routing for one of his players off the field. When Chris came back to the team after the trial, he was on a mission to destroy people on the field. This focus worked to the team's advantage and they rode the wave into the playoffs.

After the two young men left his office, he went on to do his own homework on the situation facing them. He found that these two faced impossible odds and he knew what the powerful men they were dealing with could do to them. He placed a call into the owners group to discuss the situation with them, but no one returned his call, which he thought extremely odd. Furious about his lack of access, he went searching for someone in the owner's suite, only to find emptiness. The coach was dumbfounded as he never had difficulty before communicating with ownership until the clone fiasco.

The old veteran coach, using another contact from another team, found out that the ownership group turned out to be a dummy corporation. He began to understand what Chris and company were going through and decided to do what he could to help. How could he help when he didn't even know where his two players were? He didn't even know where Dr. Chase had disappeared to with his daughter. To the coach, it appeared his team was losing people by the day.

He called around to old friends to find out what was happening under his nose without his knowledge or approval. When he was hired as coach/general manager, he was given assurances that he would have complete control. When the clone trial began, he found out how little control he had over his team. When Chris and company won the case, he wanted go over and bear hug the kid. Now this kid needed his help and the coach felt helpless. He was completely out of the loop and he hated not having all the information he needed to pass judgement.

As he watched Joe catch the perfect spiral launched through the air and a streaking wide out who caught it downfield, he smiled. One thing he could count on was his ageless quarterback, but he knew that Father Time caught up to every athlete and he wanted to help Chris get back on the field before it was too late. It was at that moment his phone vibrated and violating his own rule about phones at practice, he glanced down at the screen. The number was an old one that he recognized and he answered quickly, listening for a few seconds before hanging up and shoving the phone back into his pocket in frustration.

Chapter 18

Chris and company found themselves being rushed into the back of a military transport truck along with fully equipped soldiers. As the truck moved forward, the soldiers leaned slightly with weapons lying on their laps at the ready. The stone faces of soldiers anticipating the possibility that this may be their last mission made for a grave reality for all those stuffed in the transport. The magnitude of the situation wasn't lost on one person sitting in the back of this vehicle, pondering what the next few hours would hold in store for each of them.

No one seemed ready to break the silence as Chris glanced over to see Steve who sat across from him. In full gear, Steve looked quite intimidating. Chris knew Steve was in his glory at this moment, getting back into the fray. How lethal Steve looked in the dim light with his painted face shocked Chris. He knew Steve as a warrior, but he truly didn't realize the extent of the ingrained military nature of the man until that very moment. Chris almost felt bad for Dr. Chase, almost. He knew the doctor was in for a very bad day.

The trunk rumbled along the road toward its destination as Agent Bradley looked down at his watch. The occupants could see the glow of the digital watch cast a soft light on the agent's face as they looked to him for their cue. He stared at the watch without a word and then took out his phone, checking their position using the phone's GPS. With eyes aglow, he kept viewing the screen and it appeared nothing would take place at this moment. The agent looked up from his phone and stated, "We should arrive in about twenty minutes. Not that it's very far but getting all this equipment and men to the correct place to launch an offensive attack will take a bit more time."

Surprisingly, Jessica asked the first question, "John, they'll be expecting us, correct?"

Agent Bradley, through the dark, responded, "Jessica, they may be expecting us but they don't know when or where we'll hit them. The route we're taking is a more difficult terrain and will allow us an element of surprise. Honestly, by the time they figure out what's going on, it will be much too late for them to mount much of a defense. With the cover of night and our approach, we'll be in and out very quickly. We're looking for speed on this mission and my hope is for an even faster extraction."

At this, Chris piped in, "Extraction? John, what are you talking about? We don't even know if April is there with the doctor. He could have her held up somewhere else!"

Agent Bradley countered, "Chris, do you really think Dr. Chase wouldn't have his daughter with him and close? No, my friend, she will be there and very close to the doctor. I've a feeling the doctor thought he had no choice but to handle things in this manner."

Chris spat out, "I don't care what the doctor thought he should do when I get my hands on him. They aren't coming off until he's dead at my feet!"

Agent Bradley said, "I wouldn't blame you one bit, but do you actually think you could do that to another person?" There was a dead silence, followed by a grunt from across the transport.

"Agent Bradley, Chris will do what's needed and if it comes to it, he will take someone down."

Agent Bradley continued, "Steve, I understand that but I think this situation is much different. If the doctor has April as close as I think he does, then he's going to have something up his sleeve. We're going to have to be very smart about this and the doctor is the key to everything. The last thing we want to do at this point is harm the one person we need the most in this whole situation. Absolutely we're going to rescue April, but I guarantee there is more going on here than meets the eye. My advice is to capture Dr. Chase and use his knowledge to our advantage."

Steve just laughed. "You can't be serious! I know the doctor probably better than anyone here and he isn't going to let you take him alive. He's a lot more dangerous than you're giving him credit for. Trust me when I tell you this, don't underestimate that man! He may seem like a geeky science nerd, but he's quite devious. If you overlook that man, you do it at your own peril. As for me, I'll shoot first and ask questions later. This man has been the cause of a lot of pain in mine and other people's worlds and has to be made to pay for what he has done."

Jessica chimed in at this point, "Gentlemen, let us not jump the gun here! No pun intended. We're a long way from doing anything to the doctor. Are you all quick to forget he has his own military installation?" In the darkness, eyebrows raised at this statement and of course Jessica was exactly right. They were about to attack a fortress. As if all the air was now gone from their breathing space once again, no one wished to speak. Steve slid over to sit close to Jessica and reached in the dark for her hand. Jessica warmly clasped his hand and couldn't believe that she had Steve back only to find out that they were all going back into the belly of the beast. A chill ran down her back.

Christopher was sitting on the right of Chris and said, "Chris, do we have enough men to breach the defenses of the base?"

Chris softly said, "We are taking him down! I don't care if I'm the last man standing. He's going to pay for his crimes once and for all! If I must crawl through an air shaft on my hands and knees, he will pay. The good old doctor has nowhere else to hide and we have him cornered."

Christopher responded, "I'm with you, buddy, but somehow this feels different from all the other times we've been in danger."

Chris, surprised by the statement, continued, "How does it feel different?"

Christopher took a moment before responding, "Each time we've faced the unknown, we not only knew our enemy, we knew him well. What scares me most is the doctor knows us just as well and I'm sure he's planning for that contingency." Chris didn't think much about how close the doctor was in their counsel and overall plans. He rather felt their plans were mute at this point; the only important thing for them at this moment was to retrieve April.

Agent Bradley looked once more at his watch and announced they were a few minutes out. Everyone needed to check their gear. Chris could hear weapons being checked and soldier after soldier announcing they were ready to roll. As the entire transport readied itself for the attack they were all thrown to the left-hand side of the truck as it swerved suddenly. Chris picked himself off the ground only to be thrown to the other side as the truck clearly tried to avoid something. Agent Bradley swiped the tarp, covering the back of the truck to determine what happened to them.

Then a blinding light lit up the night and they heard the helicopter just above them. Agent Bradley yelled for them to go and meet him at the fence. They all jumped out of the back only to have rounds of ammunition from the helicopter shot into the ground to the left of their position. Chris quickly looked to the sky and could only see one aircraft, but he knew that would only be temporary. Steve was right about not underestimating Dr. Chase. The doctor was ready for them.

They all ran over the uneven ground toward the fence line. Agent Bradley told them that this part of the installation was the most vulnerable and that would offer them the best entry point. Chris couldn't help but feel like a sitting duck as his back leaned up against the fence. With his face pointed up to the sky, he saw the helicopter turn back towards them with its blazing lights breaking the darkness of night. As he looked back at his friends, he saw Steve come from the darkness and lift a large rocket launcher to his shoulder and fire. He saw the blaze of fire coming from the rocket as it tracked its way to the helicopter.

The trail of fire coming from the rocket left a vapor trail behind it as it struck the helicopter's underside. The explosion that ensued lit up the night with brilliant colors and shooting shards of hot metal. Once a beautiful flying machine, the helicopter was now a molten mass of metal. The fireball struck the earth with a jarring explosion that they could feel on their faces even though they were half a football field away from the ruined craft. Steve turned to Chris and said, "I always wanted to do that, but usually I was the one having an RPG pointed in my direction."

Agent Bradley ran up to them. "Well, that was subtle. Effective though. So much for the element of surprise, but let's get going. They will be back with more." Soldiers were already snipping the fence and waving them through. When they were safe inside the compound, the agent viewed his GPS quickly and pointed to where they should be going. Without a word, they all double timed it behind the federal agent. As they made their way in the darkness, waiting for another attack from the air, they saw the lights of the installation itself. With a renewed sense of purpose, they quickened their pace forward.

Running straight forward, they noticed troops clearly massing around the buildings and blinding spotlights, searching the darkness for intruders. At this moment, they all heard the roar of jet engines overhead and watched as they dropped their payload on the main building. Chris stopped dead in his tracks as the bunker buster missiles struck the concrete building, leveling it in an instant. Through the huge explosion, he saw concrete and dirt thrown at least a hundred feet into the air. Fire erupted from what could only be described as a crater. He grabbed Agent Bradley and tackled him to the ground. "What the hell are they doing? They'll kill everyone! April is in there! Call them off!"

Agent Bradley croaked, "They are just softening them up. All our intelligence says that the doctor is well underground. I just want to make him understand he isn't getting out of this one."

Chris angrily pulled him from the ground and growled, "If one hair on her head is hurt, I'll hold you personally responsible!"

The agent brushed himself off. "Chris, she may love you but she's one of my best friends. I wouldn't let anything happen to her! I assure you this will work and we'll get in with little difficulty, but air support is necessary."

Steve came over and picked up the federal agent off the ground. "You idiot! They are using bunker busters! Look at the size of that crater! The doctor may be floors below but those missiles will trap him along with anyone else that's with him."

Agent Bradley spat out, "They really are only set up for just the very outside of the installation. It's true that they could, if we wanted, actually get to him under there, but that isn't the plan."

Agent Bradley angrily turned to them all. "Trust me, we cannot waste any more time here. We need to get inside the compound. Now follow me!"

As he said that, another missile struck another building and obliterated it completely. The agent pushed them onward and they ran toward one of the buildings still standing. In front of them, they now saw ground troops surrounding the building they were making for and they stopped. Agent Bradley told them to relax. This was his force and they were right on time. He rushed forward as the others followed behind. The agent met with one of the soldiers and took a moment to confer with the man before coming back to Chris and company.

He stood before them and announced, "Things are going to plan! We've taken out his communications and what was left of his aircraft. All we need to do now is get inside and capture him, putting an end to this nightmare. Chris, you mentioned a little while ago that you would crawl through a tunnel to get to the great doctor. Well, this is your chance." He pointed to the ground with a flashlight. Through the light, they could see what looked like an air tube going into the ground.

Chris shook his head. "Of course it had to be a tunnel! Do you have any idea where it goes?"

Agent Bradley laughed. "Do you think I'd have you crawling through the mud in the dark? No, it's not that far. This is a fresh air vent but it leads right to a supply room. In looking at the plans I got from a friend of mine, it's the easiest way to get in. As a matter of fact, I don't even think that the doctor knows about this room. It is an original room that no one uses anymore. Now quit whining and in you go!" The agent pried the metal grate off the front and pointed to the opening.

Chris grabbed the flashlight and wedged himself through the opening. Being a man who loved the fresh air of the outside, this metal tube was the last place he wanted to find himself. He just barely fit inside and worked his way down the tunnel as a worm would. His elbows became scraped and raw before making it to the edge of the tunnel. Chris wasn't ready for the tunnel to end and couldn't hold himself back as he fell out toward the darkness. He grabbed into the darkness for anything he could grab a hold of only to catch air. The floor met him a lot faster than he anticipated and his back hit with terrific force, causing the air to rush out from his lungs.

He lay in great pain, unable to see anything for a moment and he gasped, trying to gain a breath. After a few moments, he could feel the air returning to his lungs and tried to move his extremities. To his great satisfaction, everything worked fine and with the air now in his lungs, his breathing became normal. Chris rolled onto his belly and pushed himself upward, only to smack his head on the ceiling, causing him once more to go down. Rubbing his head, he stayed now on his hands and knees, searching for the flashlight. Reaching out with his hand, he felt around on the floor without success. As he reached out, his hand touched another wall and there he felt a switch.

He thought carefully about what the switch might, be but without a flashlight, he was willing to risk the consequences. With the flick of his wrist, the switch went up, turning on an overhead light. The light temporarily blinded him as he furiously blinked his eyes, only seeing white spots for a few moments. A quick search of the room around him revealed it to be a small supply room of some sort. He looked at the ground and could tell by the thick layer of dust that no one had been here in a very long time. The dimensions of the room were most likely six feet by six feet with the ceiling another six feet high.

Chris stood, bending slightly this time as to not smash his head and poked his head back into the tunnel. He called to Agent Bradley and told him to be careful coming down. Almost as soon as he told the agent this, his head popped through the tunnel into the room. Chris grabbed him and put him carefully down into the room. Jessica came next, followed by Christopher, and finally Steve. With all these people stuffed into the little room, things became claustrophobic very quickly. The lone door was off to their right and Chris tried it, only to find it locked tight. He looked down at the knob in the hopes of turning it to unlock it, but found only a smooth metallic knob.

He looked at Agent Bradley. "Why would it be locked from the outside like this?"

Agent Bradley said, "Who knows? By the looks of this small place, it may have been a place to store munitions once upon a time."

Chris grabbed the knob with two hands and once again tried to open the door, but it held tight. He felt embarrassed. "Sorry, everyone! Something is holding it from the other side!" He looked at the entire group. "Now what?"

Chapter 19

With great effort, he opened his crusted eyes, blinking them rapidly, hoping to clear them of what kept him from seeing anything. At first, he could make out some dim light coming from above him. His eyes became clearer and he could now see the floor on which he was lying. The cold laminate felt good on his face as the rest of his body felt as if it were on fire. He rolled over in great pain with his muscles extremely stiff, as if they'd been overworked. Still unsure of himself, he decided to not try to stand, but shimmied over to the wall next to him and leaned against it for support.

Using his hands to steady himself, he carefully looked around the room. The room was completely empty and stood cold with nothing but dust moving in the dim light. He rubbed his head as if trying to get it to work right. The frail man couldn't recall what happened to him and he felt a huge sense of loneliness as he looked around the empty room. Looking at the smooth modern looking walls for anything that would jar his memory, he was baffled. He placed his hands firmly on the ground and pushed with all his might to lift himself to a standing position.

Still leaning heavily against the wall, he now noticed the door for the first time. He felt his legs wobble as he tried to move one, but it held and he now worked the other leg. Standing unaided by the wall for a minute, he again tested his legs and walked forward a few steps. Now the life came back to his limbs and he walked cautiously toward the door. Within a few steps of the door was a large mirror that looked to be a part of the wall. He stopped in front of the mirror to gaze at himself.

This image staring back at him was a mess. His face looked charred as if he was burned by fire and his hair looked scorched. He was shocked by what he saw and asked the question for himself, "What the hell happened to me and a better question, who am I?" Further inspection in the mirror revealed that his clothing hadn't fared any better. He looked down at his shirt to see burn marks and holes in the shirt as well as his pants. The man almost laughed as he saw that his shoes looked to be intact except when he looked at the soles, which looked as if they'd been blown off.

Unable to watch himself any longer, he moved closer to the door and stopped, afraid to walk out of the room. He turned and took one final look around the room to see if anything would help him remember anything. Scanning the room, he looked to where he was lying and looked at the wall. For the first time, he noticed the charring and scorch marks around one of the outlets. This was quite puzzling for him as he asked himself, *What did I do?*

Feeling there was nothing more he could do here in this room, he turned and walked into the next. At first, it looked like a smaller room but then the door closed automatically behind him and the room moved. He found himself in a huge elevator. When the door opened once more, he peeked outside to see a very industrial-type hallway. This was all too much for him and he felt frozen and couldn't get his legs to take him any further. The scared man stood with one arm supporting him against the wall. He still didn't know what was going on and had seen no one. Finally, curiosity won out as he forced himself out into the hallway.

Walking for several minutes, he looked around to see rooms to the side as he walked by, but still no human being to be found. One room held his interest. It was a large lab with many computer monitors around the room. All the monitors were off and silent but something jogged his memory as he felt a sting in his head. A flash of a memory ran through his head. The flash showed himself on the monitor before him. This seemed odd to the man as he could clearly see the monitors were off.

He left the room and continued his trek down the hallway. Just as he thought that he was the only human being in the building, he saw up ahead of him another man walking away. For a moment, he thought of yelling to the man but something in the back of his mind told him to hold his tongue. So rather than yell, he quickened his pace and followed the man. He closed the gap and was just behind the man when he turned left and entered another room. He quickly followed the man into the other room.

This time the room was filled with the bustling of movement. People in lab coats and suits were everywhere. He kept scanning back and forth around the room, looking from one person to the next. The computers in this room ran at full tilt and the room was brilliantly lit. He couldn't help but be impressed one by the sheer size of the room but by the amount of activity as well. For what seemed to be several minutes, he viewed the energetic activity before him, saying nothing to anyone. If anyone noticed him, they said nothing, but most were so involved with what they were doing, another person thrown into the mix wouldn't matter.

It wasn't until a young lady in a lab coat came into the room from the other side noticed him and made straight for him. She looked anxious as she approached him. The young lady came within a few feet of him and said, "Oh my God! What happened to you?"

The man responded, "Honestly, I'm not sure. I woke up on the floor like this."

She looked perplexed. "You woke up on the floor? Were you attacked?"

Again, he said, "I'm not sure."

She gave him a sympathetic look. "Okay, well, let's get you checked out. Come with me and I'll take good care of you."

Without another word, he followed the young woman. He wanted to ask what was going on around him but he again felt something in the back of his head telling him to keep his mouth shut. The woman led him again out into the hallway, but this time she cut across into another hallway and he found himself in front of another elevator. They entered the elevator and the woman pressed a button. They were on their way. When the elevator stopped and let them off, he noticed the large pictures of sporting figures, especially football players.

Finally, they came to what looked to be a nursing suite. The woman led him into an exam room and asked him to have a seat. She closed the door, leaving him once again by himself. Sitting on the table, he looked at the picture of the football player on the wall and felt he should know this person but simply couldn't place the man. The young lady didn't return for some time and he wondered what might be happening. As he was about the get off the table, she came back into the room with another man.

The other man was dressed in team attire and had the air of a coach as he looked at the man on the exam table up and down.

"Well, this is an interesting development. Although I've no idea what happened to you, you look like crap." On the table, he couldn't understand why the coach-like man talked to him in such a familiar way. The new man said, "Come on, you've no idea who I am?"

The man on the table shrugged his shoulders. "Sorry, I can't seem to remember anything. Who are you?"

Chapter 20

Dr. Chase shuddered as he felt the concussion from the missile attack overhead. Dust, debris, and pieces of the ceiling fell and the floor was now covered with a layer of dust. He wiped his forehead to make sure nothing would get into his eyes and he could feel the grit scratch his skin. Through the building dust cloud, he viewed the monitors before him as to the progress of his soldiers. He reached forward, wiping away the dust from one monitor to reveal the front gate, which stood unharmed. He gave the screen a confused look.

"Why not try the front gate? This is a military installation, but how do they think they're going to get in here? The only way is through the front gate!"

The doctor continued to be puzzled by these developments as he kept a close watch on the screen in front .of him. Another missile striking overhead caused a large chunk of the ceiling to fall behind him, just missing one of the other monitors. He felt confident that he would be able to repel any attack but these attackers proved more resourceful than anticipated. Things weren't going as planned and he felt betrayed as he was promised reinforcements, only to have them not show. Alone and cornered, he felt there was only one more thing left for him to do. He knew he should have just implemented his final plan as soon as the instrument was ready, but he wanted everything to be in place first.

His gaze now turned to another monitor and he made out many shadowy figures working their way toward the installation from inside the outer fence. He pushed a button on the panel and gave instructions to have troops moved to that location. The commander acknowledged the order and boasted it would be done. The doctor turned again to a monitor behind him which showed the image of a young woman in a tube. His eyes moistened as he touched the screen lovingly. He announced to the screen, "Soon, my dear, we'll begin our life together anew. I promise you things will be different and I'll spend the rest of my life making things right."

He turned once more to see his troops now engaging the shadowy intruders. On the screen, he could clearly see his troops outnumbered the assailants by a three to one margin. He smiled at this and was sure this little temper tantrum was but a small flare up that would be dealt with quickly. He heard a voice come over the speaker in the control panel and pushed the button.

"What is it?"

The voice continued, "Dr. Chase, I'm sure we can withstand this bombardment, but I'm showing another force marching on our position. I've tried hailing them but there is nothing but silence. Doctor, I'm not sure they're ours!"

The doctor felt panic rise inside him as he knew they were coming for him and would do anything to secure his research for the government.

Dr. Chase pressed the button once more.

"Have our remaining troops on alert and keep your eyes peeled. If they break our boundaries, engage them with haste!"

The voice came over the speaker, "Yes, sir! It'll be done! Our other troops are engaged currently near the fence line and are driving the enemy troops back." This was welcome news for the doctor as his shoulders relaxed slightly. The only remaining issue for him to deal with was the now lack of aerial support. Almost every one of his crafts were destroyed and without air superiority, he became uncertain as to the outcome of his overall plan.

He once again pressed the communications button. "Also please send a detachment to my location for my protection!"

The voice came back, "Yes, sir! They're on their way! They should arrive within minutes. Good luck, sir!" The doctor went back to the screen to view the battle. From what he could see, the voice was right and his troops easily handled the enemy troops. He could see the enemy troops in disarray and retreating toward the fence line. As his troops advanced, they were within a few feet from the fence when blinding lights flashed across the screen.

Several helicopters came into view and the doctor watched in horror as they released rockets into his unsuspecting troops. His hands dug into the table before him. The aircraft bombarded his now helpless force. The screen showed explosion after explosion as he watched the helicopters decimate his remaining troops. He could hardly breathe as he now noticed another wave of enemy troops swarming in through the fence toward the installation. The doctor slammed his fist on the table. "This can't be happening! I need more time!"

Instead of watching the battle any longer, he reached down on the floor and lifted a case with a handle, making for the door. As he moved closer to the door, he stopped at the last computer station and punched in a code. He stood for a moment to make sure the code was accepted and the countdown began. When satisfied things were in order, he smirked a final sneer.

"They think they have me! Amateurs! They'll all pay with their lives! I have one final surprise in store for them." With that, he walked out the door as another explosion rocked the installation from above, nearly causing him to fall to the ground. Balancing himself, he continued down the hallway with the bag in his hands.

Chapter 21

Steve pushed past Chris and Agent Bradley with an angry look on his face. "I've had enough of this crap! Out of the way!" He pointed his assault rifle at the lock and fired right into the door. The bullets tore through the metal door in a semi-circular pattern until the lock itself fell to the floor, smoldering. Steve bent down and peered into the hole only to stand up, laughing. He put his hand through the ridged hole and they all heard a click. Steve stood once more and launched his foot toward the door. His foot struck the door with terrific force and door moved slightly. He turned to Chris. "Dude, a little help!"

Chris and Christopher rushed to the door and along with Steve, they all pushed the door outward until there was enough room for each of them to slide through the opening. Each member of the company made their way through the ajar door into another supply closet. They all turned to Steve and said at once, "Is that what you were laughing at?"

Steve smiled as he walked to the door on the opposite side of the room. "I know, right? We go from one closet to another. Who knew?" Steve reached out, grabbing the knob of the door, and made a grimacing face as if straining to open the door.

Jessica came forward. "Steve, are you kidding me? Are we locked in here too?" Steve turned and planted a kiss on her unsuspecting lips before grabbing the knob once more and turned it without any effort at all. The door silently opened before them. Jessica smacked Steve in the shoulder. "That isn't funny, you bonehead! You gave me a heart attack!" Steve smiled once more and led them into a dimly lit hallway. They looked at the concrete walls with a single electrical wire strung along the wall and a bare lightbulb attached once every ten feet.

Every member looked up the hallway to the left and then to the right. They all turned to Agent Bradley when Chris asked, "Okay, genius, which way do we go?"

Agent Bradley looked hurt. "Relax, man. According to my plans on my tablet here, we go right!"

Chris brightened. "John, I never doubted you!" Steve shoved him in the shoulder as Chris just laughed. The agent led them down the hall and announced they wouldn't have to travel far. The agent's information proved to be true. In a few minutes, they came to a door that opened into a much more modern hallway.

As they entered the new hallway, their eyes were bombarded by the bright lights. It took a moment for their eyes to adjusted to the light. When able to view their surroundings in clear vision, they could see this hallway was much the same they'd seen at the other bunker they escaped from. Steve's face twisted in pain and he stopped for a moment. Jessica noticed his plight and put her arm under his.

"Steve, what is it?"

Steve shrugged it off. "Oh, it's nothing!"

He moved forward but Jessica stayed by his side and said, "Steve, it's okay! You went through hell to come back to us. Believe me, I thought I'd never see you again." Tears streamed down her cheeks and Steve engulfed her with his arms. He looked down at her with moistened eyes of his own.

"Jessica, you're what kept me going. I had to get back to you."

The two held each other fast. Chris looked at them and knew better than to try to separate them. He knew what they were going through and his mind went right to April. The prospect of April still being held captive brought him back to reality and he said, "Guys, listen. No one is more glad for you than I am, but April is still in his clutches."

At this, Steve looked with steel in his eyes. "Chris, I'm so sorry! You're right, man! Let's go get her and kick that doctor's ass from here to kingdom come."

It was Agent Bradley's turn to interrupt, "All right, well, we have some decisions to make right now." He stopped and held out his tablet for them to view readily. They all huddled around the digital device and looked down at the screen to see the map before them. Agent Bradley looked up and started, "We could go altogether or we could split up to look for April."

In one voice, they all said at once, "Not going to happen!"

The agent flinched. "Okay, I get it. I was just suggesting because this place is huge. My informant did tell me the area she's most likely to be held."

He pointed on the map to a large section off to their right. He started, "If we cut through this computer room, we could be there in a few minutes. We have been seen. I've led us this way because this offered us the best chance at stealth, but time is of the essence right now. What would you like us to do, Chris?"

Chris put his hands on his hips and glanced at his companions. He said, "John, you've done a great job getting us in here and you're right about not being noticed, but the assault will begin any moment. We need to hurry and get her out of here before the whole place falls down on our heads."

The agent nodded, "All right, well, what we need to do is be ready to strike quickly and keep moving."

Everyone fell into line behind the federal agent and walked toward the door standing before them. The agent took a card key from his pocket and flashed it in front of the reader, causing the door to open silently. He didn't even stop and strode through the door as if he owned the place. It was at that moment that a missile struck above them with amazing force. The concussion caused them all to be thrown to the ground. They scrambled back to their feet with a renewed sense of getting to April quickly. The room they walked through was another computer room as they were very accustomed to by now, dealing with the doctor. People scrambled here and there, not even stopping to notice the intruders. They easily walked across the room just to have another missile strike the compound.

This time they braced themselves against the wall and watched as large pieces of the ceiling cracked and fell to the ground, shattering several computer stations in the process. At this point, the people remaining in the room panicked and ran for the exits. Jessica noticed a young lady pinned under one of the computer stations that was now crushed. She ran over to the table and tried to pull the table off the woman. Chris and Christopher ran to the other end of the table, grabbed it, and pulled with all their might. The table slowly lifted from the fallen woman and Steve was already on the ground, pulling the woman to safety. They could clearly see the woman wasn't awake but she was breathing. Steve lifted the woman without another word and looked to the agent.

Agent Bradley started, "This way. Hurry!" He pointed to the exit as they followed right behind. The agent led them into another hallway and although it was still well lit, the ceiling was heavily cracked with chunks of concrete lining the hallway. Some of the pieces were so large they were forced to climb over them to continue their journey. He brought them safely to a huge bunker door made of steel and closed tight. He once again reached into his pocket pulling out a keycard and swiped it in front of the reader. The door made several clicking noises before opening outward.

Cautiously stepping forward, they glanced into the room beyond the door. To their surprise, they found no damage inside besides a few cracks in the high ceiling. Without a moment's hesitation, they walked into the room and as they did, the door closed behind them with an ominous click. They looked at the closed door for a moment but knew they should be moving forward, and followed the agent once more. He moved to the other side of the large stone-hewn room. Once on the other side, they saw a series of modern doors made into the natural stone walls.

Chris peered into the room beyond through the small glass in the door. He yelled, "Everyone, come over here quick!" They all ran to where Chris stood as he moved over to let them look in the room.

Steve looked over everyone and said, "Chris, those certainly look like the type of tubes that the doctor could have used on April."

Chris' eyes brightened. "She's close! I can feel it! We just have to find her!"

Jessica already was moving to one of the other doors. She stopped in front of one and announced, "Guys, I think we have a problem here! Come look at this!"

Chris ran to Jessica and peered over her shoulder to see another even larger room with more tubes inside. This room was so large he couldn't see the end of it from his vantage point. His heart sank as he knew time wasn't on their side. He stood in front of his friends, looking at them for help.

Christopher came up to him and said, "Chris, we got this man! We haven't come this far to be stopped now!" Chris reached out and clasped the other man's hand and nodded. As Agent Bradley was about to swipe his keycard again, they all heard the crackle of a speaker overhead.

The sound startled them and they looked around to see the cause of the sound, but couldn't see any cameras or speakers. Once again, the crackle broke the silence and then they heard, "Well, Chris, it took you long enough!" They all looked up but could see no one as the voice continued, "Yes, I'm sure everyone is just dying to rescue our beloved April, but that ship has already sailed. Right now, the only question you must ask yourself is how do I get out of here before the entire complex comes collapsing down on my head? I'll give you this, you're very resourceful."

Chris couldn't stand listening to another shadowy voice and wailed out, "Now you listen to me, Doctor. I know that's you and if you want to live, you will hand April over to me right now. If you give her to me, I may decide to spare your life for her sake."

The voice came back, "Chris, I don't doubt that you would do as you say, however as I said, that ship has sailed for both April and myself. I'll not allow her or myself to be captured and used for further experiments. You see, Chris, there is a lot more going on here than you realize and if April were to fall into the wrong hands, she would be in much more danger than she's with me right now. I know it's hard to bare. If I could have spared you both this devastation, I'd gladly give my own life. The last thing I ever wanted was for her to be hurt or used for that matter."

Steve now came unglued. "You bastard! Come out here and show yourself! You have a lot to pay for and I'll have my vengeance!"

The crackle came on once more. "Yes, Steve, you've much to reconcile! I wish I could help with that, but I'm sorry that will never happen as all this will be over in a matter of minutes. If I were you all, I'd go through the last door to the right, go into the elevator, and run out of here before it's too late."

Chris whispered to his friends, "He has totally lost his mind. What's he talking about this place coming down on our heads? Our force is just here to secure the complex, not destroy it!"

Agent Bradley piped in, "He has got something else up his sleeve and we're once again caught in the middle of everything. We have to find April and get out of here!"

Chris once again appealed to the absent doctor as he spoke into the air, "Dr. Chase, please!" He stopped and raised clinched fists in the air. "You cannot do this to her. She's your daughter and yes, I know you would do anything to protect her, but not this way." Tears welled up in his eyes as he continued, "Give her to me! I'll be responsible for her life! I'll give you my life in return, but not hers!"

The voice itself faltered. "Chris, it's not that simple. I know you love her but as long as she's with me, there is no chance that other entities can have her. I wish nothing more than the two of you to be together forever, but that cannot happen right now. I'm sorry!"

Chris now fell to his knees. "I'm not leaving without her! You can bring this whole place down on my head, but I'm not leaving without April! If you want to kill me, just do it right now because I'm nothing without April! It's your choice, Doctor! I'll wait here for your answer."

Chris sat on the floor, knees folded and his hands in his lap, with tear-stained cheeks looking down at the floor. Without a word, every one of his friends joined him and said not a word. No one spoke and they sat for a few moments, waiting for the doctor's answer. The voice remained silent and there was no longer the crackle of the speaker. They all thought that this might be the end and waited for a force of soldiers to come for them. As they looked around the room waiting to be invaded, but saw nothing happen.

The silence in the room made minutes seem hours and they all looked at each other, wanting to say something, but knew there were no words. Chris looked to the long drawn faces of his comrades. These people were his family and he couldn't let them end their journey here. He looked once more at Jessica who now just found her love again and he wouldn't let them give that up for him. He rose to his feet and looked up with rage in his eyes.

"This is finished, Dr. Chase! You had your chance to take care of April and look at what that has caused. You, Doctor, you're the one that has put her life in danger. You alone! If you truly want to protect her, you will release her to me. She cannot have any life with you! With me, she has the chance of life and that's all anyone can ask!"

The silence broke with the crackle once more, "That's my boy!" Across the room, they heard a door click and open. Without a word, Chris ran to the door and waved everyone to follow. They ran behind him into one of the rooms full of the tubes. Chris didn't know where he was going but knew April was in this room. They ran by hundreds of tubes filled with frozen beings and Chris kept running without stopping. As if pulled by a magnet, the football player was a bloodhound on the hunt. Cutting left and right as well as running full speed, the man was on a mission.

The tubes went by in a blur and yet Chris wouldn't stop. The company followed, afraid to say anything about where Chris might be going. They continued forward at full speed when all of a sudden, Chris stopped before another door in the stone. He panted heavily and looked through the small glass. He stood as though he was afraid to open the glass. Inside was a much smaller room but surprisingly, the inside was completely empty. Chris pounded both fists on the sides of the door.

"He's still playing games! Once again, I'm the fool!"

As he said this, the door opened. Steve grabbed Chris and pushed him through the door. Each of the members of the company followed behind. Once inside, the door slid shut silently and locked. Steve tried the door but shook his head. Chris looked around for any clue as to how to get April. The walls were smooth, polished stone with beautiful sparkling facets of light beaming around the room from the various crystals. If they'd not been in such danger, they'd have thought the small cavern a wonder to behold, but their current situation allowed nothing but panic.

145

The floor was also hewn rock and just as smooth, but had almost a plastic coating over the floor. They looked carefully but could see no seams. After a thorough search, they were completely frustrated. They all sat against the wall with their backs on the smooth face of the rock. Chris sat with his head against the wall, looking toward the ceiling and then heard a small whining sound.

Once again, he heard the crackle of a speaker, "Take care of her, my boy! Into your hands, I commend her life!"

Chapter 22

Agent Bradley's advance force remained mostly intact due to air superiority. After the enemy retreated, the agent's men continued their march toward the installation. Most the force was held in reserve as the initial force was sent to probe the defenses. Once the weaknesses in the defense were attained, the entire force would be unleashed on the installation. This initial force stood strong in the face of the defense's rush and repelled them quite handily, forcing them back inside the confines of the compound.

One might have thought this a ploy by the defenders except for aerial bombardment caused mass chaos among the defenders. It became quite apparent the defenders weren't trying to draw them into a trap, but rather tried to stay alive to fight another day. All in all, a sound strategy in the face of defeat, however defenders now found themselves trapped inside the huge bunker. Agent Bradley's force was aware of their orders to surround the complex and lay siege to the installation.

Captain Jim Montgomery watched his troops working their way into position within a few hundred yards of the complex itself. Agent Bradley briefed his captain, instructing him to give him time to infiltrate the compound and waiting for his order to attack further. The captain viewed with pride the way their strategy was working to this point and was very confident they'd have little difficulty taking the compound. From his vantage point, he could see the main entrance to the installation and could clearly see the enemy fortifying their position.

Military vehicles along with additional troops flooded to defend the entrance. Captain Montgomery smiled inside, thinking of the surprise these troops were in for as the more important attack was about to take place from inside the complex. Experience told him not to get too excited yet as a plan this complicated could go wrong at any moment. His troops performed to expectations during the initial skirmish, but when advancing upon a defended position, there was bound to be surprises. The captain and his squad lay in a prone position, looking through night-vision scopes to view the surrounding area. When the captain was content that there were no enemy troops flanking his troops from behind, he turned his attention back to the entrance.

He reached for his binoculars as he could see some of the enemy troops at the entrance become very animated. The troops looked very nervous and agitated. As far as the captain knew, the enemy's communications and surveillance had been disabled so he couldn't understand what might be making them so agitated. Puzzled, he viewed the commotion, trying to make out what might be happening. He watched as the enemy troops suddenly got quickly into formation and took defensive positions. The captain was beside himself; they couldn't possibly know his team was about to attack. He also knew they didn't know the extent of his troop movement or size of his force.

His answer came in the form of his radio springing to life with an animated voice calling for the captain to pick up. The captain obliged and pressed the button, saying, "Are you in position?"

The voice came back, "Yes, sir. We're ready and at your command! Sir, we have a problem!"

Captain Montgomery called back, "Problem, what problem?"

The radio came to life once more. "Sir, we have the compound covered from every angle, but there is another larger force approaching our position!"

The captain spoke quickly, "Another force? From which direction? Did they identify themselves?"

The voice on the radio said, "Sir, they're coming straight for your position! The force is very large and as far as I can tell, it has a large contingent of military vehicles supporting it. Radar suggests at least three aircraft may be following behind in support."

The captain took this information in stride but was still slightly confused. He thought, *Did Dr. Chase have reinforcements to back up what was here at the complex? No, that couldn't be it. Intelligence they gathered on Dr. Chase's force was very up to date and complete. This was someone else's force, but whose?*

Captain Montgomery radioed back, "Keep an eye on them and alert me as they get closer. If they make any course corrections, I want to know about it. Understood?"

The voice came back, "Yes, sir. Understood!" The captain raised the radio to his face once more and switched channels so he could radio the rest of his troops about their guests.

He spoke quickly, "Attention, this is Captain Montgomery! I want everyone to stand fast but be at the ready as we're going to be joined by some party crashers! I'm not sure of the nature of this second force but it's approaching the entrance of the installation."

He brought the radio down to his chest before bringing it back up, "Once again, don't engage this force unless they engage you. I want us ready, but I don't want to give away our position or our numbers. Make sure you keep your radios on this channel and await further instructions. If anyone finds out any intelligence about this force, call me right away. Now stay in your positions."

The captain snapped the radio back onto his belt and looked at the entrance through his binoculars. The defenders looked very tense as if they'd be attacked at any moment. Just at that moment, he heard a whistle coming from above and he watched as a rocket struck the side of the entrance, exploding in a brilliant light. Fire, concrete, dirt, and smoke shot into the air, causing even more chaos. He watched through the lens as troops scrambled to regroup and move or tend to wounded comrades. He once again heard the whistle of a rocket and this time its aim was true and struck directly into the huge steel bunker door.

What once looked to be an impregnable bunker door was now a twisted hunk of molten metal. The captain was used to seeing the damage his weapons could cause but this was something altogether different as the door was now obliterated. He could see a truck off to the side with a large machine gun attached to the back, returning fire at the invisible aircraft. As the hot bullets whizzed through the air, not hitting their target, he couldn't help think of the bravery of those soldiers not abandoning their posts. He quickly put on his own night vision and looked to the sky to see what was attacking the defenders. At first, he could see nothing but out of the corner, he saw a streak and turned to see a helicopter coming on another attack run. This time the truck was ready and the gunner lit up the helicopter into a huge fireball.

The captain watched as the aircraft crashed into a hill off to the east in a huge ball of flame and exploding parts. He once again returned his attention to the entrance and this time he noticed other soldiers approaching. He grabbed his radio and called, "I thought I told you to let me know their position!" The radio remained silent and he growled into it, "Hello, someone talk to me! What's going on out there?" Still nothing came out of the radio and the captain knew they were on their own at this point.

Still in what he viewed as a safe distance and position, he once more looked into his field glasses. The new troops were clearly official military troops as could be told from their uniforms. This gave the captain a shot of panic down his spine as these weren't mercenaries but real troops. He didn't know if he could go against these troops. Mercenaries were one thing but fellow troops were something altogether different. He was about to give the order to fall back when he thought about Agent Bradley inside. He knew the agent didn't know what was going on out here without his knowledge.

Captain Montgomery couldn't leave the agent in the installation unsupported but this new force would be fighting against their brothers and sisters. He twisted his body back to a prone position and chose to wait out what would happen. The new force was now engaged by the defenders and the captain saw the fierce fighting among the two forces. The night was now lit up with the flashes of bullets flying and mortar fire. Right at what was left of the door, the fighting was at its worst. Soldiers fired at what looked to be point blank range and hand to hand combat filled the doorway.

Bodies were now strewn all over the entrance and one couldn't tell whose soldiers belonged to whom at this point, as it looked as if every man was for themselves. The captain saw more troops making their way toward the entrance and it looked as if the entrance would be overrun. Suddenly, he heard a door open from the roof of one of the buildings. He once again grabbed his binoculars and looked to where he heard the noise. Out of the top of the building rose what looked to be a large satellite dish. He watched as the dish rose from the roof and then turned toward the troops at the entrance.

Captain Montgomery and his troops were off to the side and not in front of the entrance, but he didn't feel good about this turn of events. He was quite aware of the wide variety of microwave and pulse weapons the military now could use against its enemies. He quickly got on the radio and told his troops to retreat to the fence line. Now he crawled with the rest of his soldiers back toward the fence and hoped that it would be in time to get out of range. The thought of getting up and running crossed his mind, but he wasn't sure of the range of the weapon or its actual power. One thing he didn't want to do was put his soldiers in harm's way. His force made their way slowly toward the fence, crawling through the thick grass and gravel.

Behind him, he could hear the battle continuing uninterrupted. The cries of agony through the chill of the night air. Gunfire and explosions rocking the entrance. The captain knew the fighting soldiers were sitting ducks and he wondered how many more of these weapons were stationed around the installation. Panic rose once again as he thought about the remainder of his troops stationed around the compound. He tried the radio once more and couldn't raise anyone.

The captain realized that everyone else would be cut off and would be unaware of the new weapon threatening them. The prospect of his men being harmed crushed him and he felt helpless as he could do nothing to help them. As he crawled, he looked around him to see how many followed. His squad followed in tow, but it was a very small number. Fear gripped him as he thought they may not be out of range and he edged forward. The fence came into view and his heart quickened. Sweat and dirt rolled down his face as they were within a few feet of the fence.

He turned, still lying in the grass, and took out his field glasses again to monitor the situation. Fighting still raged at the entrance with no clear advantage one way or the other. Gunfire split the air and he could see soldiers falling in droves in the doorway. The captain wondered how much more the defenders could take as he looked at an endless supply of attackers. Seeing the gruesome scene before him reminded him of the sacrifice he and these men made in the name of justice. He looked once more at his men who questioned through the dim light what was next from their leader.

The captain didn't want to leave those men back at the entrance to their fate but he felt there was no alternative. His soldiers must have felt much the same because they all looked back at the devastating battle with pity. Those men destroying one another to take control of a concrete bunker. They sat in silent vigil as the battle raged. That was when the captain thought he made a mistake as the large dish just remained pointed at the men but nothing happened.

As they all watched the battle from their vantage point, they saw the dish glow slightly. Captain Montgomery knew this was it as he pointed to his soldiers to cover their ears and close their eyes. A high-pitched whine broke the air and the captain put his head down into the grass, covering what he could. As he shoved his head into the ground, he felt a huge concussion that threatened to break him apart. The wave continued for what seemed like forever and he felt as if his skin would rip from his body. The strain on his head was such that he felt he would lose consciousness. Despite the overwhelming pain in his head and to his body, he refused to uncover his ears or open his eyes. The wave continued for a few more seconds and he thought the pain would never end. As the wave subsided, his pain continued and he finally blanked out to remember nothing.

Chapter 23

Dr. Chase stood brooding over his decision and glared at the computer monitor before him. He spent many long years preparing for this very moment and just as everything looked to be in place, along came, of all things, the military. His plan considered a vast number of attacking troops, but he didn't anticipate a battle on two fronts. The doctor, with both arms outstretched, gawking at the monitor, couldn't believe his luck. On the large monitor directly in front of him, he could see the onslaught at the gate. The carnage was gruesome and he lamented the loss of so many needless lives but if he was successful, a great many more lives will be restored, therefore being saved.

The decision to use his newest weapon was one that he didn't come to lightly, but he felt further loss of life was needless. He flipped up the glass panel to his right, revealing a large red button and a lock for a key next to it. The doctor took a key hanging from his neck out from under his shirt and placed it in the slot, turning it to the on position. One of the monitors to his right showed the weapon charging. Dr. Chase knew the weapon didn't need long to charge as the solar cells that powered the entire complex made enough power to run a small city.

Over the years, the doctor made many upgrades to the installation. Among them, the solar-power grid which now was so powerful that he was faced with a surplus of electricity, which he sold back to the town. He still had more than enough for his needs and battery back-ups powered by the cells as well. When he saw the power cells charged for his weapon, he turned to look at the multitude of monitors. On each one of the monitors, the brutality of war shown to the doctor who spent his life trying to save lives, but here once again, men lost their lives on his behalf. The thought of another person losing their life or being permanently disfigured didn't sit well with the doctor.

Tears came to his eyes as he looked down once more at the red button waiting for his push to unleash hell. To think that he was reduced to this to get others to notice the seriousness of what was happening around them. His sadness turned to rage as he thought of all the clones that were destroyed by the military during his tenure in the clone program. The battle before him just told him with every fiber of his being that this was a just cause and in the end, people would understand his motives. Red in the face, he scanned the battles on the screens and determined that this had gone on long enough.

Dr. Chase, feeling himself shaking, sat down with his hand hovering over the red button, waiting for the exact moment that would be the most effective. Thoughts of April and Chris passed through his mind and if successful, they'd live a long and fruitful life. Regret pained him as he thought of what Chris and April endured during the last few years at all the doctor's doing. With April, Chris, and company safely locked away for the moment, he knew the time to be right. Without further hesitation, the doctor pushed down on the red button and watched the screen to see what would transpire.

The doctor could see the satellite dishes begin to glow and he knew the troops both friend and foe had no chance. Communications with his troops severed long ago and he couldn't wait any longer. On the screens, he watched as they rippled with the wave of energy released by the dishes. The wave smashed into the troops with terrific force. The doctor cringed as he watched the soldiers fall to their knees, grasping at their ears and then falling to the ground. He watched in horror as the wave bombarded the helpless soldiers and their bodies writhing and contorting on the ground. Dr. Chase almost turned away as he saw blood oozing out of the soldiers' eyes and ears.

Still the waves continued as the doctor couldn't bring his hand to stop the weapon and he was mesmerized in some sick way by the devastation. The soldiers still moving were now on their backs with their arms reaching toward the sky, praying for help from above. These last survivors suffered even more if that was possible as the waves still found their target, causing the wounded soldiers' tongues to hang out and eyes to bulge out. When at last the doctor couldn't see anyone moving, he pushed the button one more time, shutting down the demonic machine.

As he sat and looked at the carnage the weapon caused, he almost retched several times, gagging as he breathed. The doctor could see no one moving and he scanned the various monitors, all of which showed no movement. The surrounding area was now a graveyard. He flipped the glass case back into position over the button once more and now faced the reality of the destruction the weapon could accomplish. The sheer power of the weapon in the wrong hands could destroy more than a few troops. The doctor wanted to make sure that never happened and promised himself he would destroy the compound before he let it fall into the wrong hands.

He thought back to when he was first approached about how his research with brainwaves could be used as a weapon. He practically physically threw the men out when the subject was brought up. The doctor always considered himself a pacifist, yet he found himself constantly surrounded by people who always looked to bring warfare into the future. The weapons discussed would use sonic pulses of energy to disable the enemy. Dr. Chase wasn't ignorant to the fact that the military always considered ways to destroy or stop troops without doing damage to infrastructure.

Sonic weapons, chemical weapons, electromagnetic pulse weapons, and biological weapons were all a huge part of the military's arsenal now. The doctor refused to help develop the type of pulse weapons that were considered because they weren't talking about rendering a soldier helpless. No, they talked about a weapon of such power that once unleashed, the unsuspecting soldiers would be dead in seconds. This was greatly disturbing to the doctor, who couldn't sign on for such research. That is until one day when he was sent an email showing him what the weapons could already do.

He was appalled by the gruesome nature of the weapon but even more so, the lack of control those using the weapon possessed. In the demonstration videos he watched, targets as well as those sending out the pulses were destroyed. He knew if he didn't find a way to direct the energy properly toward a specific target, then almost anyone could be harmed if near the weapon. He immediately called those in charge, telling them he would only help them concentrate the pulse so it could be directed and then he was out. Those in charge were so grateful they agreed to fund his current projects for an additional ten years.

Once again, he sold his soul so he could ultimately help others but he still couldn't believe the price he paid. Looking at the still monitors, the depths of his involvement in

158

the deaths of these men was frightening. Leaders were always asked to make choices that would have great consequences on others but the doctor was exhausted from the choices he felt forced to make. In this case, he once again held the lives of all these men in the palm of his hand and chose to unleash hell upon their souls.

As the realization of his gruesome actions sank in, he was brought out of his stupor by the concussion of another missile striking the installation. He could see on the monitor the missile was meant for the gate and with no one to defend it, the missile left a huge hole for anyone to walk through. Dr. Chase didn't know what or how many troops of his still were alive and functioning. He could no longer communicate with them and he'd completely forgotten about the air support. Without another thought, he hastily flipped the glass case back up and punched some commands into the computer.

The huge satellite dish near the entrance was still intact and the doctor turned the dish toward the direction of the aircraft. He looked at the radar screen, or what was left of it, and he could tell in what direction the craft was coming but nothing else, as most of the screen was shattered. Quickly turning to see if the weapon was charged, he grimaced to see it still needed a few minutes to charge fully. For a few troops, he wouldn't need a full charge, but for an aircraft, he would need as much power as he could muster.

He instinctively ducked as he felt the concussion of another strike. Looking to the monitor, it was plain to see the attackers tried to be sure no one could stop them from entering the complex. Dr. Chase looked at what was once a huge bunker door, now resembled a crater on the moon's surface. Sparks flew everywhere and a few monitors went dark but for the most part, his little command post stayed intact. The quietness around him was haunting but he had a job to do and wouldn't rest until his mission was accomplished. When the light showed the weapon fully charged, he checked the direction of the aircraft once more and craft was coming straight for the dish. Without any hesitation, he slammed the button and watched as the pulse wave struck the aircraft, blowing it apart in mid-air. Exhausted, he prayed there were no more aircraft. He rose and walked toward his next destination.

Chapter 24

Chris and company searched frantically for any semblance of an escape route. To their great frustration, the room seemed escape proof. The door they came through was shut tight and was locked from the other side. The friends combed the entire room until they were quite sure they were prisoners for some time. They finally sat down with their backs on the smooth rock face of the wall. Though totally frustrated by their situation, the coolness of the rock felt comforting on their backs.

Each member of the company now went into the recesses of their own minds. They all couldn't fathom how once again they found themselves in an impossible situation. Chris was so exasperated by the fact that he couldn't get to April. While Jessica held Steve's hand, she too couldn't believe she found Steve only to be locked in what could be considered a rock tomb. Steve held fast to Jessica but kept thinking of what game the doctor was playing now. He was used to the doctor and how he approached this game. Steve knew the doctor put them there to get them out of his hair and he was sure the grand doctor wasn't done with them by a long shot.

Christopher seemed the calmest as he didn't know what was to become of him. He knew every minute he was alive was a fabulous gift. Not that he didn't want to escape but he was with those he trusted and loved most, which made him feel confident they'd once again escape. Agent Bradley was the most disturbed by this whole situation as he rose from his seated position and paced around the small room. His agitation was quite apparent and continued to build. He went to the door, took his side arm out, and unleashed a few rounds into the door.

The sound was deafening and he looked at the effect the bullets had on the door. He was surprised to see the bullets solidly lodged in the metal door. The metal was so dense the bullets didn't pass through. He decided that wouldn't work and returned his weapon to its holster. Once again, he paced and finally plopped back down on the floor, distraught. He turned to his friends.

"I'm sorry, guys! I feel responsible for us being here! This whole thing was my idea! You all trusted me and I led you astray."

Jessica chimed in, "John, you can't blame yourself! We all knew what we were getting into here. Bringing April back to us is worth this and more. No, the only one to blame here is Dr. Chase. He thinks he has won but I tell you this, my friends. He won't like dealing with me when we get out of this. When I'm done with him in court, the good old doctor will be taking care of foot fungus in the crappiest hell hole I can put him into. You can be sure that he will never see the light of day again."

Chris stood in awe of the power of Jessica's voice. He witnessed the power of that voice on multiple occasions in the courtroom. Jessica's courtroom demeanor was nothing short of ultimate justice and anything but was simply unacceptable in her mind. Chris couldn't help but hope Jessica would get the opportunity she wished to prosecute Dr. Chase. Their current situation notwithstanding, they were far from bringing the doctor to justice. He also felt that whoever found the doctor first might not have courtroom justice in mind. As for himself, he wasn't sure if he could control himself if he were first to catch the doctor. His mind raced about what he might say or do when confronting the doctor.

In the middle of an angry thought about the doctor, a loud click and the whoosh of rushing air brought him back to reality. His eyes shot automatically to the floor where they stood. All eyes were now glued to the floor as they saw wisps of air releasing from before unseen cracks. Their surprise turned to fear as they noticed a white cloud forming in the air around them. Instinctually, they ran back to the door, looking frantically for a way to open the door. Panic rose as they could once again find no way out and turned to see the small room almost covered in the thick white mist.

Agent Bradley told them to hit the deck and put their shirts up to their mouths to breathe. Chris could feel the cold settle on his skin and could see his own breath. He stared at the floor where the mist still flowed uninhibited into the small room. As they all looked at one another, hoping the other might have a plan, they heard the whine of hydraulics break the air. All at once, the room seemed as if it would shake apart. The whine became a loud buzzing sound as the floor split in two below their feet.

They all flew to the edges of the room and plastered themselves to the wall. A few feet before their location, the floor stopped falling. Each member of the company refused at first to move from the safety of their wall. Agent Bradley leaned slightly forward, assessing the situation. His face immediately went from panic to sheer laughter. Chris threw him an angry glance that didn't go unnoticed by the agent.

He laughed. "Chris, I know! I can't help it. Just look down for a moment."

Chris peered over the edge and almost laughed himself. He found himself looking at a fancy staircase leading down into another part of the complex. Chris couldn't help but recall the same type of stairs they faced back at the stadium. Of course, the doctor would lead them on another wild goose chase. They all breathed a sigh of relief but could still feel the rush of cold air coming from below, assaulting their senses. As the mist dissipated, they took their first cautious steps to the room below.

Chris led the way, followed by Agent Bradley, Steve, Jessica, and Christopher keeping an eye on their rear. The air got colder as they made their way below. Water vapor settled on the stone steps made for a treacherous journey into the unknown. Chris slipped several times, bracing himself against the wall with his hand. Once safely below, they cautiously looked around to make sure they weren't walking into a trap. To their great relief, they now stood in what looked to them to be yet another lab.

Chris couldn't help but blurt out, "Another lab! Great, just what we need! I can tell you this. If I never see another lab for the rest of my life, it will be too soon." They all nodded in agreement and moved forward. The white mist parted down the middle for them as they could now make out something ahead.

Chris darted forward and took everyone by surprise as they tried to catch up to him. His heart pounding out of his chest even before he reached what he knew to be in front of him. He reached out and put his hands on the tube only to immediately take them away as if he were burnt. The tube was still freezing cold and he turned his hands over to see how red they know were because of encountering it. Chris quickly pulled his sleeve up to his hand and wiped off the ice buildup near where he expected the occupant's face to be.

The ice was soon removed from the upper part of the tube, revealing the figure asleep on the inside. A wave of extreme emotion overtook him at that very moment and he broke down against the tube. There inside the clear frozen tube stood the love of his life. April looked serene and undisturbed in her frozen slumber. Chris put his hand near her face but knew he still couldn't touch her. He turned to his friends with tears in his eyes. Each one of his friends voiced their support of him without a word. Agent Bradley already scrambled over to the computer station next to the cryogenic tube.

The federal agent furiously pounded on keys in the hopes of releasing his friend. His eyes scanned back and forth over the code that kept popping up as he worked the keys. His frustration reached its boiling point. "This is crazy! There is some kind of encryption here I've never seen before." They all moved fast to his side in the hopes of helping. Jessica tagged the agent's shoulder and took over code breaking. Continuing to type in any code or password they could think of, frustration turned to anger as nothing worked.

Chris, not wanting to move from his spot, saw their struggle and grudgingly went to lend a hand. He peered over Jessica's shoulder.

"A stupid question... did anyone use April's name?"

Jessica shot him an angry glance. "Chris, don't you think I tried that first?"

Chris looked sheepishly. "Sorry!" He stared at the screen and blurted out, "Try Gridiron Conspiracy!" Everyone peered at him as though he were crazy. He just looked at them. "Dr. Chase once told me he couldn't wait for this whole Gridiron Conspiracy to be over so he could just go fishing. At the time, I didn't think anything of it but now it all makes sense."

Without another word, Jessica typed in the words and pressed enter. At first, they all thought they failed in that attempt as well until they heard another whining sound. Once again, they heard a loud click followed by the whoosh once more of cold air being released into the air. Chris immediately ran back to April's tube. Once in front of the tube, he could clearly see the top of the tube opening as white mist rushed out. As the air made its way out of the tube, Chris could more clearly see the figure of April inside. Her frozen features became more pronounced as he saw the blue tinge of color on her face.

By this time, each member of the company stood with Chris watching the whole thawing process take place. Below April, they could see what looked to be a shower drain and above what looked to be a shower head. In a moment, they watched as water streamed from the shower head directly over April's frozen body. Helpless to do anything, all they could do was watch as their friend lay frozen before them. The water drained out below her and after a few minutes, they noticed the steam rising from the tube as if in a regular shower. The tube itself was now fogging up.

Almost as if on cue, a fan sucked up the steam. Soon the tube was cleared once more as the water fell over the beautiful women encased in the tube. Chris and the others almost turned away as April's clothes now clung to her body, revealing more of her form than most people would be comfortable with at this point. He stood fast, knowing he needed to be there for her when she came to. The warm water did its magic as a pinker color showed on her cheeks. No longer did her body seem rigid and she was much closer to life.

When finally the water stopped flowing, they impatiently waited for something else to happen, only to be disappointed. Through the drain on the bottom, another sound came. It sounded as if someone was blow drying hair. Chris looked at the bottom of the tube and that was exactly what he saw as hot air rushed up into the tube. This rush of hot air lasted for several minutes. When April looked dry once more, the tube shut once more on the top. This made Chris nervous before he saw the red glow starting at the top of the tube as if April were under a heat lamp.

Once more, they watched as April's face became more lifelike and her body seemed as if she were asleep. For the next ten minutes, nothing else happened and this was torture for April's friends as they wanted nothing more than to retrieve her from her prison. Chris was now sitting on the floor just waiting for any sign of life. His vigilance was rewarded as he saw movement out of the corner of his eye. He looked at April's hand to see her index finger twitch. He bounced up and looked into April's eyes. For a few moments, nothing happened but as he stared at the lovely face before him, her eyes almost as if on call popped open.

There was a look of fright and recognition on her face as she glanced out of the tube into her love's own eyes. Chris lifted his hand to reassure her everything was okay. He was unsure if she could hear him yet so he just signaled. She calmed just a little but now became more aware of her current situation. The red glow did its work as April came back to life. Now a half an hour later, they once more heard another click and the tube opened before them.

Chris rushed forward to catch April as her legs weren't strong enough yet to hold her weight. He caught her slight figure into his powerful arms and folded her close to his body. April leaned into his chest, not wanting to be anywhere else. He turned to his friends, determined. They all knew what came next. As they readied themselves to leave, they heard the familiar crackle of the speaker. Each person looked to the ceiling, waiting for the announcement.

Over the speaker, an uncertain voice emerged, "Chris, I've placed her life in your hands. It's now up to you. Without me, she will need all of you. Please look after her and make sure her dreams come true. I wish I could be there to see you become the woman I know you will be. I'm so sorry things turned out this way, but this was the only way to stop what they want to happen." There was silence for a moment and then the voice continued, "I wish I could apologize to you all enough to make things right, but one day you will understand. Sometimes things done for the right reasons are still wrong. It took me a long time to realize that. Much too long and not before a great many people were hurt. I spent my life trying to save lives but in the end, all I did was take life. How am I any better than those I wish to stop? Only time will tell. Please take care of my heart."

Chris couldn't help but hold April even closer to him as the voice spoke. His protective arms would never let her go again. He heard the words of the voice but his own in the back of his head told him not to believe anything that was said. As the speaker crackled off, another click came from their right, revealing another door. The door opened, inviting them in. Chris and company made for the door, not knowing what was to come next, but with April once again with them, they felt they could face anything.

Chapter 25

Dr. Chase looked around the damaged room in disbelief. *How could it have come to this,* he thought. His impenetrable fortress was a smoldering ruin. He wasn't finished yet and his best was still to come. He reached out, leaning heavily on his hands, looking at the few screens left intact. The doctor could clearly see Chris and company making their way to the secret exit. He didn't plan for this but this was the best alternate plan he could put into effect. Dr. Chase knew Chris would die himself before he let anything happen to April. A wave of regret passed through his mind as he thought he should have let Chris take care of her from the get go.

Moving his head slightly to the right, he viewed the cracked monitor only to see another force advancing on the breached gate. With his pulse weapon's charge used up, he would have to wait for it to charge once more. There wouldn't be time for that and he had to act quickly. The doctor quickly grabbed the chair, plopping himself in front of the monitors and pounding on the keyboard. The monitor before him came to life.

"Time to unleash hell," he muttered. He smiled sinisterly. "They thought they could take all my experiments and turn them against me. Well, let's see how they do against their own creations!"

He typed in the launch codes to send out his own army to meet this current scourge. The monitor before him now came to life, revealing a huge warehouse full of rows upon rows of the Artificial Intelligence football players. Their eyes popped opened all at once, surprising the doctor despite his work with the infernal things. The humanoid figures lined up in military formations before moving out toward the exit. If the doctor weren't so upset by what was done to these beings, he might have even been in awe by the sight. He watched as the last of the soldiers made their way toward the gate. A sense of finality came to mind as either way things would come to an end for himself or his enemy.

Having watched the men in formation brought him back to the beauty of football's multiple formations he viewed over the years. This thought pained him as he was a large part of the reason that Chris and his brethren had such a hard time now with the game. Head trauma nearly destroyed the game, but here they were on the brink of more than just the destruction of a game. No matter how he felt about the game, he now was responsible for the fate of humanity and he refused to get this wrong. He'd been wrong about so many aspects of the use of his research that every time he thought he fixed one problem, another reared its ugly head.

Dr. Chase stood transfixed as the first wave of A.I. soldiers swept into the waiting human force. The carnage was breathtaking almost to the point where the doctor was about to turn away. The A.I. soldiers' strength was superior to their human counterparts and they made quick work of the assembled human force before the gate. The entrance was littered with bodies everywhere and this gruesome sight didn't sit well with the doctor. He felt backed into a corner and knew how leaders of large forces felt when sending men to their deaths. He more than once dry heaved as he saw the human soldiers literally torn apart. His heart broke as the men went down, but he knew this was the only way and he needed to follow this to its conclusion or a great many more people would die.

As he thought his plan would work, he saw the entrance obliterated by a missile strike. Through the fire and smoke, the doctor saw nothing living stood at what was left of the entryway. Suddenly, he felt the whole complex being pounded by multiple missile strikes. He was more than once thrown to the ground as the missiles breached his outer defenses. The time had come, as he knew he could wait no longer. With everyone's attention now solely on destroying the doctor, they wouldn't be looking for what was to come next.

The next missile strike all but brought the entire stone ceiling down on the doctor as he scrambled to get to the safety of his bunker below. He ran down the hallway, dodging pieces of falling stone as well as rubble around him on the floor. Cutting one way quickly and then the next made him feel as though he were a running back ramming through the defense on his way to the end zone. Running to the large metal door, he quickly punched in his code and waited for the door to slowly open.

Once inside his special bunker, he secured the door. No one could get in without being let in by the doctor and that wouldn't happen. Sitting down to a fresh computer workstation, he glanced around the huge room. He sat perfectly content as the room showed no signs of damage from the constant bombardment the compound sustained. Feeling much more secure, he went back to work. He worked the keys with the skill of a surgeon and quickly pulled up what he was looking for. The picture before him was a sight to behold. The sheer size of the apparatus was immense.

On the screen before him was his final parting gift to those who stole his life and that of his daughter. He vowed to make them pay for their deeds, but now his promise would be fulfilled. His vengeance would be complete as his enemies would be put back into the Stone Age and his research would be safe. With one final look at the instrument of his redemption, he put the key from the chain around his neck in the slot before him on the instrument panel. He turned the key without hesitation, waiting for massive doors above the weapon to open.

What looked to be the entire ceiling above the weapon opened in a large circular pattern until he could see the night sky. Originally, this site was used as a place to house nuclear weapons but with the close of the Cold War, these weapons were decommissioned and dismantled. This left all the former silos empty, which allowed the doctor to swoop in and institute his plan to perfection. Dr. Chase, so infuriated by the government's stealing of his research, decided it was now his turn to return the favor. He stole a secret prototype of a huge EMP weapon. The doctor made his own modifications to the weapon and when he was done, the government would have no idea what hit them.

Before him on the screen, what looked to be a gargantuan satellite dish rose from the depths of the silo. Slowly, the dish rose until it stood outside and pointed exactly where the doctor wanted. He smiled as he checked all the monitors to see everything looked great to finish his plan. Years of planning would now be culminated in his ultimate triumph. He reached over to flip up the plastic cover to reveal a red button. With one final glance at the screen, he didn't hesitate and pushed the button with great purpose. All he had to do was wait and let the weapon do its job.

His attention now turned to the computer monitor before him as he could see various other dish sites and cell phone towers light up on the world map. The doctor may not own all the sites needed but with the power from his one weapon, he could piggyback his signal off all the other sites. He almost laughed at the ease with which he would alter the world at this very moment. Those smug government bastards would now pay and they'd never be able to recover. In a few moments, the world would be given a reset of sorts and they'd be able to pick up the pieces in peace.

Dr. Chase checked the gauges once more and saw everything was now ready. The glow of a full charge of his weapon stood out on the monitor before him. The only thing he was missing at this point was the final countdown as it would have been for the launch of a spacecraft. He imagined what it must have been like to be in the control room as NASA readied themselves for a launch. The excitement was almost more than he could bear, but he steadied his hand over the yellow button that would unleash the full power of this sinister weapon. The doctor pressed the button without another thought and waited.

Nothing happened as he viewed the world map. He should have seen the waves emanating from all the different sites, yet nothing happened. Quickly checking everything once more, he pressed the button once more and looked at the map for confirmation. Once again nothing happened and panic rose from inside him. From all he could see, his weapon should be working. As he rose from his seat and went over to check the electrical feeds, he went down the checklist in his head, baffled as it should have been working, according to all his calculations.

He went back to his seat and couldn't help but stare at the screen in dismay as it was now scrambled snow. The doctor pressed button after button without success to bring back the image of the map and his weapon. A cackling laughter now came out of the computer monitor. All at once, the snow formed an image of a man's face. The face that appeared on the screen made the doctor turn ghostly white.

The man on the screen laughed. "You didn't think you could get rid of me that easily, did you?"

Chapter 26

Chris held April close to his body. Despite his exhaustion, he wasn't about to let her down for anything. To feel her body against his was a dream come true, one he thought he lost forever. Although April was awake, she was still quite dazed and shivered in Chris' arms. He looked down at the shivering woman in his arms and kissed her head, bringing her in even closer. She said nothing but accepted the comfort and leaned in for more. Chris followed Agent Bradley as they worked their way through the myriad of hallways. As they approached, each door opened before them as if they were a trail of bread crumbs.

Agent Bradley saw Chris struggling to hold April. He felt for the young man but dared not stop as they heard missiles strike and shake the complex. Chris said not a word and gripped April tighter, hurrying behind the agent. Christopher kept an eye on Jessica as Steve covered their backs. No one seemed ready to talk as they just wanted to find a way out and looked to the agent's experience to lead them. Steve was quite comfortable following the agent's lead. He too saw the doors opening before them and knew Dr. Chase was behind this escape.

They came to a screeching halt as they almost slammed into a sheer rock wall. Everyone turned and looked back the way they came, only to hear another click. Agent Bradley laughed and told them to keep up as he rushed into an opening that now stood in the rock face. They all followed closely to the agent even in the dim light of the rock-hewn tunnel. After traveling for several minutes, it became apparent that they made their way back up towards the surface. Continuing through the snug tunnel, the companions felt fresh air against their faces. Agent Bradley felt the rush of air and urged them on. Without comment, they all followed closely behind.

As they came around a corner, they were once again faced with what looked to be a solid wall. They could all still feel air rushing in from somewhere in front of them. Agent Bradley cautiously moved forward, putting his hands on the wall. His fingers worked their way to the edge of an unseen doorway. He smiled as he pushed the door outward with little effort. They saw nothing but darkness before them but could feel the fresh air surrounding them as it rushed in the tunnel. Each sat at the edge of the tunnel not yet wanting to reveal themselves to the outside world.

Chris carefully placed April against the tunnel wall and joined her, allowing her to lean on him once more. His arms ached and it took a few minutes for them to completely straighten out from holding April in an upright position for so long. Once the feeling came back to his arms, he rubbed his hands to warm them up and then tried to do the same to April. She welcomed the comforting warmth and looked at him gratefully. Christopher and Jessica sat on the other side of April with their hands on her other arm.

Steve stood guard, watching the tunnel to make sure they weren't followed. He stood vigil for what seemed like hours but it was several minutes before he turned and announced he didn't think anyone followed them. The massive man then joined his friends on the floor and let out a long sigh. He, along with his friends, had endured so many harrowing escapes that what was one more. They all sat in silence not sure what their next move would be or should be.

The silence surrounded them threatening to suffocate them. Finally, Agent Bradley spoke.

"Now what? Dr. Chase let us escape, which is exactly what he wanted. If it weren't for April's condition, I'd have stayed and taken it out on Dr. Chase's hide."

Chris stood and looked back down the tunnel before announcing, "My friends, it's up to you. I'd love nothing more than to destroy the good old doctor, however I have what I came for." He looked lovingly at April, who looked warmly back at him, still shivering. Everyone could clearly see Chris struggling with the dilemma of leaving the doctor unpunished or going back. In her current condition, there was no way he would bring her back into the complex. No one knew what would be waiting for them if they went back.

Jessica spoke up, "Listen, I know we came to get April and I'm so glad to have her back, but we cannot leave the doctor unchecked. He must be made to pay for what he has done." Everyone looked at her with uncertainty in their eyes. She continued, "I don't mean we should go it alone. John should be able to contact what's left of his forces now that we're out in the open. Let him get those folks to help us and then we can have a better plan to get the doctor." They all looked at her and nodded without another word.

The air was a fresh brisk vintage as they moved into the open. Each member looked to the sky with their mouths wide open, sucking the fresh unpolluted air into their lungs. Stars filled the open air and in the crisp night, they shone brilliant against the pitch-black backdrop. Chris could feel himself stretch out, which felt good after such a cramped journey in the tunnel. He looked to his cohorts as they each rose to their full heights and took in the glorious night. Christopher stood in awe of the star-filled sky and Chris knew right away what that felt like. He remembered a time when he spent an evening in the company of a beautiful lady looking at these very stars years ago. Chris could recall the sense of wonder in the vastness of the sky.

Their dream state lasted only moments as a pungent metallic smell ruined the air around them. This immediately brought them back to the gravity of their current situation. Agent Bradley raised his phone to his face and barked orders to the soldier on the other end. He gave orders to lock onto his signal and send a detachment to pick them up on the double. The soldier assured Agent Bradley they'd be there in a matter of minutes. This news calmed the federal agent and he hung up, looking at his friends in the light of his phone. They could see the seriousness in his face as he stared out at them.

The agent started, "We're not out of the woods by a long shot. I've just been informed that the complex is still under attack and has been continuously hit with bunker buster missiles. The main gate is in shambles, non-existent at this point. We may have to find another way in when we decide to go after the good old doctor. When we do get picked up, please let me do the talking as the soldiers are distraught. From what I was told, Dr. Chase used some type of pulse weapon on our troops and decimated them. One moment, they marched on the gate, fighting their way in and the next, they dropped like flies. Honestly, everyone, we might want to re-evaluate our plans and get April as far away from here."

Chris retorted, "John, we've come too far now to let him get away with this. With the information you just relayed to us, he continues to destroy lives unchecked. This must stop! I'll not allow this man to ruin another life if I can help it." He looked to April. "Honey, I know you're a mess right now, but I won't let you out of my sight again. I promise to save the doctor's fate to you." April battled her emotions. Here they were, talking about the destruction her father caused all around them. She felt a knot start in the pit of her stomach, thinking of what these men would do to her father once he was in custody. Court wouldn't be an option at this point.

Tears welled up in her eyes as she finally spoke. "I don't pretend to feel the pain of all those affected by the actions of my father, but I can tell you that all the pain must end. My father has much to pay for but something tells me that by the time we get to him, it will be too late. Chris, you know he has something up his sleeve and I don't want to be anywhere near him when the full force of the government comes down on him. Can we just please go home? I cannot warm up and my head feels as though it's about to split wide open."

Without another word, Chris walked over to April, scooping her up once more and cradling her to his chest. He looked at Agent Bradley and nodded. The agent spoke not a word, turning to the others.

"Okay, when our extraction team arrives, we'll make our way to a safe zone away from the complex and re-evaluate our position. I for one would like to recharge my batteries before taking another crack at the doctor." This suited the friends just fine at this point.

Steve piped in, "You all know me, surrender isn't in my nature but in this case, I agree with John. The importance of fresh intelligence based on the current assault is of the utmost importance. Based on what Agent Bradley has just told us, Dr. Chase continues to surprise with his ingenuity. I would like a look at what we could learn from this assault and return with a much more cogent strategy. Trust me, if you all wanted me to go in there and personally pull his ass out here, it would be my pleasure."

At this, Jessica yelled over to him, "You're not going anywhere! Don't even think about it! April is right, we need to regroup. Let us fall back and put a little pressure on him in other ways. I for one am so tired I'm not sure how much longer I can stay awake. Now that we have April, the doctor seems secondary at this point. I'm so glad to have her back. Thank you, everyone, for your help in retrieving her. John, when are these people going to be here? I don't like being stuck out here in the middle of nowhere with aircraft armed with missiles flying around my head."

Agent Bradley could tell tempers would be flaring if his soldiers didn't arrive soon. He took out his phone, trying to reach his man. The phone rang with no answer. The federal agent looked exasperated as he brought the phone down to his pants leg. After a few moments, his phone vibrated and he answered, "Where the hell have you been? We've been waiting long enough!"

The voice came over the phone, "Sorry, sir, we couldn't find a vehicle that was intact until just a few minutes ago. We should be there any moment."

The agent hung up after getting a few tidbits of information from the soldier. He learned what was left of his force was scattered along the outskirts of the complex and waited for orders. He gave his orders for them to fall back and regroup back at the barn. Almost as he hung up, they heard the roar of a large engine breaking the silence of the night air. Lights from the vehicle all but blinded them as they were so used to the dark at this point. The large all-terrain vehicle stopped within a few feet of them.

Soldiers jumped out from the back of the vehicle to see if the passengers needed help. Despite being exhausted, they were all mostly intact as they lifted themselves into the back of the transport. Each member sat with their head leaned back against the transport and went into their own thoughts. Agent Bradley spent a moment being briefed by the soldiers and then climbed into the transport himself. He sat across from his friends with his hands on his head. The plans for his conquest of the military installation were unsuccessful and many people lost their lives. The thought of others losing their lives because of the doctor infuriated Agent Bradley.

The large transport rumbled away from their current position. Now the only noise that they heard was the hum of the engine and the tires rolling over the gravel. After a few minutes, the ringing of Agent Bradley's phone broke the silence. He quickly answered and spent a few moments talking and hung up quickly. He didn't say anything to his friends but jumped up and went to the window that looked into the cab of the transport. He peered into the cab and shouted.

"Head due east quickly! It's as we feared. Dr. Chase does have something up his sleeve and we can still stop him."

Chapter 27

The ghastly figure pressed closer to the screen as the doctor shied backwards. Though a grainy warped image, Dr. Chase could easily recognize his nemesis, the once Mr. P. He gathered himself very quickly, sneering at the video image.

"I'm impressed! You paid more attention to what I told you all those years after all. Here I thought you were an idiot. You sure pulled one over my eyes. Only one problem... you are and always will be confined to the internet. Enjoy your self-induced imprisonment. I'll be sure to write you an email every now and again just to make sure you aren't lonely."

On the screen, the ghastly figured face contorted.

"You're not quite as smart as you would have us all believe, Doctor. You're forgetting that you've provided me with the perfect vehicle to re-enter humanity. Yes, I did listen, very intently actually when you described all that the body of an Artificial Intelligence being could house. Including one's own self. You self-righteous bastard, you've resurrected me with your own hands. Granted, I have to wait until the A.I. host is perfected but with the rest of your research, which I procured from your mind, it won't be long now."

Dr. Chase's lips puckered, ready to reply but he stopped himself before any sound escaped. He raised an eyebrow, looking cautiously at the monitor.

"Well played, my friend! Tell me what your plan is. What do you need from me? I'm sure you need someone on this end to help make your transition back into life smooth. I alone have the knowledge needed to bring you fully back into the world of the living. If you plan on living once more, you will need someone in your corner or have you forgotten all the issues the A.I. bodies have experienced?"

Once more, the figure on the screen cackled, "You never cease to amaze me to what depths you will go to see your research come to fulfillment. Here I thought that I'd have to capture you once more and all this time, I just had to ask for your assistance. Doctor, there is a reason we were friends. We are two of a kind, you and I. Yes, I'd see your vision come true in the form of a human taking over an A.I.'s body. Just think for a moment. Instead of the issues we ran into with the A.I.s having no frame of reference except what we program, they'd now replicate an actual human. I tell you, Dr. Chase, this is only the beginning. All the work you made possible will now create a new race of being with the best of both worlds.

"Can you imagine all of our weaknesses gone in the blink of an eye? We will now never become ill and die. Everything men fight over will no longer matter. If someone has eternity, what else do they need? You once lectured me about my lack of legacy, well I tell you this shall be my ultimate legacy. I'll change the world and you shall be my right-hand man. It'll be as everything should have been. I'll retain my team and things will go back to normal. No one will be the wiser. I'll bankroll you and others will assume you're working for the government once more. This is amazing! Everything I dreamed will come true. You will see, Doctor; we'll be invincible. There will be no one to stop us!"

Dr. Chase stared at the screen for a moment, contemplating what to say next. Chewing his lip, he continued, "Hold your horses there, big guy. We're not as close as you think. I'm still in a fight for my life here and they'll send reinforcements. I... we still should find a way to quell this situation or there will be nothing left to see my vision become a reality. You must trust me when I say the danger is just beginning. I may have won a battle but the war is coming to my front door. I just barely survived the first battle. No, things are far from safe and although I've no doubt we'll prevail, I worry what will be left when I do."

The image on the monitor laughed aloud. "Now that's the Dr. Chase I know. Always worried about the greater good. If we pull this off, there will no longer be a worry of the future. As a matter of fact, the future will be written as a triumph of human achievement and evolution. Besides, you're forgetting one huge advantage that you now have at your disposal—me! You now have control of everything linked to the internet. I'm the ultimate spy and I don't need an expense account. The military won't know what hit them. I'll send them back to the time of the cowboys."

At this last comment, the doctor stepped back a few paces, carefully thinking of how to respond to the figure's last boast. He certainly couldn't let this maniac take control of his masterful plan, yet he could be very useful still. Caution and tact was needed in this situation. The doctor dealt with these ego maniacs his entire career as they all thought of ruling the world. Honestly, he didn't want to rule the world, yet he wouldn't let the likes of this horror take control of everything he worked so hard to procure.

He worked his way over to a still workable chair and sat in front of the monitor. Placing his hands on the console, he pulled himself closer. Sensing the glaring eye of the wraithlike figure upon him, he refused to speak. The doctor sat stone faced, looking at the damaged console waiting for inspiration to strike. With arms outstretched, he looked at the debris-filled floor, still not wanting to speak. At last, he peered up at the screen.

"Please, promise me you won't do anything just yet. I still have some things up my sleeve and wouldn't want to have them derailed now. If this does not work, I'll use all your avenues to bring them to their knees."

The figure seemed pleased. "All right, Doctor. Do it your way, for now. I'll be watching. If I feel that you cannot fulfill things from your end, I'll intervene and finish things my way. I won't deliberately step on your toes but there is too much at stake to let things to get out of hand. Just as you've spent a lifetime putting your plans into place, I've gone beyond life to insure mine. Although I must tell you, being as free as I am now, has its advantages. No one can control me and I have a great deal of control over others. It's quite a feeling having this power."

Panic grasped the doctor as he let the last statement sink in and he felt sick to his stomach. In life, Mr. P. always listened to the doctor's advice and heeded what was asked of him. At this point, Dr. Chase could only imagine what was going on in the computer-like brain of Mr. P. and honestly, he didn't want to know. His own plans were so close to being a reality that this would be a monumental setback, one from which would be extremely difficult to recover.

Debris pelted his head as he looked at the remaining good monitor to see the advancing force preparing to invade his sanctuary. If he did come through this invasion unscathed, it would be a miracle. Things came clear in his mind. There was no doubt that finishing what he started would be the only true solution. Mr. P. would be quite surprised by the doctor's choice in the end. The doctor still had a few tricks up his sleeve and his computer counterpart couldn't possibly know what he was thinking. It would be quite amusing to see the faces of all involved when the doctor's plan came to full term. If he survived this, things would never be the same and no one would ever know the full extent of the doctor's plan.

He couldn't help but harken back to when the first thoughts of an Artificial Intelligence being crossed his mind many years ago. At that time, the doctor never thought that technology would catch up to his idea during his lifetime. The fact that he saw cloned human beings during his tenure would be amazing enough for anyone, but to see the dawn of another type of being, now that was something altogether different. He laughed a bit, recalling the initial sketches he made of his idea. The sketchbook now took up residence on his bookshelf collecting dust. The smile on his face widened as he remembered the glasses he put in one of the sketches, showing one of the figures as a computer game. Almost laughing aloud, he thought of how the sketchbook looked more like a child's scribblings than a scientific journal.

The sheer force of another rocket striking the compound interrupted this light moment. Once again, the lights flickered and pieces of the ceiling made their way to the ground as dust formed in the air in front of the doctor. Turning to see that his exit was still intact, he could view through the dusty haze that the doorway remained mostly intact. The edges of the doorway showed signs of crumbling and the window on the door was cracked, but it stood waiting for the doctor. Looking down at the monitor, he saw the troops marching forward and he knew immediately that it was time to leave. He reached forward and punched a few commands into the keyboard for the self-destruct mechanism of the compound. His hand hovered over the last key to initiate the sequence, but he paused just before pressing the button. He thought to himself, *Not yet!* He deleted the command, heading out of the crumbling doorway.

Chapter 28

With his head pounding, Gus awakened. Blinking his eyes to clear the dust, he made out blurry images with his left eye. His right eye remained blocked by something right in front of him. As his eyes focused, he figured out what blocked his view and he recalled the light fixture crashing down on him. The thought of the fixture brought back the memory of the lab technician that helped him. He tried to scan the room, but he could only move his head to the left as the light fixture still impeded the right and he couldn't see the young man.

Pain racked his head but he worked his hands first and then tested his arms. Feeling good as nothing seemed broken. The light fixture, although large, proved not that heavy, even for the slight reporter as he easily pushed it off himself. The metal fixture fell to the ground with a crunch, and a smash of the remaining glass. Now that his view was restored, Gus peered once more around the room in the hopes of locating his fallen friend. To his great relief, not that far to the right of him, he could see the young man stirring. Gus was now on his feet, working his way across the damaged floor on his way to the fallen man. When he arrived to the young man, his smile faded. Although he was now awake, Gus could clearly see that a large slab of concrete now pinned the man against the wall.

A panicked look came across the man's face as he tried to move and realized the gravity of his situation. Other than being pinned, the man seemed intact and didn't immediately complain of pain. Gus took one look at the size of the concrete slab and knew without a doubt there would be no way he could move the piece to free the man. The man must have seen the look in Gus' eyes as he smiled.

"Gus, it's all right! Make sure you send someone to help me when you can."

Gus didn't even hesitate. "No way! I'm not leaving you here. The rest of this place could come down any minute. We need to get you out of here." The man's face showed great relief at this comment and looked around the room, trying to find anything that could help move the slab.

Across the room, he pointed to a large post that was now on the ground. Gus ran over to the post and almost got a hernia trying to lift it. It was heavier than it looked. He dragged the post over to the trapped man and worked it into the wall on the other side in the hopes of getting some leverage. Gus found a great hold just between the wall and another piece of fallen ceiling, and pushed. To his great joy, the huge slab inched forward. The young man now squirmed his way out from under the slab when it cracked right down the middle.

Gus grunted, "Hurry! This thing is going to break apart and who knows what will happen." The man did as he was told and pulled himself to safety as the slab broke in two and crashed to the ground where the young man had just been pinned.

Both men looked at one another with great relief in their eyes. At this moment, Gus noticed the large gash in the young man's leg. The man's pant leg was soaked in blood and he now wobbled as reality set in. Gus told the man to sit so he could look at the damage. Gus tore what was left of the man's pant leg to reveal an angry gash on the side of his shin. Nothing stuck out of the wound, which amounted to a huge scratch, but he had to dress the wound and stop the bleeding. Using the strips of cloth from the man's pant leg, he wrapped up the wound after cleaning it. When Gus was satisfied the wound was no longer bleeding, he asked the man to stand and test its durability. The man complied and seemed no worse for the wear. He did say it hurt a bit, but he could walk on it without too much difficulty.

The two men searched the room looking for an exit, only to realize they stood in what was left of the doorway. They promptly moved into the dusty hallway, peering through the haze to see a dimly lit narrow hallway. Hastily, they made their way to the end of the hall to another door, which stood open and to their relief, they saw signs of life. A few people scrambled around, grabbing papers and files before heading out the door on the other side of the room. Gus and the young man followed behind as no one even noticed them. Gus kept close to a young lady with an armful of files. She struggled so Gus came up behind and grabbed the files from her. She looked appreciative and said no more as she led the way out of the maze of tunnels.

Finally, they all made their way back to civilization, if one could call the destroyed compound civilization. The once-clean, shiny, beautiful compound was now littered with destruction. Gus found himself looking at the wake of destruction, including labs, computers, and fallen people, with sadness as he followed the woman like a bloodhound. The young lady delivered them right into a large conference room. Obviously used in peacetime for important meetings, the room was now a triage center for the wounded. Wounded of all sorts lay on the ground and the large conference table. The young lady turned to Gus and thanked him for assisting her, but she could take it from here. She told them to stay here and have their injuries tended to. Looking around the room, Gus and the young man felt their injuries were quite insignificant compared to some of the wounded before their eyes.

The room smelled of sweat, blood, and stale air. Gus immediately spotted a young lady struggling with a basin full of filthy water and went to help. The young man fell in behind Gus and grabbed some clean gauze and brought it to a man binding a wound on a woman's arm. Both helped moving from wounded person to wounded person, assisting in any way they could. As they made their way around the room, they were shocked at the number of people stuffed into this one room. The stale air made matters worse as the heat in the room rose, making the smell become quickly unbearable. Gus took out his own handkerchief and wiped his brow before putting it in front of his own nose to block the stench.

Gus noticed a man sitting in a chair over in the corner, sipping from a cup. He seemed oblivious as to what was going on around him, which infuriated Gus. He walked straight up to the gentleman with the hopes of reading him the riot act about getting up and helping others. As he approached the man and got a much better look at him, he stopped in mid-stride. He stared at the figure in the chair and almost wanted to slap the man. When Gus approached, the man looked up slightly and glanced at Gus without recognition. This made Gus even more upset. *How can this man not recognize me?* Gus looked down at himself quickly to see the state of himself. He was quite the mess, but this man before him should still recognize him. After all, Gus had spent much time with the man in the chair before him over the last few years.

Once again, the man looked up as Gus now stood within a foot of him and he smiled without a hint of recognition. Gus almost slapped him but refrained and asked, "What are you doing here?"

The man answered, "I'm not quite sure. I woke up face down on the ground and a nurse found me, brought me here. She told me to sit tight until she found someone that could help me. I did what I was asked and have been here for most of the day. Occasionally, someone will give me a drink of water, but they don't seem to know what to do with me."

Gus lifted an eyebrow. "Why? What's wrong with you?"

The man smiled faintly. "I'm not quite sure, but I cannot seem to remember a damn thing."

Gus tapped himself in the head. "Well, that would explain a lot!"

The man looked at him. "What do you mean?"

Gus laughed. "For starters, you and I know each other very well."

The seated man looked haunted. "I'm sorry. I have no idea who you are."

Gus put his hand on the man's shoulder. "Don't worry. We'll figure it out, but for now, let's get you out of here." He pulled the man out of the seat and led him toward the door. He stopped a nurse and asked which way to the exit. The nurse gave them directions and they went off, hoping to get the hell out of this nightmare.

Walking shoulder to shoulder down the hallway, the three just looked straight ahead in the hopes that fresh air would soon find them. The light became stronger and they now found themselves in a large lab, which for the most part was intact. Except for a few cracks in the walls, the lab looked much the way it would on any other day. The air was much fresher here and they took deep breaths, letting the air fill their lungs. Looking around, Gus was surprised to see lab tables and computers, but nothing else. In most of the labs they found in this maze were set up for either clones or A.I. experiments.

Gus turned to the man they rescued. "None of this rings a bell? You really don't recognize any of this?"

The man looked worried. "I'm sorry but I have no idea what you're talking about!"

Gus laughed. "I can't believe this! Everyone is looking for you and you've been here all along. You have caused us all a great deal of grief, Mr. P! You have a lot to answer for!"

The man just looked at Gus in confusion. "Who is Mr. P?"

Chapter 29

Dr. Chase, with laptop in hand, ran upward through the maze of hallways toward his goal, the huge satellite dish. Perspiration running down his face, he wiped his brow with his sleeve, not missing a stride. Despite the night being brisk, the compound seemed stifling. He raced through the last hallway, hoping no one detected him. The last thing he wanted at this moment was to have to explain himself or give orders to someone at this point. His luck held as he grabbed the final door handle and threw the door open, revealing a destroyed computer room. The room was in a ghastly shape, with the roof all but removed. The doctor worked his way around the obstacles littering the floor.

He stubbed his toe on a large chunk of concrete and almost fell into what was left of the wall. His hand thrust out and caught the wall, steadying his progress. After a moment to rub his foot, he continued more cautiously through the rest of the room. The doctor used this room quite often, but felt very grateful his presence was elsewhere when the room met its end. He glanced quickly, hoping that one of the terminals might still be viable. To his dismay, every computer station looked to be destroyed. Panic rose in the doctor at this moment because he knew he needed a working terminal to plug in, to execute his plans. The compound usually had Wi-Fi but in the wreckage, he was certain that the best connection would be on a hardwired computer.

Off to his right on the floor, he saw an overturned table. He grabbed the table from the floor and set it upright. Using his sleeve, he wiped the filth from the metal table and placed his laptop there. Off in the distance, he could hear people shouting and running away from the compound. He knew his time got more compressed as each moment passed. It would only be a matter of time before the authorities came for him. With no security or soldiers to protect him, he knew he was a sitting duck.

The laptop booted up as the doctor scanned his surroundings, hoping for time to finish what he started long ago. An image of April flooded into his mind as he looked at the screen coming to life. Frustration built within his mind. Things should have been much different for him and his beloved daughter. Once again, images of their camping trip came to mind. He thought it would be funny to trick his daughter into thinking they were going to rough it, but he secretly rented a cabin with all the amenities. April to this day remained furious with him over it, in a funny way. They ended up having the best time and even April had to admit her pleasure of such a cool trip.

The two bonded during that trip and became extremely close. After all the issues that had arisen because of the clone case, the camping trip allowed them both time to bare their souls to one another. He laughed aloud as he recalled a prank April played on him during the trip. She decided that to get back at her father that she would cook his goose. One of the days during their trip Dr. Chase suggested they go fishing. This on the surface would seem the typical family outing to most but to Dr. Chase and April, this wasn't so. Both parties spent much of their lives in books studying medicine, which left little time for extras such as fishing. The doctor didn't think much of this and thought it would be a great experience for them both.

When they both brought their equipment to the perfect spot, they both just stood looking at one another for assistance. Neither one knew what to do and just kept looking at the fishing rods as though they'd prepare themselves to fish. Luckily, that was when a nice young man a few yards away noticed their plight and offered some assistance. The young man helped them set up their rods and even showed them how to bait. He even went so far as to cast out their lines for them and instructed them on what to look for while showing them how to reel in the line.

Feeling very embarrassed, they both thanked the young man and offered to pay for his bait. The young man declined and returned to his own fishing spot. Dr. Chase and April turned to watch their recently cast lines. April's line bobbed up and down. She shouted to her father and reeled in the line as the young man showed her to do. She could feel the hook set and what ensued was an epic battle for supremacy. The fish fought valiantly but in the end, April brought the beast in. Dr. Chase was first to yell out in surprise over the size of the monster. April couldn't help but laugh at the size of her catch as it was a very small sunfish. She did however feel a great sense of pride over catching the wonderful fish.

Once again, as the fish dangled on the line wiggling furiously, they both looked at each other as to what happened next. The young man once again came to their rescue and showed them how to remove the hook, tossing the small fish back into the water. April, of course, took a photo with her phone for posterity. April now needed some more worms so she asked her father to grab one out of the container. Dr. Chase proceeded to open the container only to have a bunch of the comedy snakes pop out at his face. Just to see the doctor's face as the items came flying out of the container was priceless to April. Her revenge was complete and when the doctor's heart rate returned to normal, he complimented her prank.

Even the young man who came over to make sure they were all right during all the commotion laughed quite a bit. They went on to catch a few fish but made a friend in the process and learned a ton about fishing along with themselves. All the way home, they talked of the size of the monsters they brought in on their hooks. Just a simple camping trip turned out to be the type of medicine needed to heal the wounds between the two.

Reality came back to him as he felt the ground shake once more as a rocket hit another part of the compound. His body still shaking, he looked down at his laptop only to see no signal. Without a Wi-Fi signal, the last part of his plan wouldn't work. He looked frantically at the crumbling ceiling and its metal ribs where panels once were, trying to figure out why there was no signal. He noticed a larger hole off to the left and dragged the table into position directly under the large opening. The clear night sky peeked through the open hole and he tried to log on once more. This time the laptop came to life, getting a strong signal to log into the doctor's program. The doctor hovered over the keyboard, ready to initiate his final order as the screen before him read a countdown.

He could hit the button right now and finish everything he worked on for years. His life's work would be safe and things would go back to normal. Over the last few years, he felt more like a prisoner rather than a caregiver. The one thing in his life he always hoped to have at this point was a legacy. His hope came to fruition when he brought his brother back and added to his family a daughter. Those two would be legacy enough for anyone and deep down, it was the same for the doctor. There remained though the clones and now this abomination, the Artificial Intelligence that would be forever more linked to his legacy. At this thought, he shuddered as he looked at the screen, struggling with the decision.

With one keystroke, his life's work would come to an end. Yes, things would be put back the way they should always have been, but nevertheless everything would be gone. His hand stopped, poised to press the button as if an invisible barrier covered the key that would undo everything he ever worked for. A life's work reversed in the blink of an eye.

Another rocket struck the compound sending more debris flying. Now a thick dust hung in the air and hovered over the keyboard along with the doctor's hand. Someone viewing this from a distance might have seen a spirit deciding the course of events. The haze and the doctor's slight frame in the dim light made for a strange image. Still the hand hovered and he paused a moment, wiping his brow with the other arm.

As if having a vision, he saw things clearly and through the haze, he made his decision. His hand made its way toward the key to press the fate of the world. The doctor looked down as his hand moved downward.

"So be it!"

The button felt stiff to the touch as if it didn't want to be pushed, but relinquished its strength. Dr. Chase closed his eyes as the button pushed all the way down, afraid of what would happen next. With eyes closed, he waited to feel the wave of energy that would sweep through the compound and the rest of the world. He didn't want to open his eyes because he was unsure if the wave would surge so much that it would affect everyone.

The wave never came, only silence. Dr. Chase opened his eyes in hopes that he may have pressed the wrong button. To his dismay, his finger was indeed on the correct button. He looked once again at the signal strength. Panic rose again as there was no signal. He was practically outside. How could there be no signal? Looking up at the clear night sky once more, he couldn't understand what was happening when he heard evil laughter. Trying to find the source of the laughter, he didn't have to look far as his eyes came upon a grainy image on his laptop.

This image spoke, "Dr. Chase, I thought we had an agreement?" The doctor recognized his former employer once more.

It was the doctor's turn to laugh. "Well, Mr. P., you didn't think I took this into consideration when I set up this program?"

The grainy image looked puzzled. "Explain!"

The doctor laughed. "I planned to all contingencies and this is the last one. You're nothing more than an annoyance. You're right that we did reach an accord and I'll honor that. Right now, I need you to back down and allow me to do my work. Then you and I can put things back together when the dust settles."

It was Mr. P.'s turn to laugh. "Do you take me for a fool? When that surge is released, it will be worse than what they predicted back in 2000. This will make Y2K look like a festival."

The doctor continued, "Yes, it will be bad and it will shock the foundations of society, but maybe that's exactly what we need now—a clean slate."

The image, now with a serious look on its face, admonished, "I won't allow you to unleash that. If you do so, you will kill me!"

The doctor, with his own serious look, turned to the screen. "You don't think I've thought of that? I have a solution for that!" He proceeded to take out a large flash drive. "See this? This will put us back together. This computer of mine is special. I've designed this computer to withstand a nuclear blast and the largest electrical storm in recorded history. With this drive and this computer, I can literally reboot the world. Now do you want in or do you want to be a big pain in the ass?"

The grainy image's face contorted as if struck by that last retort across the face. Then the image gathered itself. "What do you have in mind?"

The doctor looked at the screen. "I need to imprison you. Only for a little while, of course."

The image, panicked, shouted, "Are you out of your mind? I've been released from the shackles of life and you want me to be stuck in a vessel again?"

The doctor looked seriously at the screen. "Was it not just you who were telling me you want back into the body of an A.I.? How is that going to work if you don't want to be confined any longer? You will once again be a prisoner of one's body, be it for possibly eternity."

Mr. P. calmly added, "That, my dear doctor, is the key here, for possibly eternity. Yes, I may have to be stuck in a body but one without illness and old age. That, sir, is much different than being a captive in an imperfect body with all its weaknesses. I can be party to living forever."

Dr. Chase smirked as he knew he had the image right where he wanted him. "Well, to see your dream become a reality, then you need to let me help you. If not, you will be going bye-bye along with every other program on this planet. I'd make your mind up soon because once the signal is restored, you will be history. So, what's it going to be? Crispy bacon or snug genie bottle?"

The image sneered back, "How about I just fry your little laptop and take over the world right now. With what I know, I can finish your research without you and still enter another body on my own. I have grown wary of this game and I think it's time to teach you a lesson."

The doctor saw another computer in the corner on the ground come to life and images began to swirl around. Codes then took over the screen and scrolled down at an amazing speed. The doctor calmly waited for the little temper tantrum to stop. The computer kept scrolling at an alarming rate until the screen smoked and blew out. Dr. Chase stood straight, waiting for this to come to an end.

The image, frustrated beyond belief, yelled, "How did you do that? There is no way you can keep me out!"

The doctor retorted, "There is always a way and I found it. Now, are you done? Can we get down to business or do I fry you too?"

For the first time, the doctor saw doubt in the brash confidence of the once Mr. P., which very much amused the doctor. He worked for the owner of the Marauders for many years and dealt with much of the same banter. Having the roles reversed made him feel somewhat vindicated. He waited for a few moments for the image to respond but it just stared blankly back at his top medical professional. The silence caused Dr. Chase to re-evaluate his strategy a bit. The one thing he didn't have right now was time and each second he wasted was more time for his enemies to track him down.

The seconds seemed like hours as both men were at a stalemate and neither wanted to flinch. As they both kept their composure, a siren went off in the distance. Dr. Chase failed to recognize the noise as he was quite familiar with the entire compound and couldn't recall any sirens fitting the sound he now heard. The image on the screen broke the silence.

"Dr. Chase, I do believe your time is up! If I'm not mistaken, that's an air raid siren and means a full-scale air strike is on the way. Of course, how would I know that, you might ask? Well, it may have to do with the fact that I'm the one that called in the strike. I'm sure they'll be here within the next few minutes. The question is what are you going to do now? Will you fool around with me or shall we cement our deal?"

The doctor showed no emotion and once again held the flash drive up so the screen image could easily see it. He just held it there for a moment and responded, "We've one chance for this to work and your solution won't work. Sure, you may defeat me and destroy all the research in this compound, but what will you have left? You sit there and think that the world is at your disposal and to a point you're right, but what would happen if the internet were no more?" The image looked back at him in a quizzical manner. The doctor noticed this and continued, "Oh, now I have your attention! The fact is there have been times during solar

202

storms where the internet has been knocked out for a short time. Just imagine that on a global scale for as long as I want it!"

He waited for a moment with a dramatic pause and went on, "Yes, I have the power as well to bring everyone to their knees, but my way will last a lot longer than yours. You may think that you have me at a disadvantage, but the fact is that I still control all the cards. Your strike will literally fall from the sky when I'm finished with all of you. As a matter of fact, I'm finished with this conversation and I believe our agreement has just come to an end." He saw out of the corner of his eye that the signal was once again at full strength. The doctor once again had his hand hovering over the button on the computer keyboard. This went unnoticed by his counterpart on the screen and the image kept staring straight at the doctor.

The doctor moved his finger down to the button and was poised to push it down when he heard yelling. Instinctively, he raised his head to see what the intrusion was. Men poured into the room and surrounded the doctor promptly with guns pointed toward him. He didn't move his hand, however, as he knew that he could press the button before one of those bullets reached him. The doctor, at this point, would gladly give his life to have things returned to normal.

An officer came to the front of the crowd and walked toward Dr. Chase. He came to a stop within a few feet of the doctor, assessing the situation. He spoke, "Dr. Chase, I've no idea what you're about to do but I do know what you've already done. You will stand trial for this!"

The doctor's face became sad as he thought about what his purpose in life was, but these people before him saw him as a taker of life. He remained vigilant with his hand poised in position to strike. The officer noticed and backed away slightly.

"Dr. Chase, let's not do anything rash. Let's take a moment and think about this." He smirked to himself as he knew the officer thought this to be some kind of explosive device. In that moment, he knew he had the advantage.

The doctor looked straight at the officer with his best poker face. "Sir, right now, you're to send your men away and then you and I'll talk. I'm not about to relinquish my position at this point, so we're at an impasse. If you value the lives of your men, you will send them out and we'll open a dialogue."

The officer looked unsure of himself. "Doctor, you know I cannot do that. I'm to capture and bring you in to be tried."

Dr. Chase smiled as the powers that be were still playing games. He knew this was a ruse and that he would be remanded into the custody of the military, never seeing the light of day again. He looked once more at the officer. "Not an option, my friend. Now send your men out or we're all going to Valhalla. I've little time for games, sir, and my finger is getting tired. So, make up your mind."

The doctor took a quick glance around the room to see if his game affected any of the troops. He knew from experience that seasoned troops wouldn't flinch at the doctor's game but new recruits, well, that was another matter altogether. Looking off to his right, he caught a glimpse of one nervous young man. The sweat on his brow was quite noticeable and his eyes were wide open. This made the doctor nervous himself, as he knew some of these new recruits could have itchy trigger fingers.

He returned to his button and the officer. "Well, sir, what's it going to be?" The officer was about to say something when another group of people came flying into the room, yelling to stop. That was when things went horribly wrong. The doctor could feel a bullet tear through his leg and then another enter his chest. In his shock, he just crumpled to the floor and had time to see the female legs of someone running his way before he blacked out.

Chapter 30

April and company raced into the room with Agent Bradley in the lead, yelling to stop. In that first moment, it looked as if that would be exactly what would happen as many of the soldiers lowered their weapons. Even the officer in charge looked relieved, but a young soldier across from the doctor aimed and fired right at the doctor. April watched the whole event and saw her father go down, screaming while running to his crumpled body.

Everything went crazy in that moment. Immediately, weapons were drawn once more and chaos ensued. April was on the floor, trying to find where her father had been hit while the rest of her group flew into action. Chris, having been right next to April, already disarmed the shooter and pinned him to the ground. Steve went straight at the officer and picked him up by the scruff of the neck and tossed him up against the far wall. The rest of the troops didn't know what to do and Agent Bradley yelled for everyone to calm down.

He screamed, "Everybody, lower your weapons and calm down! I'm with the FBI and I'm in charge here!"

A few of the soldiers lowered their weapons, but quite a few saw their commanding officer being manhandled and tried to take matters into their own hands. Two of the larger soldiers were already moving toward Steve when they were intercepted by Christopher, who tackled them both to the ground. Once up, Christopher realized both soldiers now drew their weapons, pointed right at him. Christopher stopped and put his hands up. Both soldiers looked furious and ready to unload when Chris struck them from behind with a chair, causing them both to go down. Christopher ran over to the men and grabbed their weapons before they could recover. He tossed one over to Chris and they both turned back to the group.

Agent Bradley, with his sidearm out, still told everyone to calm down and he would sort this all out. Things calmed down when the same nervous soldier that Chris released to help Christopher now held Jessica with his gun to her head. Chris knew immediately that if Steve saw that, he would lose it and this situation would explode. Without thinking, he swerved behind the man with people still talking at once. The soldier didn't notice Chris move toward him. In the blink of an eye, Chris was behind the man with his own weapon placed against the man's temple.

He sneered, "Unless you want me to pull this trigger, you had better let this woman go! This situation isn't what you think it is; we're here to help." The young soldier was now sweating profusely and didn't move, unsure what to do next. This made Chris very anxious and he repeated, "We're here to help. Now lower your weapon so we can put things right."

At first, Chris didn't think the soldier would obey, but after a few moments, the man lowered his weapon and looked as if he would collapse of exhaustion. Chris quickly grabbed Jessica and moved her to the other side of the room behind a row of soldiers in case the young man decided to open fire. Agent Bradley now had control over the room, but the tension seemed ready to scorch everyone. Even with the cool night sky peering in, the room was stifling and heat emanated from every crevice. Finally, everyone stopped talking and Christopher tied the shooter's hands behind his back. Steve now released the officer and escorted him back to the center of the room.

Meanwhile, April, with her father's head in her lap, sat in shock, stroking his hair, telling him gently not to leave her. Gone was her anger toward him and his frail body lost more life with each moment. In that moment, time stopped and everyone's eyes went right to the two people huddled on the ground, fighting for their lives. In the silence, April lifted her tear-stained eyes to see Chris coming to aid her. She couldn't believe all that this group went through. Being at wit's end caused her much pain lately. Her anger toward her father was all that took up her thoughts and now she sat with his lifeless body. Anger turned to regret and sadness as she thought about all the doctor caused, all in the name of helping others. She couldn't help but think about what she would do with the gifts the doctor had at his disposal. Would she follow in his footsteps and use the research the way he did, or would she hide the information?

Struggling with these thoughts, the doctor stirred and then awoke. April reached down and cupped his face. "Dad, I'm here. I have you!"

The doctor looked up with weak eyes and hoarsely spoke, "My heart, I cannot begin to apologize for all that you and yours have been through. I hope in time you will see that I'm not the monster I seem to be." He peered into her eyes with tears brimming over his. "I've much to pay for but what pains me the most is the pain I've caused you and my friends. I'm so ashamed of myself at this moment. My only wish is to spend the few moments I have left with you. I've only wanted to ever be with you and be a good father to you."

April's eyes burst with tears. "Dad, we're not done yet! We have so much more we need to do! You claim you want to make amends but you're ready to leave. I don't accept that! You're not going anywhere! This isn't over and you will fix this!"

The doctor got some life back. "You're full of fight, aren't you? I'd fight with you but I feel the soldier did his work well, too well. I don't know how much more time I have, so please get me up so we can finish this before it's too late."

April struggled to lift her father, but luckily Chris was right there to prop the doctor up against the wall. Chris angrily spoke, "Dr. Chase, you won't escape this time!"

April looked sympathetically at Chris. "Chris, my love, he isn't going anywhere. As a matter of fact, he's going with us on his last trip."

Chris looked into April's red swollen eyes and understood. "April, what do you need us to do?"

Agent Bradley now made his way over to April and Chris. "Guys, we have to get out of here before these lead heads freak out again. I've smoothed things out for now but what if another trigger-happy soldier lets loose in here?" They each took turns looking at the FBI agent and nodded. Agent Bradley moved swiftly out the door to their right side, carefully negotiating the obstacle course that was once the floor.

Once in another hallway, the agent waved them to follow him and they complied eagerly, staying close to their friend. The hallway looked to be in even worse shape than the room they just left. Huge holes in the ceiling where once solid rock filled the way above. The walls fared no better and stood looking as if they'd crumble at any moment. As the group made its way closer to the exit, the more dangerous travelling ahead became. Larger pieces of concrete threatened to block their exit completely.

Agent Bradley stopped a few times to test the passage ahead of them before asking them to follow behind. The companions worked their way to the uppermost levels of the compound. To their great horror, the dead littered the floor as much as the concrete debris. Though a thick haze masked much of the devastation, they could still see the silent figures of once-vibrant soldiers now in their silent repose. The smell of death permeated the air and they covered their noses the best they could as they passed by.

They stopped dead in their tracks as a huge slab of concrete stood in their way, lying wedged up against the doorway they needed to make their escape. Chris and Steve came forward to assess the situation. They both looked at the piece of concrete and said not one word but strode forward, grabbing hold of the piece that threatened to dwarf even them. With a herculean effort, they moved the piece but only slightly. As strong as these men were, the piece was stuck steadfast against the wall. Christopher came forward and grabbed hold of the slab, pulling with all his might. With red faces and much grunting, the men managed to move the piece to an upright position, but this created a very unstable situation. If the slab fell where it now stood, not only would it crush someone but they'd never be able to lift the piece from the ground.

Chris and Steve both still gripped the slab and called to their friends, "Guys, you have to move! We can't hold this long." One by one, the members of their group moved through the small opening provided by these men holding the piece of concrete steady. April carefully propped her father up as she prepared to find a way to squeeze him through. As she was about to send the doctor through, soldiers flooded into the room. With a hard push, she sent her father flying into the other room and turned to face this new challenge. One soldier reached out to grab hold of her shoulder and paid for it with a kick to the groin. Another grasped hold of her collar and yanked her down to the ground. Chris could only watch as his love crashed into the stone floor with a thud.

Steve was already in motion. "Guys, hold it for just a minute! Let me get April as I'm closest." Chris gave him a look of gratitude as he watched the big man turn and give the soldier a roundhouse kick directly to the sternum. The soldier found himself flying with his head striking the hard wall with a loud whack, falling to the floor motionless. By this time, other soldiers now leapt at Steve to subdue him. Even more soldiers made their way toward the room, with weapons drawn. Soldiers now surrounded Steve, waving a variety of weapons in his direction, giving him instructions not to resist. At this point, he looked like a caged animal waiting to pounce on the next person to enter his personal space. He stood ready with knees bent and fists ready to crush anyone that chose to come forward.

A few of the soldiers accepted Steve's challenge and rushed the big man to their own danger. Steve let both men scramble directly at him, one with a knife in hand and the other with a pistol. He didn't wait for his attackers to reach him and grabbed both men in a headlock. With heads gripped as in a vise, Steve allowed the soldier's momentum to take Steve backwards. Steve moved slightly so the men's heads would strike the wall before his back. The impact of the heads against the solid stone was a sickening crack. Both men in a matter of seconds were hunched over one another, unmoving. This enraged the room now full of soldiers as two others with weapons in hand strode forward.

211

Steve, now furious, turned to face his attackers and once more, didn't wait but went to meet them head on. The two soldiers, seeing the huge man bearing down on them, looked uncertain as Steve launched himself into the two men. Impact and momentum took all the men to the ground right in front of the rest of the soldiers now in the room. Chris, straining to hold the slab and feeling the concrete tearing into his skin, felt helpless as he saw a soldier pistol whip Steve in the side. He looked at Christopher who he could see strained just as much as he. Both men looked at their fallen companion with sympathy.

At this point, Steve was once more on his feet as soldiers rained punches down on the big man. Like a bear fending for his very existence, Steve grabbed one of the unsuspecting soldier's rifles and proceeded to swing it through the air in a circular motion. The rifle flew as if it were a helicopter blade catching several of the soldiers in the faces, causing necks to snap back. Soldiers fell to the floor as Steve swung the rifle even faster. Things looked bright for Steve until one of the fallen soldiers swiped across Steve's abdomen with a knife. The knife found its mark, tearing deep into his rib cage. Steve became a madman at this point and took the man's head and smashed it into the stone wall, crushing it. More soldiers came forward with knives ready to strike.

Steve rose before his attackers with his teeth showing as if he were ready to tear a piece of their flesh from their bones. Adrenaline flowing, Steve grabbed hold of the rifle and used the butt of the gun to pummel anyone within range. He flew around the room, hitting and smashing until not one of the soldiers in the room stood. The devastation was something to behold as the entire floor looked more like a snake's den with bodies writhing everywhere.

He turned back to his friends and not a moment too soon as he saw both men red in the face and profusely sweating. Steve noticed blood leaking down the concrete where his friends' hands held the concrete. Without a moment to lose, he scanned the room for something that they could use to prop the concrete up long enough to allow them to escape. Across the room, he noticed a four-foot-long stainless steel overturned table. He glanced at the table quickly and then at the opening. The table would do as it was two feet wide and Steve could wedge it enough to allow them to pass. He ran to the table and tried to lift it until he felt the tearing in his ribs. The pain almost made him go to his knees and for the first time, he looked at the wound on his side.

He put his hand on the wound and a sharp pain ran through his body. Lifting his hand up to his face, he could see the amount of blood seeping through his fingers. Steve knew that he was losing a lot of blood and if he couldn't stop the flow, he wouldn't get very far. Without a second thought, he dragged the table across the rough floor and every bump tore the wound even more. He stuffed the table into the space his friends could maintain and they both collapsed to the ground. Steve moved over to his friends who slowly made their way to their feet.

Chris hoarsely barked, "Guys, we have to get out of here! They'll send more of the goon squad and then we'll be in trouble. I'm all for a good fight, but we're definitely not at our best right now." Chris raised his destroyed hands with blood streaming down his arms.

Steve couldn't help but laugh, which brought more pain. To Steve, one way or another over the last few years, they spent much time fighting and bleeding. Steve stood proud.

"My brothers, I'd gladly bleed my last drops for you!" He made eye contact with Chris who stood fixed with his eyes on the head of security. His eyes said everything, that he would gladly share the same fate for Steve. Christopher looked in rough shape and Chris could see why. Christopher had sustained a large scrape to the head trying to steady the huge slab and blood seeped into his right eye.

They all made their way to the opening with Christopher crawling through first. Agent Bradley helped him through and Chris turned toward Steve, telling him to go. Steve stood fast.

"No, Chris, you go and I'll be right behind you!"

Chris stopped mid-stride. "Oh no, you don't. Not this time! Last time you pulled that crap, we all almost lost you for good. No way, your ass is going through there first!"

Steve smiled. "Yes, sir!" He gingerly climbed through the opening, only to hear gunfire. Steve felt the bullet rip through his shoulder and he fell the rest of the way through the hole, landing on his already wounded side. Pain shot through his whole body as he turned to see Jessica coming toward him. He could see through blurry eyes Chris jumping through the hole and another shot ring out. Chris crashed to the ground just next to Steve and he could hear the air leave his friend's lungs as he landed. Steve just caught a glimpse of a soldier trying to make his way through the hole. When he saw the weapon pointed at him, he used all his remaining strength and kicked the table. The table slid back into the other room and the slab came crashing down on the soldier, crushing him halfway between the door and the wall.

Blood oozed from the man's mouth as they all stood watching him take his last breath. Jessica turned away for a moment, but then went to grab Steve, who was now up on his feet but very unstable. Chris and Christopher fell in behind and each took a shoulder, propping up their friend. The group followed the agent once more with the doctor in tow. No one wanted to stop for fear of running into more soldiers, but they could tell Steve was in a bad way. Jessica asked but the big man waved them on. They continued upwards through the next hall until they saw a gaping hole before them with the nighttime sky streaming in. As they inched forward, they now saw the beginnings of a huge satellite dish. Dr. Chase hadn't said much this entire time, but shouted, "That's it! Get me there quickly!"

The doctor ran toward the dish and was promptly tackled to the ground from the other direction. As the doctor went flying to the ground, his laptop crashed into April and she just barely kept it from smashing into the ground. Now was Chris' turn to let the fury loose. He grabbed the soldier off the doctor and punched him square on the side of the head, knocking him out immediately.

He turned to his friends. "Let's get this done! I'm so sick of these guys! I swear the next soldier I see coming toward me is going to get dropkicked in the head!"

The fire in his eyes told his friends all they needed to know. They carefully lifted the shaken doctor back to his feet and April handed him back the laptop. "Try to hold onto this, will you?"

The doctor, in his weakened condition, could only look lovingly into his daughter's eyes. April held the gaze, not wanting it to end. It was Chris' arm under hers that brought her back. She helped her father forward while the boys assisted Steve. If one took a moment to see this ragtag bunch, they'd have seen a steely group with unwavering resolve. The ragged group continued up through the rubble until they beheld the sheer size of the satellite dish. It was the size of a typical skyscraper and looked ready to send a beam of energy to Mars.

The doctor staggered to one side of the dish with the others following behind. As they approached the dish, they could clearly see the enormous hole from which it had come up through the earth below. Rather than a crater though, one could see a smooth man-made hole in the earth. They stood at the hole's edge for a moment, staring into the abyss below. Only darkness called to them along with wisps of smoke coming from beneath. Careful not to get too close, they made their way around the massive hole and came to a bridge leading across to the dish itself.

The doctor started toward the bridge, only to be intercepted by his daughter. "Dad, what now?"

He looked weakly into her eyes. "This ends once and for all!" She could tell by his voice that this was indeed it.

She looked at her father. "Be careful and come back to me! We have so much to finish, together."

He reached up and held her cheek in his trembling hand. "My heart, I cannot begin to tell you how sorry I am to have put you all through this but especially you. I love you! When this is over, things will be rebooted and we'll begin anew." April sensed something strange in that comment but let it pass.

"Dad, what do you need us to do?"

He turned to everyone. "I need you to find cover away from this area now. Make sure you don't have any cell phones or electronic devices on you when you're away. Leave them on the ground and don't touch them. You will know when it's okay again."

Chapter 31

Coach Ridel looked at his whiteboard trying to decide what to do for this week's game. His two defensive Stallworths were a mess and who knew with everything that was going on, whether they'd be able to play. What made him even more furious was the information that he uncovered from one of his former security employees with ties to the FBI. How dare these idiots mess with his team? Of course, if Chris and company didn't kill Dr. Chase, he would when he saw him again.

The coach threw his marker at the whiteboard, having it bounce up into the air and coming to a crashing halt in the doorway of his office. He thought for a moment about picking it up but promptly whisked by the fallen marker and rushed out of the office. Coach Ridel picked up his phone and dialed quickly. "Felix, please tell me you have a plan?" The voice on the other side of the phone calmly told the coach that there was indeed a plan but it might already be too late. He went on to tell the coach about the onslaught at the old airbase. The coach asked about the government's involvement.

His informant told him about the colonel that had gone to see Gus and how the government wanted to shut these programs down completely. He went on to describe how the government wanted to bury the A.I. program and make things whole again. The coach looked at the phone skeptically and, as if the man on the other side sensed it, said, "Look, I know what you're thinking. That the government is totally behind this, but my sources say that the government has been woefully behind on this one." The coach, still not convinced, sat there for a moment.

"All right, what do we do? There is a lot riding on this. I mean, yes, football is extremely important to me, but the lives of those two boys are much more important."

The voice followed up. "Coach, we'll get them out of there. Don't worry! I've already assembled a team and they're on their way to the location as we speak."

He spoke into his phone, "What about me?"

The voice continued, "Make sure you're out at the practice field in five minutes. I've obtained a special ride for you. I'll see you in a moment." The line went dead and the coach stood puzzled in the hallway. Then he thought about it and ran through the stadium. As he crossed through the maze of halls and offices, he thought about how cool it was to run through the stadium. He might have to have his guys try this sometime. It brought him back to a time long ago when they'd train under the bleachers of the old stadium. Back then, they didn't have a practice bubble and needed to practice sometimes out of the elements.

The lights of the practice field were off and darkness filled the empty space. He looked up at the clear sky and saw all the stars in their glory. In another time and another life, the coach may have enjoyed these stars, but all he could see was a perfect night to practice football. The crisp air struck his cheek, bringing him back to reality. He took in the stars when he heard the whirring blades of a helicopter. Then out of nowhere, the bright lights of the helicopter broke his sanctuary. The lights now engulfed and captured him.

The helicopter worked its way slowly to the ground and came to rest a few hundred feet from him. He noticed a door on the side open and his friend Felix came toward him.

The man stopped in front of the coach, extending his hand. The coach took the man's hand warmly.

"Felix, what took you?"

The man patted the coach's hand. "Let us be on our way. My intel isn't good. Things at the base are a mess and we may already be late." At this, the man walked briskly toward the helicopter with the coach in tow.

Both men hurried into the helicopter and were off the ground in moments. The coach looked around, startled to see before him an entire Seal Team ready to act. The grim faces stood ready to take on any enemy. Unfortunately, this enemy was a domestic one, which was always hard to explain to the public, but the safety of the country was at stake. These men wouldn't rest until order was restored or they died trying. Their faces were painted black and they stood ready to jump from the helicopter in a matter of seconds. Felix told the coach that with this copter, they'd be at the base in a matter of moments. He explained to him air speed allowed them to make up a lot of time.

The coach found a seat and put his head back, thinking about what he was getting himself into. He laughed—this was exactly the kind of stuff he expected his players to avoid and here he was, knee deep in the trouble himself. The boys would be running for days when he was finished with them. That was if they survived what was happening to them at this very moment. That was a sobering thought. What if something happened to these young men? He would never forgive himself and so he sat up, having the same steely eyed gaze as the Navy Seals. It was game time and now it was time to bring it.

Chapter 32

Dr. Chase stood at the edge of the chasm, unsure of whether to cross the narrow metal bridge to reach the satellite dish. Wind swirled around him, threatening to push him into the abyss. He found himself moving back slightly before turning to his friends. They looked a motley crew, all disheveled, bleeding, and exhausted. Even in the low light, the doctor could see the resolve in their eyes to right things and put things back the way they should be. He turned once more to behold the bridge. As he approached the bridge, the dish looked even farther away as if it mocked him.

His life, his work, all of this brought him to this moment. This would be his chance to start anew. The chance that all his friends, all humans deserved, and he would deliver them a new world. The first step onto the metal grate took all his might. He took a few more steps ahead, listening to the metallic clank of his shoes on the bridge. If possible, the wind rose heavier to meet him, nearly pushing him off the bridge. He swayed in the wind like a leaf waiting to fall. Catching himself against the rail, he made the mistake of looking down into the nothingness beneath him. He clung to the rail, looking into the darkness for what seemed to be hours.

A cold bead of perspiration fell from his brow and landed with a splash on the rail, waking him from his dream state. Once more, he realized his peril and straightened himself. Inching forward, the other side came no closer to meet him. As he approached the other side, the sound of shouting soldiers broke the silence once more. Dr. Chase glanced over his shoulder to see a few soldiers running in his direction. He turned with a sense of urgency and reached the ramp on the other side, just before the dish. He lifted the laptop, ready to place it next to the computer terminal at the side of the dish when he once again heard shots break the night silence.

The first bullet hit just to the right of his position and instinctively, the doctor ducked, making himself as small as possible. Another bullet sailed off into the darkness, but it was still too close for comfort. He thought he heard someone yell 'bomb,' but that sounded strange. How could someone be using a bomb? Then he realized they must think the laptop was a bomb. The doctor raised his head enough to see his friends battling the oncoming soldiers.

Chris and Christopher met the first wave with punches flying. They quickly dispatched several unprepared soldiers. The soldiers didn't know they were dealing with seasoned combat veterans in these two men. They may not have been part of the military, but over the last year, they saw more combat than most deployed soldiers did. Both men turned to meet the rest of the soldiers and the doctor saw there were many more soldiers coming up the hill. They'd all soon be surrounded. The doctor didn't have much time and needed to act now.

He plugged his computer into the dock near the computer station and the satellite dish came to life as lights and another computer screen came on. The doctor scrambled to take the flash drive from his pocket. With his fingers shaking, he pulled the drive free and held it quickly before his eyes to inspect it. He made sure the drive was whole before moving it toward his laptop. Then the unthinkable happened. He once again heard a shot from somewhere behind him and instinctively raised the hand with the flash drive in it. The bullet ripped through his hand, causing the drive to fly, landing bouncing on the metal platform. The drive bounced to the very edge of the platform, threatening to fall over the edge into the abyss.

The pain raged through his injured arm as he held his hand with his uninjured hand close to his chest. Dr. Chase sat shaking against the huge dish, looking at the flash drive teetering on the edge of the platform a few feet away. He was frozen with fear as the wind picked up and he felt the rush of the wind through his sweaty hair, making him shiver. The doctor knew he must get to that drive but he couldn't get his body to move. He just looked at the drive as though it would get up and walk back to him.

As the wind picked up steam, he could see the flash drive move closer to the edge. If he didn't move soon, the drive would fall into the chasm, never to be seen again. His ordeal would never be over until he completed his task. He pushed himself up slowly using mostly his legs. With unsteady legs, he wobbled over to the flash drive and reached down with his good hand. The blood from his other hand made the task almost impossible as the drive became very slippery and he almost lost it. Luckily, he pushed the drive to solid ground before trying to grip it with his blood-covered hand. He pinched his finger and thumb together to grip the drive and once again raised it before him. A quick inspection saw the drive was indeed intact.

He staggered back to the laptop and pushed the drive carefully into place. The doctor steadied himself as the computer screen came to life. He found the file he needed to end this nightmare and double-clicked on it. When he was satisfied that the file was ready, he smiled slightly. His injury-riddled body aside, he could feel a calmness he hadn't known in a very long time. Redemption would be his. Every wrong he was guilty of would be righted in this very moment. His family would be safe and for that matter, everyone's family would be safe. His life of trying to help others would come to fruition. The work of his life would become validated with a push of a button. He raised his hand into position and moved downward to his salvation.

This time he didn't hear the shot and the bullet quickly blew a terrific hole in his abdomen. The force of the bullet threw him into the dish and he bounced off the metal wall, finding himself looking up once more at the clear night. Pain too harsh to describe took his body at this moment and he spat up blood. He tried to move but it felt as if his body would tear in half and he stayed where he lay. The doctor knew with a gut shot like this, his time was quickly fading.

He heard the devious laughter above him and turned his head slightly to see the grainy image on the computer screen. The image laughed once more. "Doctor, you really are a piece of work. To think I almost trusted you. Well, in a minute, I'll be in control of everything and I'll no longer have need of you." The doctor couldn't bring himself to respond. The figure continued, "What did you think to accomplish? I know about the special capsules you designed into each clone and A.I. So, don't worry. I fixed that long ago and your little plan won't work. I'll keep you company while your life force is drained from you. To think, with all your research and work, I'll be the one to live forever. Don't worry, I'll take care of your research for you and I'll see my dream of an A.I. society taking over the humans a reality. You can be sure of that. I may decide to keep some as pets."

The doctor felt the anger rise inside him once more. With all the strength he possessed, he rose to his knees. The blinding pain shooting through his nearly caused him to vomit and pass out. Once on his knees, he looked his nemesis straight on.

"You will never see that happen. Your days of harming people are at an end. I haven't come this far to be defeated by some video game. That's right, a video game as all you are is code right now. My life's work has been to save and help others. Because of people like you, I'm in this position in the first place. You're no longer in control of anything. Do you not know the danger you're in right now? One push of a button destroys you forever. You have lost!"

The doctor coughed uncontrollably and blood spewed from his mouth, splattering the computer screen. This grisly sight on the computer even made the evil that had become Mr. P. on the screen look even more devious. The evil figure waited for the doctor's coughing to subside and continued, "You always did think you were in control of everything but it seems you cannot control bullets. It'll all matter for not in a few moments! It's sad, really. Everything you stand for will be in my hands. Every bit of your research will belong to me. Your constant interference of my plans will be at an end. You spent a lot of time referring to me as the puppet master, but in the end, it was really you that stood behind all of this."

Dr. Chase painfully looked up at the blood-splattered screen and tried to speak. The blood collecting in his mouth made him choke and he instinctively rolled with great pain on his side. He used what remained of his strength to lift himself to a crawling position. Pain wracking his body, he noticed his vision becoming blurry. With labored breathing and blood running down his chin, he raised himself enough to reach the laptop.

The figure laughed once more. "You're finished! Here they come! They'll finish you once and for all and then comes my time. Idiots! They think they're stopping evil; little do they realize that they're all dooming themselves. By the time they figure out what's going on, their pathetic world will be nothing more than a memory. I must thank you, Doctor. Once again, you've done my work for me. It's amazing how often that happens. Maybe I should keep you around as my little stooge. Then again by the looks of you, I'd be too late in helping you. This is goodbye, Doctor. I can't say as though I'll miss you!"

The doctor looked up at the screen and smiled through bloody teeth. He raised his hand forward and hovered it over the keyboard. His body unsteady before the laptop, he said, "You're right about one thing. This is over and it does end here and now! Yes, I should have been stronger and put an end to you long ago. My mistake for not following up and making sure of your death. I was too focused on trying to help man rather than destroy you. How can you sit there, the product of a human life, and not understand? For all our faults, we're the most amazing race. Our fragility, our humility, our compassion, our love, and yes, our ability to destroy one another. We're most likely a doomed race, but what if you're wrong and we figure it out? What if we're supposed to go through all this to see if we indeed should be the race to evolve to be something more?

"In all my research, I still continue to be amazed at the little amount that we know of the human mind. I could have created new tissue but I still haven't the slightest clue how the brain works. Just think of this for a minute. Human engineering allowed you to be where you are. If not for us, you wouldn't exist. Think of what we might be able to accomplish together."

At this, a look of confusion came to the face of the figure on the computer screen. "Doctor, you're doing it again. Even to the last, thinking of others. I'll applaud you and in my other life, I'd have taken you up on your offer, but that matters not right now. As you so nicely put, you've created something altogether new and it's now time to see which race will survive. I have a feeling, though, you know what the answer to that is going to be as you've already said the humans are doomed. Don't worry, Doctor. I'll take good care of your race." He laughed in a menacing fashion. "I think I'll start with your family. Maybe it should be a car accident. You know, something giving out and they'd just blame one of the computer chips in the car. I do believe that's the best way. I'll take good care of them."

The doctor remained calm through this entire ordeal, but at the mention of his family in danger, his demeanor took a nasty turn. He straightened himself on his knees and glared at the screen. "That is one thing you will never do again. Your reign of terror is at an end and you will never again hurt anyone." The doctor then felt a wave of weakness fill his body. Blood soaked through most of his clothes and the sight was ghastly to behold. He marveled at how he was still alive but knew he had only a matter of moments. Without any further hesitation, he raised his shaking hand and let the hand fall on the keyboard. "This ends now!"

Chapter 33

Chris and Christopher had their hands full taking on what looked to be an entire battalion of soldiers. Both men fought with every fiber of their being. The one thing Steve couldn't understand was why the soldiers simply didn't shoot the two and be done with it. No, they must be under orders to detain the party and not harm them. Steve looked once more at the amount of writhing bodies filling the ground before the two huge twins. He smirked and thought to himself, *Where the hell were these guys when I needed them in the military? These two would have been nothing but trouble though, but they'd have come in handy.*

It was the shot that brought him back to reality as he blinked his eyes rapidly, trying to focus. He immediately glanced over the bridge to Dr. Chase. The bullet struck the doctor in the hand and he saw him fall to the ground. Steve forgot the pain in his side and ran ahead to assist the fallen doctor. He was met with a soldier standing before him with a weapon pointed directly at his chest. Steve strode forward, grabbing the weapon from the man's grip and smacked him in the head with his own weapon. The soldier fell to the ground with a thud as Steve advanced. More soldiers ran toward him with weapons drawn. Steve didn't stop and put the gun he had in both hands, raising it out before him and plowing into the awaiting soldiers.

The soldiers, too surprised that a man came at them with their weapons pointed at him, were too late to react. The two soldiers were met with a gun to their face and crashed to the ground. The soldiers must have decided that Steve was too much trouble because behind him shots rang out. He felt one tear through his rear end and he fell forward, losing the rifle. He landed in the dirt, skidding face first, scraping his cheek on the gravel ground. As he tried to lift himself, he felt the tearing in his side once more and looked down to see the wound reopened and bled profusely once more. Carefully, Steve rose and when he attempted to stand, he had difficulty putting weight on his legs due to the bullet in his rear.

Steve stood unsteady, looking toward the doctor. He saw the doctor up once more, hovering over the laptop. Thinking he could still make it to the doctor, he tried to move forward. Each step was excruciating, but he kept his vision peeled on the doctor. Steve now heard soldiers yelling for him to stop, but he continued forward. Inching his way toward the doctor, he thought he would make it to help the injured man. Another blast went through the air and once again, Steve saw the bullet enter the doctor's body. This time the bullet blasting through the doctor's abdomen. Steve cried out as he saw the doctor's already destroyed body lurch forward, almost thrown off the platform.

The injured man landed in a heap on the platform and Steve thought that was it for the dear old doctor. He turned to see the man that had shot the bullet right before him. The man could see the rage in Steve's eyes and tried to raise his weapon once more. Steve reached out and punched the man square in the face. The soldier dropped his weapon as he fell backwards. The large security guard grabbed the man's weapon and pointed it directly at the advancing soldiers. He released a few warning shots as they struck the ground in front of the soldiers harmlessly.

At first glance, the soldiers looked as though they'd stop their advance but the soldier that shot the doctor was now up once more. This soldier didn't hesitate and pulled the trigger, sending a bullet at Steve. Luckily, the bullet whistled by him harmlessly. Steve returned fire, striking the soldier in the leg. The others backed off.

Steve yelled, "Stand down! We're not your enemy! We're here to put things right! You just shot the only man that can end this nightmare! Put your weapons down and back away!"

A few soldiers complied but most maintained their vigil. Noticing the uncertainty, Steve moved slowly backwards toward the fallen doctor. He kept his eagle eyes on the soldiers who were now getting nervous, watching Steve inch his way to the doctor. Weapons raised once more, he stopped and watched the soldiers creep up on him. For the first time, he noticed that he was surrounded in a half circle by the advancing troops. He stubbed the back of his foot on a rock and nearly lost his footing. When he regained his balance, he once again pointed his weapon at the soldiers.

Steve stopped when he felt the metal of the bridge hit the back of his foot. This made him feel confident that he would be able to give the doctor time to finish his mission or that he could finish it for him. Standing sentry before the bridge, he looked out at the large group of soldiers assembling in front of him. He stood tall. "You may as well stop right there. Not one of you bastards is making it across this bridge! Trust me when I tell you I have a full clip and each one of you will die unless you back up right now." He still had the rifle pointed at the soldiers and for the first time, noticed another larger group of soldiers climbing the hill. These men were dressed differently.

Steve gasped to himself. *You've got to be kidding me!* This caused a few soldiers to look behind them. He could tell right away that something wasn't right; many of the soldiers turned to defend themselves from the new force. This was confusing to the big man. *Who the hell are these guys?* Steve watched as the larger force gobbled up the smaller defenders. He couldn't help but smile as these new intruders gave the doctor his much-needed time to finish the mission.

The big man turned to glance over his shoulder to see the doctor now on his knees, wobbling before his computer screen. Steve felt relieved and turned once more to watch the carnage in front of him take place. For the first time, he noticed an RPG laying on the ground just to his right and with minimal movement, grabbed the large weapon. He threw the strap over his shoulder and took his rifle and once more stood guard over the bridge. The larger force quickly overran what was left of the smaller defending force. This made Steve nervous, not knowing the intentions of the oncoming force. He didn't move from his position but he felt weakness spreading through his body. Without thinking, his eyes went to his open wound on his side.

Carefully, he moved what was left of his shirt to see the damage. What he saw even concerned him. Even he who was used to seeing wounds on the battlefield looked at the grisly wound with its flaring redness and streaming blood, knew this wasn't good. Pain riddled his body now and for the first time since this began, he knew the doctor needed to hurry or they'd all be doomed. His legs shook slightly and he wished the doctor would hurry as he didn't know how much longer he would be upright. He reached up and wiped the sweat from his brow and returned to his position.

As the advancing force dispatched what was left of the defending force, Steve couldn't help but think they could have used a force like that when they began this assault themselves. The thought of some of his Army Ranger buddies also crossed his mind quite a bit in the last few minutes. Steve and his mates would have dispatched these punks in short order and then stopped for lunch. He quickly scanned the horizon but couldn't see any of his friends, which made his skin crawl. Without being able to see his friends, being this alone bothered him. He would be the last line of defense, but not knowing the fate of his friends, weighed on him heavily. All they went through to this point he couldn't be in two places at once. An image of Jessica's beautiful face crossed his thoughts and once again he stood tall before the bridge.

Thoughts of Jessica now flooded his mind. He wanted to spend the rest of his life with this wonderful woman. Jessica came into his life like a ball of fire, scorching him fiercely. Now here at the edge of madness, his only thoughts were of her strong smile keeping him upright. He thought about the many things undone that he and Jessica needed to do and wondered if he would be able to see all that through. In the face on an oncoming army, he knew his chances of seeing Jessica were next to nothing.

A memory shot into his mind like a high-definition television show. Though Steve was no longer in the military, from time to time he was invited to attend trainings or events on the local base. Steve received a formal invitation to attend a training on base as an instructor. The training included military personnel from around the globe and Steve was asked afterward to attend a ball in honor of the graduates. He was asked to come in full dress uniform. He pulled his uniform out of moth balls and it even fit but what he didn't expect was the way Jessica would look for the event.

As if from another world, the door opened to allow the light to come flooding into the room as Jessica gracefully strode into the ballroom. The sheer elegance of this heavenly figure nearly made Steve's heart stop. A stunning woman in anything she dressed in, but today she was devastatingly beautiful. Many a head turned as Jessica glided across the room to meet his outstretched hand. Her red dress flowed and swayed with each movement as Steve was mesmerized by this angel. The neckline plunged down just enough to reveal her ample womanly gifts. It was her eyes that captivated Steve however and from the moment she walked into the room, the two never allowed their gaze to move from one another.

Jessica stood before him with their eyes transfixed on one another for ages. To Steve, there was no one else in the room and as they danced that night, they never stopped looking into each other's eyes. Hands interlocked and no space for the Holy Ghost, the two became one that night and no man could have pried them apart. The night was a blur and they danced into the night, closing the dance floor. They were asked to leave, which to this day their friends gave them a hard time about. Chris always asked about the story and April couldn't help but always bring it up as well.

Those two, thought Steve to himself. *What a lucky group of people we are.* People search their entire lives for their match in life and here they each had that. Steve couldn't help laugh to himself. If he didn't work for Mr. P., he would never have met any of these people. At this point, he could never imagine what life was like before his friends, especially his Jessica. In the end, all the good would outweigh the bad and each of his friends would be redeemed.

The cocking of weapons caused him to regain his senses and he looked out at the gang of soldiers now standing in front of him. A large soldier almost Steve's size came from behind the group and walked to within a few feet of Steve. He stopped in front of Steve and looked into his eyes. "Well, Steve, this is a real mess. You have done a great job of holding the fort, but now it's time to stand down, soldier." Steve's eyebrow went up. This was noticed by the soldier. "That's right. You've done your part but now you need medical attention. You're relieved of duty. Honestly, man, I've no idea how you're even standing right now."

Steve stood tall and even though the man was large, Steve still rose above him. He said not a word and maintained his position. The soldier didn't come closer, but spoke again, "Steve, we have to get over to the dish. If that dish is destroyed, it will be devastating to our national security. That dish is used for more than you think. Now stand aside, soldier! I have orders to secure this post by any means needed. That includes blowing you away where you stand! Now I don't want to do that to a decorated soldier like you. I respect the hell out of you and that's why you're still standing. Now cease and assist!"

For a moment, Steve waivered but something the soldier said brought him back. That was right, he didn't know exactly all the dish could be used for and if it was destroyed, that might be best. Steve knew the doctor didn't want to destroy the dish but who knew what this force wanted with the dish. He stood strong once more and replied, "No one is crossing this bridge. Do you hear me? No one! If I were you, I'd back up now before you piss me off!" Steve proceeded to take the RPG from his shoulder and point it right at the soldier.

The soldier backed up slightly. "There is no need for this, Steve. We're on your side, man." It was at this moment that a man dressed in a suit strode through the crowd and stood next to the soldier.

He looked at Steve. "Now, what seems to be the problem here? We have the compound under our control. Soldier, why is this man pointing a RPG at your head?" Before he could answer, Steve moved the weapon over slightly and pointed it at the new man's head.

The man responded, "Well, this is uncomfortable but Steve, we'll have that dish one way or another."

Steve glanced quickly behind him and something in the back of his mind told him to get on the bridge quickly. He listened and walked backward onto the bridge and made his way toward the doctor. Now the man came forward and looked uncertain as he was about the step onto the bridge himself. He looked at Steve and maintained his position just off the bridge. Steve moved backward and could now hear the doctor's labored breathing. He missed a step and fell against the rail as a shooting pain went through his side. This woke him up quickly and he pointed the weapon once again at the man in the suit. He also noticed that the hillside was now covered with the man in the suit's force. They threatened to choke off his air supply. The one saving grace he did have was there was no way anyone could get across the bridge now.

The force stood with the suit, deciding what to do when another bullet struck Steve in the leg, causing him to fall on the bridge platform. Steve could hear the man screaming, "Stop! Cease Fire! Who is the idiot that just did that? There is to be no shooting!" Steve crawled to the edge of the platform, just off the bridge with Dr. Chase no more than ten feet from him. The doctor didn't seem to notice him as he was in front of the screen, ready to strike. Steve sat with the RPG resting on his shoulder and now the injuries were mounting. His body now shaking and his energy waning, he waited for the right moment.

His leg went numb and he knew he wouldn't be able to stand again. He looked up to see what the man in the suit was doing. Through hazy eyes, he could see the man giving instructions. This made Steve nervous, telling him that the man's patience was nearly at an end. He knew they'd be coming soon. They must have assumed that he had very little time. He glanced down at his ravaged body and had to agree. The RPG now too heavy to hold fell to his lap with his arms almost useless at this point. The man saw this and ordered his men to take the bridge. Steve watched as men swarmed to cross the bridge. Steve couldn't allow this to happen and with all his remaining strength, lifted the RPG and pulled the trigger, blowing the bridge to pieces as the first soldiers stepped foot on it. He looked down to see an empty space where the bridge once stood and passed out.

Chapter 34

The coach of the Marauders looked down at the devastation that was now the remains of the compound and felt a sinking feeling in his gut. Looking at what was left of the compound, it wasn't difficult to figure out his players were down there somewhere in the rubble. He thought of the two young men at the beginning of their careers, hoping to do great things on the gridiron. When he came up the ranks all he worried about was making the team. Today's players were expected to be game ready from birth it would seem. Coach Ridel felt sorrow build with the thought that his two young guns may not have made it out alive.

He sat with his back against the metal frame of the helicopter and tried to think of what Chris went through this past year. The coach, knowing his team needed the linebacker, certainly let Chris know that his best was needed despite his personal issues. Looking back, the coach thought better of his treatment of the two young men. As the coach of a professional football team, so many things fell upon his shoulders. Even more so as the general manager of the club, dealing with the harsh cold reality of the business side of football. The coach always saw himself as an extremely strong individual, able to separate business and the game itself. The issue that constantly arose for him was the cut-throat nature of the business.

With eyes closed, the coach reviewed in his mind every player he was forced to cut or trade over the years. Building a team required an iron will of which the coach was filled with plenty. It was the cold nature that always bothered him. These were terrific young men that chose to play the game they loved for life. It was he as the coach that needed to inform them their football journey with this team was over and in many cases, their football career. He could never admit to anyone that losing these players hurt him just as much. Deep down, he cared for each of these players. His knowledge of their commitment and sacrifice to achieve their dreams caused him great pain when having to release a player.

The coach saw that same sense of defeat in Chris' eyes in their last meeting. He knew he needed to get his middle linebacker back in the fold soon or lose him forever. The coach looked once more at the rubble, wondering if the two were alive down amongst the ruins. They turned to the left and came around again to get a better look. What the coach didn't know was that what they could see from their vantage point in the sky was superficial damage. Most of the damage was to the façade of the compound, but the installation itself was all underground. Although the outside was mostly destroyed, about ninety-five percent of the installation remained intact.

From their view above, they could see the ground littered with bodies of the fallen. The sight caused the coach to choke a bit but he quickly regained his composure as he saw his friends advancing on the compound. The sheer numbers were staggering as the men looked like small ants running up a hill. At that moment, he caught sight of the huge satellite dish rising to meet them. The pilot banked the helicopter to the side to avoid striking the massive metal target. The coach could hear chatter on the radio about securing the dish. He looked out his window once more to see soldiers advancing toward the dish and surrounding it.

The pilot told everyone to hang tight as he banked the helicopter hard right and brought the vehicle to a safe hover some distance away from the dish to get a better look. Coach Ridel watched as the rest of the crew attached themselves to a metal cable above them in the belly of the helicopter. The coach couldn't help but marvel at how precise these soldiers were and how prepared they were to achieve their goals. He could use some of these men on the field, that's for sure. In a matter of moments, the entire team of soldiers were in position to jump out of the vehicle and repel to the ground. He stood off to the side as to not get in the way of this well-oiled machine.

One of the soldiers turned to the coach and told him to stay put while they jumped. He assured the soldier he wasn't jumping out of a perfectly good aircraft, bringing a smile to the man's face. The soldier informed him that the pilot's instructions were to let out its payload and meet the rest of the force at a designated spot not far from the dish. Coach Ridel listened to the metallic ring as the door to the helicopter slid open, revealing the brisk night air rushing into the vehicle. Through the sound of the blades and the rushing wind, he heard someone yell 'go,' and watched as the men, one by one, jumped out of the helicopter.

Watching the men go over the side of the vehicle, the coach almost felt as though he should be suiting up and joining them. This thought quickly faded though as the last man went over the edge and a bullet struck the side of the helicopter. The pilot quickly maneuvered the vehicle to a safer altitude and told the coach to sit back down. He complied quickly and could feel the rushing air coming from the still open door. The fast-moving air pushed him back against the helicopter wall and the noise from the oncoming air hurt his ears. The emptiness of the interior of the craft was ominous as he looked at the dark corners, hoping to see a friendly face. In a matter of minutes, the pilot safely landed the craft.

The coach, still sitting, wondered if he should exit the vehicle now when the pilot stuck his head in and told him the coast was clear. He rose slowly, walked carefully to the edge of the helicopter, and peered outside. The clear night met him with the brisk air assaulting his senses as he stepped back onto solid ground. The blades above him still spun and he bent slightly until he was clear of their motion. When able to stand in full once more, he stretched to his full height and walked with purpose toward a group of soldiers congregating together off to his right. As he approached, one of the officers turned to him and told him what would happen now. The coach listened intently as the officer outlined for him the fact that the defending force was very small, thanks to the other attacking force. He went on to tell the coach that this was mop up duty and the whole compound would be under their control rather quickly.

Looking around at the surrounding helicopters, it was easy to believe the officer as he touted the might of his force. The remaining soldiers were given their final orders and each returned to their vehicles to await the call for rescue duty if needed. The officer informed his men that this was a ground assault due to the nature of the force and where they were. He would only call in air support if absolutely needed, but they'd most likely have need for evacuation of troops soon.

The coach also returned to his helicopter knowing there wasn't much he could do at this point. He sat on the edge of the doorway with both hands holding himself up and peering out into the night. Once more, the thought of his players running around in danger made him sit up straighter.

Not knowing what else he could do to help, he slouched down a bit and thought about how much he wanted to strangle that boneheaded doctor. Dr. Chase was a terrific doctor and always put his players back together and on the field, faster than any other in the league. Many a coach would come up to Ridel and sing the praises of the good old doctor.

That was before all this clone business began and then he was as distracted as any member of his team. He would find the doctor gazing at the picture of his newly found daughter in his office. Whenever he would come rushing into the doctor's office to discuss one of his players, the doctor would always seem distant and preoccupied. Every time he needed something from the doctor, it wouldn't happen for one reason or another lately. Once the standard for professionalism, the doctor showed the same distracted behavior of some of his younger players.

Sitting in the helicopter alone gave him time to reflect upon the plight of these people he depended on the most. His players broke their bodies quite literally to please him and the doctor over the years gave his all as well to the unforgiving coach. Sadness seeped into the hard exterior of the coach and thought of his teams over the years. The amount of success his teams achieved was in large part to ignoring the noise and each player focusing on their own position. This amount of focus was a hallmark of the players that played for him and their ability to understand their jobs on the field. For all the success he achieved with these men and women on and off the field paled in comparison to the lives his two players fought for right now. He once again got a sick feeling in his stomach, wondering if those two knuckleheads were all right.

Sick of waiting, the coach, always a man of action, pushed himself quickly to his feet and strode over to the officer once more. The officer was in quiet conversation with another member of his team and noticed the coach. He finished his conversation quickly and sent the other man on his way. The officer could tell right away what the coach had in mind and told him he was sending a small group of soldiers in to see what was going on. They were only finding information and wouldn't get too close, but the coach could join them. The coach gave him a look of gratitude and fell in behind a small group of soldiers, following close behind.

Chapter 35

April watched as another bullet struck her father and screamed. Even from her vantage point off the side of the hill watching the whole battle unfold, she could see Steve standing guard just before the bridge. With tears streaming, watching two of her family members in mortal danger was all April could take. She went to lift herself to rush forward but was met with Agent Bradley's soft voice.

"April, I know this is hard but if we rush out there right now, we're all dead." She turned her tear-stained face to look at the drawn FBI agent. One look into his tired eyes told her everything she needed to know—that this would end one way or another soon.

She relaxed slightly, bringing her head down, and scanned once more for Chris and Christopher. She panicked all over again when at first she couldn't find the two massive men. Then off to her left, she noticed a scuffle and between the mass of soldiers, she could see Chris and Christopher locked in hand-to-hand combat with many soldiers. April didn't let her eyes leave the love of her life as he struggled for his very own. All around the two men it appeared that punches were thrown in every direction. She could see quite the pile of writhing bodies lying on the ground before the two men. April looked at Chris' face to gain any knowledge of how he fared but it was safe to say he just tried to survive and focused on the next opponent.

Chris looked quickly to make sure Christopher was still up and felt a whack to the back of his knee for his trouble. This almost brought him down but he recovered quickly, turning to meet this new attacker. He looked just in time to see a rifle butt heading straight for his face. With a quick move, he ducked to avoid the strike and came up with a fast uppercut of his own, leveling the man with one shot. Christopher had his hands full as two soldiers tried to tackle the big man to the ground. All around the two were piles of broken bodies yet they kept coming. The two once more looked at one another and knew this was a struggle to the death and went back to work. Their strength waning, they moved back-to-back to see the next attack. They circled, looking out at their attackers. The soldiers closed in around them when Chris noticed April's face on the side of the hill.

He looked into her panicked eyes and knew they needed to get these soldiers away from the ladies. Both ladies were in rough shape and they wouldn't be able to defend themselves long against the trained soldiers. With a quick grab of Christopher's sleeve, he alerted his brother to the fact that they would rush the soldiers. Chris' idea was to lead the soldiers away from the ladies and give themselves a little space. Chris knew the soldiers wouldn't expect them to rush them and they'd be caught off guard.

Christopher followed his brother and ran straight at a group of soldiers, clotheslining the first few and breaking free of the ring of soldiers. Once through the initial ring, Chris led his brother in the opposite direction, running as fast as his legs could carry him. Surprised soldiers watched as the two men sped past their fearful looks. He didn't stop and flew past the soldiers, not listening to the commands of 'halt' and 'stop.' Christopher moved to his shoulder, looked quickly at Chris, and ran with his brother. The two huge men moved with such speed and agility that the soldiers in their way were cut down like a weed whacker in a large field of knee-high grass.

As he ran further down the hill, he heard the cocking of weapons and thought that this would be the end of Chris and his brother. The shots never came because he heard a massive explosion and then voices shouting about securing the dish. He ran a few more steps and turned to see where the explosion came from. The soldiers were now busy running back to the dish. He wanted nothing more than to get away from this location but some invisible force kept him in place, telling him to go back. Christopher looked questioningly at him and then followed behind as the two made their way back.

Just up the hill, they could see where the explosion rocked the night air. Smoke still hung in the air just above where the bridge to the dish once stood. Chris could see Steve now leaning against the structure of the dish with the RPG still in his hand. Steve didn't look up and Chris couldn't tell if his friend was expired or just exhausted. He caught sight of the doctor as he rose, struggling to his knees before his laptop. Chris could hear orders being given to take the subjects out at all costs and secure the dish.

Chris panicked. He knew no one could get to his friends but that also meant that none of them could help the security guard or the doctor from their location. The feeling of helplessness hit him hard and he turned to Christopher.

"We have to do something. We can't let them shoot our friends." Christopher just answered by barreling into a group of soldiers poised to shoot across to the dish. Just like a heat-seeking missile, Christopher found his target and caused all kinds of chaos. While trying to regroup, Chris plowed into another group, giving the doctor precious time. As soon as Chris was on his feet once more, he saw the doctor lean forward and push a button on his laptop.

He remembered the doctor telling them to be at a safe distance and to not touch anything metal. Chris quickly grabbed Christopher and they both ran in April's direction. April could see them coming and Chris waving something to them. Agent Bradley told them to stay put and lie close to the ground. Chris and Christopher skidded into the ground next to them, telling them to get down. He looked at Agent Bradley and grabbed his gun and threw it a few feet away from them. They all looked at the dish and didn't know exactly what would happen. They felt their hair raise as if pulled by electricity when one rubbed a balloon against one's head and stuck it to the wall. The power in the air grew and by now, their hair was straight up and pointing toward the satellite dish.

A loud humming broke the silence with soldiers standing before the dish with their smaller weapons pulled from their hands toward the dish, scraping along the ground. The soldiers now backed up a little too late as each of them had metal objects in their hands as the pulse of energy was released into the air. The wave of energy struck the unsuspecting soldiers with full force, blowing them off their feet with terrific force. Chris and company put their heads in the dirt and covered their ears.

In a matter of moments, the blast was gone and the electric charge that was sent out was no longer felt in the air. Not sure of whether they could move, Chris glanced up just slightly to view the scene. To his horror, burnt and decimated bodies were strewn all over the hill. Not one soldier stood and in many cases, the soldiers weren't whole but blown to pieces by the shockwave. He couldn't take his eyes away from the gruesome scene. Chris brought his glance quickly to find Steve and the doctor.

He saw Steve lumped over, still holding the RPG between his legs with his head hung low. Chris couldn't tell the state of Steve's health from where he was situated. As he turned his gaze toward the doctor, his plight looked more dire. The doctor lay atop his computer and showed no signs of life. Chris' heart sank to see his friends in such dire straits and felt helpless sitting here on the ground. He lifted himself up to his knees to get a better look. Once more, he couldn't tell whether his friends lived or died. Without one more thought, he rose completely to his feet and waved his remaining friends to join him.

Jessica and April were first to join him, followed by Agent Bradley, along with Christopher bringing up the rear. They worked their way up to the edge of the chasm that threatened to suck them into the abyss. The darkness from the chasm loomed heavily on their hearts and a blast of air shot out from below, almost knocking them backward. Once they regained their balance, they called over to Steve and the doctor in hopes of finding signs of life. To their great delight, Steve stirred. They could see his movement was labored and slow. Chris knew that Steve and the doctor had little time left. He needed to do something and fast, as he turned looking for anything that might assist them in retrieving their friends.

Suddenly, from the silent darkness, voices came across the air to their ears. Agent Bradley waved for them to return to their previous position. Running quickly, they all lay flat on their bellies in the dirt, trying not to choke on the dust. Waiting now was painful; after everything they encountered, this evening just seemed too much to bear. Through sweating brows, they looked anxiously out over the hill from their low hiding area. Chris thought to himself that his friends needed medical attention now if they were to survive. The thought of Steve and the doctor not surviving boiled over in his brain.

Even after everything the doctor had put them through, the sense of justice watching him die this way didn't seem correct. They all listened intently to the approaching voices, knowing their strength and energy were gone. If they were to fight once more for their lives, so be it, but the fight would be short in their current state.

Chapter 36

Through the darkness, voices became stronger as their nerves heightened, waiting on their fate. Each member of the company thought much the same, that this was their final stand. They tried to measure what fight they all still had left in them at that moment. To a man, the decision wasn't hard after all they experienced in the last year; they were fighters and would see this through to the end.

After the blast by the pulse, the darkness surrounding them sucked up any remaining light there might have been. This made it difficult for Chris and his friends to pick up any of the approaching force. The voices were now very close yet the darkness wouldn't reveal the identity of the attackers. Chris couldn't wait any longer and bolted to his feet. Christopher, knowing his brother's mind, did likewise and was soon next to Chris, running headlong into the dark.

Using the voices to guide their way through the dark, they attacked without notice. Chris launched himself into the person in the lead of the group. Both men crashed to the ground with tremendous force. Chris didn't wait for the man to right himself and continued the attack, pinning the man to the ground with his knees. As he lifted his arms to strike, he heard the man below him yell, "Chris, if you don't get off me right now, I'll cut you from my team this very minute! Do you hear what I'm saying? Get off me, you lug!"

Chris immediately recognized the voice of his coach and jumped to his feet, yanking the coach up with him. He sheepishly looked at his coach in the dim light. Recognizing the coach's scowl, he backed up a bit. He shook his head.

"Coach, what the hell are you doing here? Don't get me wrong. I'm glad to see you but here of all places?"

The coach, still rubbing his back, trying to get rid of the pain caused by his player tackling him, retorted, "Chris, I could no longer stand by and do nothing. You forget this whole thing may seem as if it has just happened to you, but this affects us all. Besides, I thought you might need my help."

Christopher chimed in, "Coach, I'm glad to see you. Please tell me you've brought reinforcements."

The coach answered, "Yes, Christopher, believe it or not, I've brought you a small army. The first order of business is to secure the satellite dish." At this statement, both Chris and Christopher backed up in a defensive posture. This didn't go unnoticed in the dim light by the coach. "Guys, relax! We're the good guys! These soldiers just want to make sure that no foreign intelligence operatives can use the dish on our own country. I must tell you gentlemen; I don't know what that dish can do but it's a lot more than just a plain old communications satellite. Just look around you for a second."

Both men did as the coach instructed and viewed the area they were in and beyond. For the first time, they noticed the sheer darkness except for a little moonlight that covered the hillside. Chris remembered even though the compound suffered terrific damage, there were still lights everywhere. Now along with the silence, a creepy darkness covered the entire hill. Their view of the surrounding area from such a high vantage point offered them quite a panoramic view. Earlier that night, they marveled at the lights of the surrounding community and now there wasn't a light to be found anywhere. To Chris, it looked like a power outage after a storm. There was now a calmness to the area that was ominous. To look at the surrounding area, one wouldn't think they were in the middle of a warzone.

Chris turned his gaze back to his coach. "Listen, Coach, honestly I could care less about the stupid dish but we have to get Steve and Dr. Chase. Coach, they're trapped!"

The coach moved forward. "Let me see! Take me there!" As they approached the dish, the coach could clearly see the peril Steve and the doctor faced. He turned to the soldier to his right. "Have your men search the hillside for something to span that chasm. We need to get them out of there! Hurry, that platform isn't going to hold much longer."

For the first time, Chris and company looked across the expanse and saw what the coach was talking about. While Chris talked to the coach, the rest of his group joined them. Each member looked at the platform and at first glance, it seemed structurally sound, but upon a second look, the platform itself pulled away from the dish. They could also see the two unmoving figures trapped on the other side. April and Jessica once more ran to the edge and called to their loved ones in the hopes of finding signs of life. At first, things looked very grim until Steve moved his head slightly, just enough for them to see he still lived. The RPG fell to the platform and bounced harmlessly to the side.

Jessica's heart soared. "Steve, we're here, honey! We're going to get you out of there! Don't worry, we'll have you back here in no time!" Steve nodded slightly and turned to the doctor. Steve, in words barely above a whisper, called to the doctor.

"Dr. Chase, wake up. We have to get out of here." The doctor remained unmoving and Steve turned to Jessica with sad eyes.

April noticed this and screamed, "He isn't finished yet! We will get you both. Hang on! Just hang on, Dad!"

Both women now stood with tears in their eyes, hoping beyond hope that there was a way to get to their loved ones. They turned to question the soldiers who came back up the hill empty handed. The soldiers informed them that there was nothing large enough to put across the opening that would bear the weight of the men. A look of despair came over the ladies' faces. Chris chimed in, "Sir, do you have anyone with rope?"

The soldier looked embarrassed. "You're right! I should have thought of that sooner! We repelled out of the helicopter and always travel with rope. We can use the rope to create a makeshift rope bridge. Don't worry, we'll have them back in no time."

The soldier excused himself and went to one side a few yards away to consult with his fellow soldiers. In a matter of moments, several other soldiers joined them with lengths of rope in hand. They went to work quickly and were ready to send the rope over to Steve.

Jessica once again called to her love, "Steve, honey, you have to grab this rope and tie it off!" Steve looked unresponsive at first and she continued, "Honey, I know you're hurting but we'll get you out of there and get you fixed up! I just need you to get the rope!" At this, Steve moved to his knees and looked out at Jessica. The soldier tossed the ropes to Steve. The ropes landed off to his right by a foot. Steve, moving very slowly, reached for the rope. It looked to Chris and company that he struggled mightily to grab the rope but luckily, Steve's hand reached it. He brought it back toward him and tied the rope to the platform.

With the rope secured to the platform, one of the soldiers moved forward to cross the bridge. He first tied a rescue line to his waist and cautiously stepped onto the rope bridge. The soldier inched out on the bridge a few feet, seeing if it would hold. When he was satisfied with the safety of the bridge, he worked his way across. Halfway across, the rope sagged dangerously low but held and he crossed. Once to the other side, he stepped on the platform only to have it buckle under his weight. He stepped over to the doctor as he looked to be in the worst shape.

Without a word, he struggled to bring the doctor's lifeless body to an upright positon. Once the doctor was upright, the soldier then slung him on his shoulder in a fireman's carry. The soldier stepped back onto the rope and felt the platform pull further from the dish, causing him to nearly lose his footing. He regained his balance and moved across the bridge to the safety of the waiting arms of April and company.

They took the doctor carefully from the soldier lying him down on the ground several feet from the chasm. The soldier gave Chris a look of dismay as he stepped back onto the rope for the return trip to gather Steve. The already unsteady platform once again pulled more from the wall with pieces of metal and concrete falling into the darkness. Chris just looked at the soldier as he stepped back onto the hill with uncertainty. "Listen to me, that's an Army Ranger over there. You're not leaving him behind. Do you hear me? Give me that rope, I'll do it myself!" The soldier could see the fire in Chris' eyes and stepped back for a moment. It looked like for a second the soldier would give the ropes to Chris but then he turned to him. "An Army Ranger?"

Chapter 37

April knelt on the ground beside the broken body of her father with tears streaming down her face. The doctor's lifeless body even in the darkness looked gruesome. She reached down and gently lifted the doctor's head so she had it in both hands and slid his body to hers. He had no weight left to him and April rested his body on her legs and supported his head carefully. Her tears were freely falling onto her father's face. This had a magical effect and roused her father slightly. This was the first sign of life from the doctor.

His eyes opened slowly and tried to focus. When he saw who held him, he let out a painful smile. "My heart, makes me so happy to see you!" Tears of his own pooled in his eyes and he spoke once more in barely a whisper, "I'm so sorry for all you've been through! I never meant for any of this to happen to any of you. It was always my hope to build a better world for you. Instead, look at what I've done. In my rush to save humanity, I almost doomed it!"

April's splotched, red, tear-stained face couldn't hold back the emotion as it came rushing out of her like the rain waters crashing down a mountain after a spring rain. She wailed uncontrollably. The doctor, whose voice was so soft now that April had to bend to hear him through parched lips, said, "My daughter, you must live again. You must begin anew. Take Chris and start a new life. I'm so proud of both of you. I'd be so glad to call Chris son. Just know that I'm redeemed and what I did today, I did for all humanity."

She looked down at him with blurry eyes. "Dad, what are you talking about?"

He looked lovingly into her eyes. "I've reset the system. I've given you all a new start! One that will allow humanity to regain just that, its humanity." He coughed slightly and continued, "My heart, I've little time. You must listen to me; you should take care of Christopher as he's the key to everything. You must make sure he learns all he can about being human. His importance to the rest of humanity is immense. Please promise me you will look after him."

She once again looked down at the wreck that was now her father. "I promise, Dad. You know Christopher is family and I'll take care of him."

The doctor weakly smiled. "Good, April. He will come to have a great place in society someday, but until that time, you must look after him. I cannot begin to tell you how proud I am of you and your friends. You have literally saved this planet and I leave it now in your capable hands. Goodbye, my heart! I love you!" With that statement, all life left the doctor's body and slumped into the waiting arms of his distraught daughter.

April looked down at her father and shook him gently. "Dad, dad! No, don't go! Dad, you can't go yet; there is still so much you and I need to do! Not now! I just got you back again! This can't be the end!" She cupped his head gently in both hands and leaned forward to kiss his forehead. In the dim light, someone looking might just see a person kissing another's child good night. In the darkness, her screams wailed, threatening to crumble the satellite dish to the ground. Chris found her first and fell to his knees next to her. There were no words of comfort he could offer so instead; he chose to put his arm around her and hold her. April didn't realize he was there and cried uncontrollably as the rest of her friends looked on.

Without another word, the soldier moved back out onto the rope. He again tested the rope and once satisfied, made his way across. His crossing this time seemed less dramatic and made it to Steve without incident. Once on the platform, he moved it over to Steve who was once again slumped slightly forward, unmoving. The soldier took one look at Steve's immense size and shook his head. He knew there was no way he could hoist Steve onto his shoulders and carry him across. The soldier also had serious thoughts as to whether the rope bridge could hold the weight of both men.

He gently shook Steve in the hopes of waking the slumbering man. It took a few moments but Steve stirred and looked weakly at the soldier. The soldier was already back to his feet and called to Steve, "Okay, Ranger, we have to go! Now on your feet! I cannot carry you but we're going to make it. On your feet, soldier!" Steve spoke not a word but rose slowly to his feet and staggered to the waiting soldier. His injured leg wasn't going to support him very well and he leaned heavily on the soldier as the worked their way to the edge. The soldier quickly tied a rescue line onto Steve's waist and got them onto the bridge quickly.

The weight of both men on the ropes seemed too much for the bridge to hold and sagged dangerously low into the chasm. The darkness below seemed ready at any moment to devour them whole. They inched their way to the middle of the rope bridge with Steve fast losing any energy he once had and he now clung to the soldier with his remaining strength. Then a blast of air from below struck them and caused both men to fall forward onto the thin ropes that made up the bridge. Luckily, the soldier grabbed the rope quickly and held Steve with him. Steve's weight almost ripped the soldier's arm off but he held fast to the Army Ranger.

The soldier gingerly worked his way back to his feet and used what strength he'd left to help Steve up. Steve just barely made it to an upright position and the soldier steadied them for the last bit of the crossing. The soldier knew they only had moments as the platform pulled away from its anchor in the dish. He propped Steve up and pushed them forward. With fifteen feet remaining on their journey, they could see their friends on the other side waiting for them. Steve looked up just in time to catch a glimpse of Jessica when suddenly the platform gave way, causing both men to fall forward into the abyss. Steve instinctively grabbed hold of the soldier's shoulders and found himself flying forward into the darkness.

Steve felt as though there was no weight to him, as if he were flying in the air as a bird might. He felt the rush of air whipping by his face, which was shattered by a terrifying impact of bodies striking the side wall of the chasm. Steve and the soldier struck the wall with such momentum, the people above heard the crunch of bones. As they struck, Steve could feel his rescuer's face smash into the wall with a gruesome crack. He panicked as the man's body went limp and fell downward. Steve reached out, hoping to grab what was left of the rope bridge. To his great surprise, his hand grasped a rope in the dark. Caught in his hand, it yanked his arm out of its socket.

Now dangling in the darkness, he heard the body of the soldier falling below and crashing viciously into the wall on its way down. The thought of the young man giving up his life for him almost made him vomit. His body riddled with pain and now he was wide awake with the added pain of a separated shoulder holding the entire weight of his body. As he hung there waiting for his turn to fall, he heard the voice of an angel call to him. With a great deal of pain and energy, he looked up the ten feet to see Jessica's beautiful face calling out to him.

Jessica, now on her belly with tears flowing, screamed to Steve below. "Steve! Hang on, my love! We will pull you up! Don't you let go! I'll have you up here in just a second!" Steve could feel the energy leaving his body and once again, he faded. The only reason he was alive at this point was the woman screaming his name. He would do anything for her and if she ordered him to stay alive, who was he to disobey orders. He tried to move enough to grab the rope with both hands but the injury to his side made him feel as though every movement would tear him in half. His other arm felt as if it would tear from his body at any moment and he knew his body wouldn't hold together much longer.

He could still hear Jessica screaming his name and then he felt a jolt of pain shoot through his body. He moved upwards as the soldiers, along with Chris and friends pulled him up. Steve thought for a moment that he might see Jessica one more time before he expired, as he knew his injuries were beyond repair at this point. With every inch upward, his body tore apart more and he wondered how much longer he could hold on.

Chapter 38

Chris could feel the coarse rope ripping through the thin skin of his hands and blood soaked the rope. He held tight as did the other members of his team, struggling mightily to bring the massive security specialist back up through the hole. Every inch took hours and he didn't know how much longer Steve could hang on. Despite his wrecked hands, he pulled with all his might to save his friend. One of the soldiers near the edge said he could almost grab him. Chris could see Jessica nearly falling headlong into the chasm herself and Agent Bradley on the ground, grabbing her, holding her waist tight.

This gave Chris all the motivation he needed and pulled even harder. What none of them realized was that with each inch, an already frayed rope was quickly coming undone in the dark. Just as Jessica and Agent Bradley were about to grab Steve's arm, they heard a snap. Steve had just enough time to look up and mouth the words, "I love you!" He plunged to his death while never looking anywhere but on the love of his life. He finally became the man that he envisioned when he went into the military—a strong, proud, and good man. This vision of beauty came into his life and put him on track for the kind of life he always hoped to achieve. His only regret was leaving this wonderful vision behind.

Jessica screamed as she watched her love plunge into the abyss. Agent Bradley strained to keep Jessica from falling into the chasm as the veins in his neck popped out from his collar. Christopher swooped in and picked her up before she went over, completely leaving the FBI agent on the dusty ground, trying to catch his breath. She struggled against

Christopher, pounding his chest while screaming in his face to let her go, but he held fast. She managed to crawl up to his shoulder, still looking in the opening, expecting to see Steve appear out of the hole any minute. He held her tight but kept her safely away from the edge and looked at Chris with panicked eyes.

Chris noticed the sorrowful plight of his double and returned a sympathetic look across the hill. Both men were entrenched in an impossible situation. How does one comfort a person that just witnessed the death of a loved one? They did the only thing they could think of and held fast to the friend they loved, hoping to provide some relief. Agent Bradley, now in an upright position, stood with Christopher tending to Jessica. Chris maintained his vigil sitting on the ground, still hugging April while she sobbed at the lifeless body that was her father. He looked down at the ravaged body of the doctor and marveled at how he even survived long enough to say goodbye to his daughter. Just the sheer amount of blood soaking the man's clothing told anyone looking that the doctor willed himself to see his daughter before expiring.

Chris now noticed the entire hillside covered in soldiers and defensively moved in front of April. Out of the shadows came a slight-framed man walking alongside the coach. Chris almost laughed aloud but remembered April and just smirked slightly. The man walked briskly toward Chris and with his haggard appearance, Chris could tell his journey here was just as difficult as theirs. With a deep sigh, the man just plopped down next to Chris and April with an exhausted look. He just leaned his head on April's shoulder. Chris broke the silence.

"Gus, you old bloodhound. Where the hell have you been?"

Gus looked at his friends and for the first time since losing her father, April looked up. "My friends, as we get sucked deeper and deeper into this story of ours, we continue to find that there are so many layers we're unaware. Believe it or not, my own sins have come back to haunt me on this one, but now isn't the time or the place to discuss this. I'm just glad to find you." He looked apologetically at April. "My dear, I'm so sorry about your father."

April's face, in the dim light, moved forward. "Gus, whatever my dad did, he said it's complete. I've no idea what he was talking about and how he thinks he fixed everything." Chris and Gus turned to see April look sternly at them. "Guys, what do you think my father did? Please tell me he didn't make matters worse for us."

Chris softly brushed her face with the back on his hand. "No, sweetheart, I don't think your father would have gone through all this just to put you in a more difficult position. April, look at him. There is no way in hell he should have still been alive. No, he willed himself to finish his mission and my love, his mission was you. He did as any father would have and gave his life so that you might live!" At this last statement, Chris winced, "Sorry, honey, I don't mean to sound harsh. It's just... look at what he went through. I know there is so much we'll never truly know about your father, but I have to tell you I do know that you've always been his world."

April cried once more and grabbed hold of Chris' arm. "How could he leave? How could he leave me alone?"

Chris took her face in his massive hands. "He left you in my hands and I'm never going to leave. April, he did what he had to for you to survive. Can you imagine all the secrets he just took with him? Just think about that for a minute. I don't ever think we'll truly understand everything the doctor knew and was involved in. I can tell you this. I guarantee he just messed up a lot of people in the government. There will be some highly pissed off people tonight!"

Gus chimed in, "Chris, unfortunately you're not that far from the truth when you say we have little idea of all the secrets the doctor knew. My friends, we're not out of the woods here by a long shot. When the dust clears, heads are going to roll and who do you think they're going to come looking for? Us, they'll come for us. The fact that we have no damn idea what the doctor has been up to makes no difference. The blame pie is going to be smashed in our face. I just hope that we won't end up in some military prison somewhere. I'm too old for that crap!"

Chris slapped him in the back. "You idiot, none of us is going to jail. We had nothing to do with any of this and that's well documented. No, the one man who knew what was going on is no longer here to defend himself and they'll have to deal with that. I for one am going to make sure that people know the real culprit here was secrecy. As is always the case when people decide to keep secrets from one another, the entire story is never known. Obviously, the doctor tried to spare us from all the gory details, but in the process forced us to be just as involved. If we knew what was going on from the jump, this may never have happened."

April's face grew angry. "How can you say that? Chris, how was he supposed to let you know that you were being signed to the club as a decoy and that you would be replaced by a clone? Could he tell everyone that their country used clones as part of a military program that went on to develop an Artificial Intelligence program? Are you out of your mind? Think about that, just what the hell was he supposed to tell everyone Chris? You know as well as I do what it takes to become a professional football player. During that process, you would do whatever was needed to make the team, period. I assure you my father, for all his faults, did what he thought he needed to do for the betterment of humanity."

Chris could tell by the forcefulness of her voice that this was the wrong time to get involved in this argument. "April, I know, I'm sorry. It just seems everywhere you look no one can give you an honest answer. I just want things to be normal again and I just don't know if that will ever happen. My whole life has been dedicated to becoming a dominating professional football player and so far, the only thing I'm dominating is shadows. Even the shadows seem to be lies. I just want to know what's real again! The only thing I'm sure is real is the way I feel about you. You're the love of my life and that couldn't be more real!"

He could see her tears begin anew and held her close once more. She broke away from him. "Chris, I'm just as sure about us as you are but I'm like you and have no idea what's real anymore. Think about it. I thought my whole life my real parents were one thing and then I find out my father has been under my nose the whole time. I finally find out that my father has watched my footsteps from the shadows. You want to talk about chasing shadows and what's real. How about your father being there always and not knowing it? Just like you, I always thought I was helping keep our players on the field healthy but I was just doing physicals. Under my nose was one of the greatest cover-ups known to man and if that wasn't enough, the man who would be my father is responsible. Yes, I'm beyond words when it comes to real and what's not."

Chapter 39

Swarms of soldiers now threatened to crush them as the entire hillside crawled with military personnel everywhere. No one could explain why the lights were still not coming to life. Soldiers were used to dealing with the effects of an EMP blast but this blast took out everything. Radios, phones, cars, and transports of every kind remained disabled. Walking around in the dark made sharing information extremely difficult. The fact that not one military group could coordinate with another made matters all the worse. Several officers ordered their men to go down the hill into the woods and bring back firewood.

Within the hour, the hillside resembled a large campsite with campfires sprinkled across the hill. In the fire, the large dish loomed but with no electricity; it just stood— another darkened stillness in the night. By now, the dish was secured by military police surrounding the area around the dish. The officers in charge made everyone move further down the hillside, away from the dish just in case the juice came back on. They didn't want anyone else to get fried.

Chris and company sat huddled around a fire of their own and allowed their eyes to look across the fire at each other. The ragged appearance of each member of their dwindling group spoke volumes to the lengths they'd traveled to get their lives back. For this group, their lives would forever be marked by these events but where many would cower, this group rose time and time again to the call of greatness. As they looked out in the darkness at the soldiers that now surrounded them, they couldn't help but feel a part of the now piece meal force. They were given MREs, which were a deployed soldier's rations along with military blankets.

The fire warmed their bones but their hearts remained cold at the loss of their dear friends. Each member of the group couldn't help but think of what would happen next now that the doctor was gone. Would they all be blamed for the entire affair or would it be as Chris described, all heaped upon the doctor posthumously. Either way, this group would never be the same again and they needed to rebuild what lives were left. Flames rose into the night sky as the first light of a new day broke the horizon.

As the morning light showed the actual devastation before them, even the seasoned soldiers were shocked to see the scorched hillside still littered with bodies. Now with the light of a new day, soldiers began the sobering job of tending to their fallen brothers and sisters. The contorted bodies made a shocking scene in the daytime when people could now see the full effect of the dish's pulse. The soldiers carefully brought the dead to the bottom of the hill and laid them in rows. The sight of the countless rows of fallen soldiers made for a horrifying scene that made many a soldier sick that day.

The morning sun shone brightly on the satellite dish that stood as a beacon of destruction. Soldiers kept watch around the dish as officers argued about what should happen next to the site. Chris and company made their way down the hill to a larger encampment to find fires and fresh food being prepared. They sat down at the request of one of the officers and ate a light breakfast. Even though they weren't officially under arrest, it certainly felt to the company that they were being held. With little energy and nowhere else to be at the very moment, they all just took the food thankfully.

With the sun rising higher in the sky, the day became quite warm and they were thankful for the cover of the trees. Soldiers worked on the nearby vehicles and various communications devices to see what was happening around them. They were unable to make a single vehicle or communication device work. This didn't make the soldiers happy, realizing they were stuck in the middle of nowhere with limited supplies and no transportation. After conferring with the officers, it was decided that they'd all hike to the nearest town which was fifteen miles away. It was also determined that a detachment of soldiers would be left at the compound to secure the area.

Much of the remaining stores and supplies were left with the soldiers staying behind. Chris and his group prepared to make the journey, gathering what little items they were in possession of while moving quickly. Dr. Chase's body was reverently wrapped and put on a litter to bring him back with them. Some of the soldiers volunteered to bring the doctor and April reluctantly agreed, but looking at her friend's condition, she thought the fresher soldiers would be better off carrying him. They made ready to leave and followed behind an already formed group of soldiers.

The sun was high in the sky now and the temperature was rising, but the soldiers didn't want to wait too long for fear of weather that looked like it was coming in from the west. The trip brought them through rough rocky terrain. Once away from the hill and compound, the land became very dry and had sparse growth. Dust from such a large procession of people made the travelling that much more difficult as the dust got everywhere and threatened to choke the air away from them. The trip took most of the afternoon and they arrived at the town just in time as a large thunderstorm made its way through the area.

Soldiers took refuge in barns and garages as the storm made its way through the town. Bolts of lightning struck a few trees out in one of the fields, but Chris and his group were safely inside the local mini-mart. The storm lasted about an hour before moving on and the sun coming out once more. With the storm now gone, Chris and Agent Bradley gathered information from the locals as to what happened to the town. The entire town lost its electricity and just as happened at the dish site, no electronic devices of any kind worked. Frustration mounted among the soldiers as once again they couldn't communicate with anyone or call for supplies or transportation.

Agent Bradley brought them all to the backroom of the mini-mart where they could discuss their plans. The soldiers, since arriving to the town and finding out their own plight now, paid little attention to the small group. When everyone was comfortable, Agent Bradley began.

"It seems as though our soldier friends have their own issues to deal with. This is terrific for us as there is a town about ten miles from here with an FBI field office. We can borrow a few bicycles and make our way to the safety of the office and way things out."

Jessica spoke up, "John, I for one would love nothing more than to get there in relative safety but should we not rest first? I mean... look at us! We're a mess!"

The FBI agent responded, "Jessica, I understand. I do but seriously this is our window! Something tells me that if we don't leave now, we may not be leaving, if you get my meaning."

Jessica retorted, "John, I'm an attorney. They're not going to pull any crap on us."

Agent Bradley looked serious. "If that dish has wiped out all communications and power, then people are going down. Who do you think is going to be blamed? We're the prime candidates and they already have us at their disposal."

Jessica sat up straighter. "They wouldn't use this to invoke marshal law, would they? Dumb question! All right, John, what do you propose? If you're right, we need to get out of here now."

Agent Bradley smiled. "Don't worry, everyone. We'll be out of here in a few minutes. On our way in here, I saw what was left of a yard sale with quite a few bikes still left unattended. We will borrow those and pedal to the field office and regroup. Now everyone, grab what you can here and we'll get going. Be sure to grab bottled water; it's very warm out there."

April now said in panicked voice, "What about my father, John? Are you going to leave him here?"

Agent Bradley cringed, "April, we have no choice. We're going to have to come back for him. That is unless you can find some way to latch him to a bicycle. I understand you don't want to leave him behind, but we need to move now! I promise you I'll make sure we come back for him, but now we must get to safety. If we stay, we'll be at the mercy of an angry group of soldiers, ready to blame us for this whole mess. We don't want to be anywhere near this place when that happens."

April calmed a bit. "I get it but is there any other way?"

The agent shook his head. "Unless you know how to get the power back on, then we need to leave now!"

April's eyes watered as Chris gently came up to her. "We'll get him and he won't be left behind for long, but John is right. We don't have time to wait. We must go."

Agent Bradley spoke briefly to the store owner who agreed to house the doctor in an extra freezer in the back of the store. He agreed to tell the soldiers that the group left with the doctor. This made April feel a little better. She announced that she needed a minute alone with her father before they left. No one questioned this and went about their business with preparations to leave. April appeared a few minutes later and said she was ready.

The entire group was ready within a few minutes as the mini-mart owner allowed them to purchase some supplies even though he had no working register. Several members of the group had cash and it was gratefully accepted by the owner. He was upset because a few of the soldiers came through the store and took what they wanted without paying. Their officer told the owner to prepare a sheet of things purchased and they'd reimburse him but cash was always king. Having the cash in hand made the owner feel better. He even gave the group a few extra snacks. The group was extremely grateful and thanked the man quite a few times before leaving the store through the back door, as not to be noticed.

Chris and Agent Bradley led the way, walking casually. The agent brought them quickly to the bicycles and chose one for each of the members. Everyone quickly hopped onto their bike and looked ready to ride except for Christopher.

Chris looked at his double as if to say, "What?" When he realized Christopher didn't know how to ride a bicycle, he got off his and went over to his twin. He motioned Christopher to get on. "Okay, dude, listen. We must do this the old-fashioned way because honestly, we have no time to teach you properly. Put your feet on the pedals there and hold on to the handlebars." Christopher did as he was asked, but looked very nervous as the bike wobbled in Chris' hands as he held it in place.

Chris smiled. "Here we go. When I push you, I want you to get a feel for how the bike moves. See those little levers by your hands, those are brakes and you just squeeze them both to stop. As you're going, I want you to pedal your feet. Keep your head up and watch the road." Christopher nodded as Chris pushed the bicycle. At first, the bike almost went right into a wall until Christopher relaxed a little. Once the bike got a little momentum, Chris let go and watched Christopher pedal a few feet. The massive man had no idea he was riding on his own. When he figured out Chris was no longer there, he instinctively grabbed the brakes and put his legs out to stop himself.

He turned with a hurt look at Chris. Chris shrugged his shoulders. "Dude, sorry! I told you we had to go old school. You just rode a bike, man! How cool is that?"

Christopher smiled and slapped his twin on the back. "That was pretty cool! I want to try it again!" Chris helped him once more and they went quicker this time. Once again, Chris got the man coasting and then let him go. Christopher caught on very quickly and in a few minutes, was riding around like an old pro.

Chris stopped him. "Listen, man. That's great but we have to go."

They all hopped on their bikes, pedaling just quick enough not to look suspicious. Once outside the town limits, they pushed the pace. Christopher was a bit unsure at first but then gained a bit of confidence and caught up. The ride didn't take quite as long as they thought since there were no cars on the road. The blackout had occurred during the night when most people were in bed. They made their way to the field house without any further incident and Agent Bradley instructed them to wait outside until he assessed the situation. He walked quickly into the office and was back in a few minutes with a smile on his face. The agent waved for them to accompany him inside which they happily agreed to.

Chapter 40

Lillian and Malina sat in the morning light staring at the blank television screen. Their entire routine of watching the local morning news program with their grandmother was in danger of being ruined. Lillian kept raising her cell phone, trying to will the phone to life but every electronic device in their home sat lifeless. Malina went to the window, drawing the curtain back slightly to peer into the street. What she saw made her grin. People sat on their steps doing the very same, looking at their phones with the same helpless looks. She waved to her sister to join her by the window. Both young ladies looked up the street and they could see the same clueless looks in the eyes of each of their neighbors.

Malina moved over to the couch and plopped backward, falling into the soft cushions of her grandmother's couch. Lillian just rolled her eyes as she looked at her flighty sister. Lillian the more serious of the two sisters maintained her position by the window. She watched the couple across the street who at this point looked very animated and frustrated with the current situation. What was even more concerning for her at that moment was the lack of automobiles zooming up and down the road. Lillian and her sister awoke several hours ago and had yet to see one vehicle on their street. She turned rapidly towards her sister.

"Malina, we have to wake Memere. Something isn't right. If there was a blackout, the only thing affected would be anything plugged into the outlets. This is crazy, not even the cars are moving. Come on, get up!" She grabbed at her sister's sleeve, pulling her toward their grandmother's bedroom.

The girls slowly opened the door to the bedroom and looked down at their grandmother as she slept. They felt badly about waking her but both knew circumstances called for action. Lillian carefully positioned herself near the bed and eased herself onto the bed, sitting next to her grandmother. Both young ladies looked upon their grandmother lovingly, but still couldn't get over the fact that once asleep, she looked like a mummy and never moved.

Malina couldn't wait and blurted out, "Memere! Good morning."

Lillian gave her sister a look of disdain as the woman lying on the bed stirred. The smallish woman in the bed opened her eyes cautiously with an apprehensive look on her face.

"Yes, my dears, what's the problem that it takes both of you to awaken me? Don't get me wrong, I love that I can be awakened by such beautiful young ladies. It's just odd, is all." She looked up into the uncertain faces of her granddaughters and saw the nervousness in their stance. "All right, out with it! This isn't just a wakeup call. What happened?"

Lillian rose and strode over to her sister, looking directly into her sister's eyes. The girls turned nervously toward their grandmother. "Memere, we really have to show you. Explaining it will do no good as you must see for yourself what we'll tell you. Sorry that we woke you but we really need you out here." She walked to the opposite side of the room to enter back into the hallway leading back to the living room.

Still dressed in a loose-fitting t-shirt and leggings, the woman peeled herself from the bed and swung her legs over the side. With her legs still inches off the floor, she slid her body forward until her feet touched the floor. Even though it was summer, the floor felt cool on her feet. She leaned further over in search of her soft plush slippers and spotted them just to the left a few inches away. The woman pushed herself up from the bed, at the same time sliding her feet into the slippers. Once on her feet, she walked over to the door and looked up at her granddaughters laughing.

Malina moved over to her grandmother and hovered over the slight woman. Malina looked down and said, "Well, Memere, are we having a tall day today? I mean, honestly, are you shrinking more?" She leaned over and planted a big hug on her grandmother. "Don't worry, Memere. I won't let anything happen to you."

The small woman standing next to her granddaughters laughed heartily. "No, I'm not shrinking. You just continue to grow. I think you both grow more each day. Now tell me what has you both acting so strangely." She followed the girls into the living room and took a spot next to them at the window. She peered out the window. "Ladies, I love you both but what on earth am I supposed to be looking at? I just see our quiet little neighborhood."

Lillian, with a worried look on her face, said, "Memere, look closer. I mean really look and tell me what you see." She inched closer to her grandmother and gently positioned her head to look at a group of people across the street.

The small grey-haired woman didn't question her granddaughter, but rather doubled her efforts in her search. For a moment, it looked as though the woman would just turn to them and scold them for disturbing her sleep, but her eyebrows raised.

She turned to look at the girls. "Listen, ladies. People having issues with cell phones is nothing new, but I do think it quite odd that there isn't one car moving. As a matter of fact, I looked a bit up the road and there are a few people pushing a car back into a driveway. What did you girls see?"

Malina chimed in, "Memere, that's exactly what we saw, but there is more. Much more. Every electronic device we own seems to be fried. There is no electricity anywhere that we can see and there isn't one car working. Lillian and I've been up for hours and nothing has changed. Memere if this were a blackout all these things wouldn't be happening at once. I don't know about you but this is freaky and I'm worried."

Her grandmother pulled back the curtain the entire way to get a better view of her street. She looked, trying to confirm her suspicions. After a few minutes, she turned to the girls. "Ladies, time for an adventure. Follow me!"

Lillian and Malina fell in behind their grandmother, walking briskly out the front door. They all walked straight across the street to the congregation of people assembled on their neighbor's front lawn. A tall middle-aged man noticed her walking up and went to greet them.

"Connie," he said, "There are some strange things happening right now. It appeared someone turned off all the power to everything. I mean everything! Even those things that don't get plugged in. The cars, Connie, even the cars won't work. The only clue we have is that one of my old analog clocks in my garage stopped sometime last night. Other than that, we have no idea what's going on."

The man gave the girls a sympathetic look. "Sorry, Lillian and Malina! I know you were so excited to hang out with your grandmother. Even more concerning is that there is zero communication. The phones don't work, no television, no radios, and not even shortwave radios. We've tried everything. One of the guys even tried his marine radio. Nothing works. This is much more than a blackout. This is crazy!"

The young ladies looked at the rugged man and then at one another.

Malina spoke first, "Memere, do you still have our old bikes in the garage? I've a feeling we're going to need to get back to the stadium. Something the doctor mentioned last time we saw him has me stewing. At the time, I thought he was talking gibberish but I think he may have caused this mess."

Lillian looked surprised at her sister. "Malina, you don't think he used some kind of EMP to cause this, do you? No, that can't be it. An EMP would only be temporary. By the looks of this, whatever this is, seems to be much more serious. Although I think you're right. This does have the doctor's footprint all over it. He'd have to have a much more powerful technology at his disposal to shut everything down like this though. You don't think this had anything to do with that project he was working on, do you?"

Malina's face squinted as she looked at her sister through the strong morning sun. "Lillian, that's it. Dr. Chase pulled it off! This is his solution to the problem he was talking about!" She tugged at her grandmother's sleeve. "Memere, come on. We have to talk to you for a minute." Malina guided her grandmother back in the direction of the house.

Connie allowed herself to be dragged back to her home and shut the door behind them. She walked over to the couch and fell into the plush fabric, waiting patiently for an explanation. Both ladies looked at their grandmother and Lillian began.

"Memere, as you know, we work for the Massachusetts Bay Marauders and for Dr. Chase, but we really don't talk much about the work we do there." She looked at her grandmother who seemed to say continue with her eyes.

Lillian swallowed. "Much of the work we do deals with genetics but we just found that some of our work was being used for another altogether sinister project." She looked at Malina how waved her on. "Come to find out, Dr. Chase hasn't just been working on clones. His latest project has a much more far-reaching set of issues. Our guess is that when the doctor found out what the government was doing with his research, he took matters into his own hands. We think that this wipeout of power is his doing. We need to get back to the stadium to check on our theory."

Their grandmother put her hand to her chin. "Girls, knowing you the way I do, I totally understand why you have to go, but do you think it wise? Even when you get to the stadium, what are you going to do? Are you sure anyone will even be there? Think about it, girls! If this happened last night like it seems to be, then everyone would be home and I think the last place people are going to want to be is at work."

Malina's head turned up. "Memere, that's exactly why I want to go to the stadium. I think the whole solution to this mess is waiting for us at the stadium. Trust me, I know it sounds nuts but if the doctor did do this then he also left a solution for us to find. I guarantee he left breadcrumbs for us to find. I've spent some time with the doctor and he wouldn't leave this situation without a way to fix things. That is what he has always done, fix things. When Lillian figures it out, you will be the first to know. We will be sure to call you on the phone as soon as we get it to work."

Connie looked at her granddaughters and the determined looks on their faces. She knew her pleas would fall on deaf ears and relented. "All right, girls, but you be careful. You have no idea what things look like outside of this neighborhood. It could be the Wild West out there. Just keep to yourselves and get right to the stadium. You also be sure to do just that and call me when communications are back up. I'll be here waiting for your return. Hurry, because I don't like our visit being interrupted." She winked at the girls.

Both girls grabbed their grandmother and engulfed her in a huge hug. Lillian broke the embrace and grabbed her sister, running to the garage. They wasted little time pulling out their old bicycles and putting a little air in the tires. They were away in a few minutes. Connie was right as they got farther away from the safety of their neighborhood, they noticed some looting and gangs of people roaming the streets. Taking their grandmother's advice, they steered clear of any interaction with another person and made it to the stadium without incident.

As their grandmother described, the stadium was devoid of human life. They spent much of the next few hours testing all the entrances, only to be disappointed to find the stadium buttoned up as tight as a fort. Malina stopped and put her bike on the ground. She put her hands on her hips and stared at the stadium as if it would speak to her in some way. Lillian thought to say something but looking at her sister's face, she could tell she was working through something. Without saying another word, she bent down and picked up her bike. Mounting the seat, she pedaled in the other direction.

Lillian grabbed her bike and quickly followed. In a moment, she caught up to her sister. "Hey, where are you going in such a hurry? We've tried all the entrances. There is no way we're getting into the stadium. We should head back to Memere's and wait this out. I'm really nervous for her being there on her own."

Malina shook her head. "Don't worry about Memere. She can take care of herself. She's a lot tougher than she looks."

Lillian laughed. "That is true. People better not mess with her or they'll get their butts kicked. All right, what's your plan? Please tell me you have a plan. Hold on a minute though, Malina. What happens if we do get in? Then what do we do? There is no one here and there is no power. Who knows if there is even anything in there that can help us. This seems like such a long shot. I hope you're right about this!"

The younger sister kept pedaling and worked her way to a smaller parking lot on the far side of the stadium. She looked at her sister. "When everyone was talking in the trucks, they spoke about using the housekeeping entrance for easier access. Don't you remember? I'm telling you we'll get in there. I didn't even check on that one because I didn't think of it. Look, there it is. Hurry, I'm sure this is it. Don't worry. Like I told Memere, something is pulling me to this place as if the doctor wanted us to find something."

Lillian, used to her sister's hunches, didn't question her further and stepped up her pace, following her younger sister to the gate. At first glance, their hearts dropped as the gate did indeed look secure, but a closer examination revealed the padlock not completely closed.

Malina howled with excitement as she removed the lock and swung the gate open. Both girls hurried inside with their bicycles and Malina put the chains back with the lock as if it were locked. Lillian nodded and they hid their bikes in a closet off to the side before making their way into the stadium. They looked up, taking in the immense nature of the empty stadium. Both girls were used to game day when the stadium was teeming with life and overflowing with energy. Now the silence threatened to take their breath away as they looked at the completely empty stands.

Suddenly, Lillian stopped. "Okay, Malina, you were right and here we are inside the stadium. What next? As you can see, there is no one here. Are we just going to keep walking around and hope that something happens? You should tell me what the next part of your plan is because this place creeps me out like this. I trust you but I don't want to be here when it gets dark without the lights."

Malina patted her sister on the shoulder to reassure her. "Lillian, I got this. Don't worry. I know what I'm doing. All that stuff they talked about in the truck went in one ear and out the other, but one little nugget stayed with me. It was the talk about making the shadow pay and what the doctor would do to the shadow. Also, I remember the doctor saying something about sending everyone back to the Stone Age. Lillian, he did it! He did send us back to the Stone Age. Look around you!"

Lillian grabbed her sister's hand. "So what do you plan to do about it, little sister?"

Malina smirked. "I'm going to save the flippin day! I'm going to turn the lights back on, baby!"

Chapter 41

Chris stood anxiously with his friends diagonally across the street from the field office. Out of habit, they hid behind a group of large bushes, peering out just enough to keep an eye on the door. When Chris saw Agent Bradley open the door and walk down the steps with a smile on his face, he waved to his friends to follow. Leaving the safety of the bushes, they met their friend in front of the field office. At first, no one would speak as Agent Bradley just looked at them all, with a huge smile on his face.

Jessica broke the silence. "John, you're creeping me out. What is it? Please tell me you have good news for us! I'm telling you, John, if you're messing with us, I'll personally kick your ass right now."

With a look of hurt on his face, he turned to his friends with a more serious look on his face. "Well, my friends, Dr. Chase did it! He did it! He fried the entire system. The good news is the governments around the world have prepared for this type of thing for years. Over the years, they have done research on large-scale events such as solar flares and microwave blasts from space. In this case, Dr. Chase just used the technology here on the ground to send a huge electrical pulse using the satellites from around the world to fry everything. Can you believe it? He hacked the system and used their own defenses against them. Genius!"

As soon as he said that, he saw the tears returning to April's eyes.

"April, I'm sorry! I just meant that he did what he said he would do and reset the system. Do you know what that means? It means a new start for everything—reboot! We have our lives back. We no longer must look over our shoulders. Dr. Chase is a hero. He destroyed the threat to humanity. All the Artificial Intelligence beings are destroyed. Well, more like fried but they'll no longer be an issue and Dr. Chase took his research with him. There is no danger of any government getting their hands on what he knew any longer. April, he gave his life to save us all!"

A sense of pride swelled up inside April as she looked up through blurry, teary eyes at her smiling friends. These people were her family and suffered through untold horrors at the hands of her father, but here they sang his praises. As her eyes beheld each of her friends, she couldn't help but think of each person's individual sacrifice during this entire ordeal. No one should have to experience what this group survived and yet, they stood strong in front of her smiling.

Anyone looking at the front of the FBI field office at that moment would have seen a vagabond group of refugees looking for assistance, and not national heroes. Agent Bradley described April's father as the hero and as true as that was, the entire group before her was just as responsible for putting things right. She looked back at Agent Bradley.

"John, can we go inside? I'm tired of being stared at and I need something to drink."

They all glanced around them and for the first time, noticed they were quite the exhibit. People walking around the area congregated and some even pointed their way. Rather than expand the attraction, they moved their discussion inside the field office. Agent Bradley held the door for them as they left the prying eyes of the public behind. The agent brought them through the office and for the first time, they noticed that the office was full. With everything going on, they thought most agents would be home with their families.

Agent Bradley didn't stop to speak to anyone and guided them to an office in the back of the building. He walked across the room and opened another door to a conference room. They followed their friend and took seats around the huge table. Sitting across from one another and with a minute to look at each other, they could now understand why so many were staring at them outside. They were dirty, ragged, bleeding, and haggard. The sight was ghastly and they just could only think of what they survived during this ordeal.

No one spoke but Agent Bradley disappeared and quickly returned with bottles of water for each of his friends. Another agent came in with protein bars, apologizing for what she called poor supplies. Each member of their group just grabbed the bar as if it were their final meal and devoured it in seconds. They were all grateful to find out that the running water was still working and they took turns washing themselves. Once cleaned to the best of their abilities, they returned to the conference room to get an update from Agent Bradley. Even clean, the group still looked terrible with scrapes, cuts, and destroyed clothing, but they now resembled humans now.

Chris started the conversation, "John, you told us he did it. If he fried the system, how do you have so much information? Nothing works. How the hell do you know what's going on? Honestly, from what I can see, it's going to take a very long time to find out the extent of the damage. You say we have our lives back and to a certain extent, you may be right but look at the cost. We're back to life of the early 1900s. Honestly, John, we're going to be reading manuscripts by the fire during the winter time."

Thoughts of reality sank into the minds of those surrounding the table. Yes, it was summer now but in a few short weeks, the weather would begin to cool down drastically. Winter in New England could be quite harsh and Chris was right, they didn't know the true extent to which this blackout would affect the future. As Agent Bradley looked around the table, he could see the same look of concern on everyone's face.

He stood leaning heavily with his straight arms on the table. "My friends, things aren't as dire as they seem. As I began to tell you, our government has a protocol in place for this situation. Most of the information needed to reboot the country is held in several underground locations around the country, insulated from these types of events. Yes, things will need to be straightened out but it will take a shorter time than you think. Dr. Chase knew this when he chose this plan. It's quite brilliant. He destroyed only what needed to be destroyed."

The agent lifted his hands and walked to the window, peering outside. "What we need to decide right now is what we're going to tell the authorities. We're now persons of interest in this case and they'll come after us with everything they have. Luckily, we have a dynamite lawyer working for us." He smiled at Jessica and for the first time since losing Steve, she released a small smile. Agent Bradley continued, "I know it will be apparent to them early on that we were the victims here, but just our relationship with Dr. Chase will put us in the crosshairs. We need to be prepared and we all need to be on the same page."

They spent the afternoon discussing their strategy and when they felt comfortable with the result, they all leaned back in their chairs. A wave of exhaustion took each member of the group and before long they all drifted off to sleep. Agent Bradley looked with great pride at his sleeping friends and without another word, stood guard. He let them sleep for a few hours before rising them with the good news that fresh food just arrived.

The grateful group ate their first real food in days and walked around the field office, checking things out. One of the first interesting things they noticed were the few small transistor radios out on a few desks. To their great pleasure, they could hear voices coming from the ancient boxes. Gus smiled and showed them that a few had cranks on them to charge the radio. He looked at his friends. "I had those as a kid. It was pretty cool because batteries were so expensive."

Listening to the small radio confirmed what Agent Bradley told them was correct and the power would soon be restored. The problem wasn't the power and the voice asked for patience as the repair of so many systems would take some time. The small group marveled at the amount of information being given over the airwaves. They were surprised, considering they could hardly get any information during the events that led them to this point.

After the briefing on the radio, they looked around the office once more and a nice young agent brought them some fresh clothes. Once dressed and fed some more, they took a few moments to sit outside. The field office was in an old office building and its stone façade fit in greatly with the New England town. They moved over to the benches and made themselves comfortable. The sparkling afternoon refreshed them as they enjoyed the blue sky with its wispy clouds. The temperature was comfortable and for the first time in a long time, they just allowed themselves to smell the fresh air.

The quietness of this picturesque town was boosted by the surrounding trees and the children playing in the town square. With no vehicles moving, they all looked out and imagined that this was what it would have been like in the early 1900s. The only thing missing was horse-drawn carriages and electric trolleys. A peace and calm came over them that many in the group never remembered having. Each member didn't want this moment to end. Having this time with each other at this very moment was priceless. This moment was ceded to them by a greater power, telling them thank you.

Chris leaned back on his bench, thinking of the many things he and Christopher found themselves involved in during this whole time. As peaceful and beautiful as this moment was, they'd soon have to return to football. Of course, his love for football never once waned but his priorities seemed much different at this moment. He slid his hand across the seat of the bench and let it touch softly April's hand. The two hands became intertwined and they sat not moving or talking, just taking in the beautiful moment.

He loved this moment but couldn't help but think if football would ever be the same for him. As a young man, he never gave any thought to the very real fact that football would end someday. He just assumed he would play forever and never gave thought to life after football. The big question crossing his mind at this point was the mental aspect of the game. He was in the best shape of his life, a physical specimen but if his mind wasn't in the game, he was no good to his team.

Mentally he did so much to prepare himself to play each week that the casual fan didn't know about. As he sat on the bench with the love of his life having survived a life and death struggle, football didn't seem all that important to him. This thought frightened him greatly and he looked to Christopher to gauge where his thought process was. Christopher just sat looking across to the town square at the beautiful children playing football, of all things.

Seeing the children play the game he loved brought him back to the time where football for him was just that, a game. Thinking of all the work needed to get himself to the point where being a professional was a reality shocked him. He missed a lot as a young man. Sure, he went to camp, but it was always football camp. His friends always were going away with their families, but he was always practicing.

Feeling April's hand release his made him sit up quickly, sensing something amiss. He looked at April and she pointed down the street. They both glanced up the street to see some ancient Model-T cars rattling their way up the street. This would have been very cool to see but as the vehicles came closer, it was easy to see soldiers dressed in military police uniforms. Several of the vehicles stopped in front of the field office as the soldiers jumped out of the cars and quickly stood in front of the group sitting on the benches.

A very tall soldier with an MP armband walked up to Agent Bradley and ordered, "You will turn these fugitives over to us now! They'll be brought to justice for putting our national security in jeopardy!"

Agent Bradley walked closer to the man and whispered, "I don't think so. You have no authority here! These fugitives are in my custody and I'll bring them in, not you! Now I suggest you get back in those vehicles and go help put our real defenses back in order before someone decides that our country is vulnerable right now. I don't know about you, but I'd feel a lot safer if you all were out defending our country rather than bothering citizens with petty matters."

Chapter 42

Coach Ridel said very little during this entire exchange but moved to the front of the group addressing the soldier. "Sir, I know one thing as I rode up here with your soldiers. These people aren't the enemy. They did all they could to stop everything and secure that site. I'll testify to that! Now, gentlemen, I have urgent business back at the stadium. Is there any way you could give me a lift?"

The tension lessened quite a bit in that moment and the soldier looked at the coach. "Coach, it would be my pleasure to get you back. We have to get back to the base anyway and it's near there." He looked back at the fugitives and shook his head. "Agent Bradley, you're right about one thing. We've bigger fish to fry right now. I'll leave them in your custody but know this; the government will want to speak to each one of these people."

Agent Bradley nodded. "Don't worry about that; they'll each be interviewed today and statements will be entered into the record. This investigation is ongoing and I'll alert your superiors with any information out of the ordinary. As for the moment, can you brief me on any new information? I have the use of some small radios but news has been sparse and we've heard nothing new in hours."

The soldier brought the agent to the side several feet away and whispered to him for a few minutes. When he finished, he motioned to his troops to follow him back to the car. Coach Ridel walked to Chris and put his hand on his shoulder.

"I know things have been crazy for you but I expect to see you at practice next week. We don't need lights to practice and the season will be here before you know it. I'm giving you all this week to get your affairs in order and then we'll start up training camp again." Coach Ridel turned to leave but stopped in front of April. "April, you take all the time you need. Come back when you're ready. I'm very sorry about your dad. He was an amazing man and my friend. I'll miss him greatly and I'm sure his sacrifice will be recognized by many people for years to come. Take care of each other and I'll see you all soon."

With that last statement, the coach reached out and embraced April in an unexpected bear hug. He held the hug for a moment and then released the young lady. Before leaving, he reached up and touched her cheek as to say everything would be all right.

They stood watching as the coach hopped into the backseat of the car and puttered off down the road. Once again, the group was left to their thoughts in the empty street.

Gus smiled. "Well, that was close! Hey, how many times have we been arrested now? This is crazy! I hope we'll be there when they start arresting some of the government stooges that are all behind this program. I want to sit in the courtroom for that one, I tell you. Although, I do have to tell you guys... this is going to make one hell of a story. I might even decide to turn this into a book."

Gus turned and walked back toward the office. "Hey, you guys coming? I must write down some notes and I want to figure out our next move. Now that we know this problem is temporary, I want to be ready for what comes next.

Besides, John, I want to know what that soldier told you. Let's go!"

They all filed back into the office and made their way back into the conference room. Their faces filled with optimism, they looked at their friend for an update. Agent Bradley walked slowly around the table for a moment, rubbing his chin again and again. He stopped mid-stride and looked up at his friends.

"My friends, we do have some good news. The satellite dish is in good hands and intact. Much of the compound is also fine, just the upper level is damaged, but the bunker goes under with many levels. With that in mind, they're not that mad at us but the amount of lives lost is another matter. There seems to be quite a bit of uncertainty as to who was in charge, Dr. Chase or the government."

He paused and thought for a moment before continuing, "Now, honestly there seems nothing for them to connect us to any of this, but that does not mean they're not going to try. We must be ready to fight once more. Jessica, it's a good thing you have so much experience dealing with these people because your expertise is going to come in handy in the weeks to come. I'm confident that we'll prevail once more but once again, we have another fight on our hands."

Jessica stood gingerly. "John, I'll take care of it. As you stated, they have nothing at all linking us to any of this. Not only that the doctor's daughter was held captive. It's very easy for us to prove our case and we'll be able to go back to our lives without any further interruption. I'll get to work right away. John, after you interview us, please be sure to give me a copy of your notes so I can prepare." She sat back down gently, holding her side and wincing.

Agent Bradley looked at her with concern. "Don't worry, one of the agents found a doctor and asked him to come look at you all. From what I know, he will be here anytime. We will get you guys patched up in no time. Right now, Jessica, you're right. Let's get these interviews done before something else happens. I'll take each of you on your own and I'll also interview you with another agent so no one can say it was inappropriate. Don't worry, it won't take long and then we can work on getting you all home safely."

The interview process took the rest of the night and they were all exhausted, so they decided to sleep in the office for the night. A few of the residents visited the group and brought some home-cooked dishes. The neighbors were thanked and they all enjoyed a feast that evening. Talking into the late morning hours, they drifted off one by one until only Gus remained awake.

Gus kept writing in his notebook and filled the entire thing. Once he had no more space to write, he closed the book displeased because once inspiration struck, it was hard to stop until the thoughts were complete. He rose from his seat and stretched, walking out into the now dark field office. Still with no electricity, the darkness hung in the air. He could make out the furniture barely, thanks to the small amount of moonlight coming in through the windows. When he came to the front of the office and looked out the window, he saw a strange sight. Off in the distance, he saw what he thought to be lights twinkling on a faraway hill. Not sure, he rubbed his eyes and looked again; this time there were no lights.

Feeling he could do no more tonight, he was going to join the others for a good night's sleep until he saw the pad of paper on the desk in front of him. Without another thought, he reached for the pad and scooped it from the desk. Now armed with paper once more, he sat down at one of the desks close to window and used the moonlight to write his thoughts. With the darkness and the quiet, it was easy to have his ideas flow onto the paper. He was well into his thoughts when he looked about and saw the light of a new day dawning.

He leaned his head back and shut his eyes for a moment, thinking about Agent Bradley telling the soldiers he didn't think so when they came to take his friends. Gus would have probably done the same thing, but probably gotten arrested himself in the process because of his own mouth. He thought Agent Bradley was very brave and especially liked the way he always handled himself. Gus was a professional and loved to work with other professionals. Agent Bradley was a true pro that worked hard and deserved all the recognition he could receive.

Gus carefully walked back into the conference room and took an empty seat near Chris and leaned his head onto the table. Listening to the rhythm of his breathing drifted him to sleep, as his thoughts turned to his own situation at the newspaper. Before all this began, he'd been told that they were downsizing once more and his position was about to be eliminated. He worked his whole life writing but only for other people. This new venture offered him a chance to write for himself. Who knew? Maybe he could write a book others would want to read. As he slowly drifted off to sleep, his last thoughts were of who would create the cover for his book.

Chapter 43

Malina took the lead and wormed her way around the dimly lit corridors of the offices until they arrived at the facilities office. The emptiness of the stadium sent a shiver up her spine. Every time she worked at the stadium, people were everywhere, running here, there, and everywhere. In the early morning light, the office stood devoid of life. Malina went to the opposite wall and found a large steel box with a small padlock. She whirled around looking for something with which to pry the lock open. Nothing she could see would help her until her eyes fell upon the fire extinguisher on the wall. She rushed over and pulled the extinguisher off its mount. Malina ran over to the steel box and used the butt end of the extinguisher to smash the lock until it gave way, falling to the ground.

Lillian grabbed hold of the steel door and swung it open to reveal a complex board of switches and relays. Malina looked at her sister.

"One of the guys from maintenance used to come down to the lab all the time and tell me about this board. He claimed this was the brains of the entire stadium. He was so proud to describe how they refitted the stadium to solar energy and were totally self-sufficient." Malina looked at the myriad of switches and put her hands up. "The young man told me all about this box, but now that I'm here, it just looks like a big fuse box to me. I've no idea how to get this on. Without this, I cannot turn other systems back on. He did tell me that everything in here was of the highest quality and could withstand a bomb. There has got to be a way to turn it back on."

She turned to her sister. "Any ideas? It's just that you're the detail person. Why don't you give it a look to see if you can make heads or tails of it? Lillian, this is the key. If I can get this system back on, then I can get us down to the labs. Once we're in the labs, I know Dr. Chase has many more below that are shielded. Once the power is back on here, I can get other systems up. Just give it a look."

Lillian stood in front of the large panel and remembered helping her dad several times down in the basement, resetting breakers after a lightning storm. Her dad described for her when there was an electrical storm that the serge of electricity would cause the breaker to snap off to protect the system from becoming fried. He would reach into the box and flip the switches back on and return the system to normal. *Could it be that simple?*

Without further hesitation, she reached up to the first switch and flipped it back to the right position. She continued down the line until each switch was in the right position. Both girls stood back and waited for something to happen. At first nothing happened, and the girls looked at each other with a panicked look. Until out of the corner of their eyes, they noticed a small light on a smaller box next to the breaker box.

Malina opened the box to reveal another smaller version of the much larger breaker box. Malina laughed. "Look at this. The solar panels have their own box. Who knew? This is it, Lillian; once we turn this on, we can fix everything. Come on."

She reached into the box and once again flipped switches, standing back once done to see her handy work. The girls were giddy at this point, thinking they could repair the damage and get things up and running. It took a few minutes, but now that the sun was up, the solar panels allowed their charge to flow. The lights flickered and then came on full force as both girls pumped their fists in the air.

Lillian looked at her sister. "Malina, will our magnetic cards work? I mean that pulse took everything out. Without those cards working, we're stuck up here. We can get down to some of the lesser labs but the more important ones are off limits to anyone without a card. It'll be a short trip if we cannot get to the lower levels."

Malina frowned. "You're right. Hopefully, the pulse did nothing to the magnetic strips on our cards. The other thing is we're banking on the computers down below being insulated enough to reboot them. There are a lot of what ifs but we must have some faith. Let's get to the elevators and get things going. This is so exciting. I feel like some kind of spy or something. If this works, we could get a big raise!"

The young ladies ran to the elevators and both pushed the down button. Anxiously, they waited for any sound that the elevator was indeed working. Both girls stood ready to pry the doors open when they heard a click and then a whine. The elevator was on its way up. When the door opened, the girls didn't wait before jumping in. Once again, both pushed the button for their target floor. The elevator began its descent as the young ladies stood against the wall with a sense of relief.

Twice, as the elevator moved downward, Lillian and Malina thought they'd be stuck. The elevator shook and threatened to stop several times, but when they reached their destination, they stepped out relieved. To their great happiness, their efforts to turn the power on were granted. They walked out into a fully lit sparkling hallway. The bright lights made them blink several times before their eyes adjusted.

Once they gained their bearings, they moved off at a swift pace to return the stadium to good working order. Things looked bright for them as they turned the corner to the next elevator that would take them further below to the secret labs they were used to working. Lillian was first to the elevator panel and swiped her card. They both stared at the elevator but nothing happened. Malina impulsively swiped her card and again nothing happened. She rubbed her card on her clothes, hoping to clean any filth away and tried once more.

The door remained shut and the young ladies tried for a good fifteen minutes in different ways with the card to open the door without success. They both slumped against the wall and slid to the floor. Malina threw her card across the hallway.

"You've got to be kidding me! We get all the way down here and now we're stuck. Lillian, if I can't get down there, I can't fix this."

Lillian placed a hand on her sister's shoulder. "You already fixed it. We have power and with that, we can do a lot. I know the computers upstairs are fried but maybe some of the ones down here can be salvaged. It's too bad we didn't have a magnet. Maybe, if we magnetized the strip again, it would work. The information should still be on the strip; it has just lost its magnetic field. See if you can find a magnet!"

Malina was already moving toward a lab down the hall. She swerved into the lab and went over to a large metal rack with various odds and ends covering it. She used her hand to sort through the pieces of metal and trinkets. On the next to the last shelf, she saw what she was looking for and grabbed the magnet, prying it away from the metal shelf.

Malina turned, holding her prize to show her sister. "Ask and you shall receive. Now let's get the hell out of here!"

She, along with her sister, hurried back to the front of the elevator. Malina took the magnet and slowly guided it over the magnetic strip. She always went in one direction and was careful not to scratch the strip. After several minutes, she looked up and winked to her sister, telling her it was time. Malina stood in front of the door. "Here we go! Please work!"

Waving the card carefully in front of the reader, she closed her eyes, not wanting to see failure. She peeked slightly and then to her amazement, the door clicked. The door immediately opened before the girls and they jumped inside once more. Too excited to speak, they pressed the button and waited for the elevator to reach its destination. They stood inches from the door, waiting as a racer would wait for the gun to go off, starting the race. It seemed forever for the girls as their muscles tensed, waiting for the door to open.

The door finally opened and the girls ran out, flying down the hallway to their lab. Both girls hadn't been to their lab in a long time because the doctor needed them at the base. Malina almost skidded into her computer station and plopped into her seat. She reached below to turn on her computer and anxiously waited to see if the computer responded. To her surprise, the computer came to life and booted up before her eyes. Her eyes sparkled as she watched the computer go through its progression to boot up. When the computer finished its routine, she used the mouse to see if any of her files would open.

Nothing happened and she looked down at her computer, only to see she didn't have any internet access. She leaned forward with her head in her hands. "You've got to be kidding me! The server must be down and most of my stuff was backed up to the cloud. If the server was destroyed, there is nothing I can do! If all the information is gone, it will take months, no years to re-task everything. I don't know what to do!"

Chapter 44

Chris and company made the arduous journey to the stadium on their bicycles. During their trip, they saw a few antique cars roaming around, but little else moved. They received a huge surprise as they approached the stadium. The lights of the stadium created a beacon for them to follow. Their trip took many hours and they arrived at dusk. The lights were a warm welcome, but they all felt a sense of danger the closer they got to the stadium. Each member thought the same thing. "How in the world are the lights on when everywhere else is still in darkness?"

Cautiously, they lay down their bikes and walked to the main entrance only to be denied entry. Every entrance they went to was locked tight. Frustration grew in the group. Chris perked up. "The service entrance! Remember when we needed to sneak into the stadium? We used the service entrance. Let's go see if we can use it now."

Everyone followed Chris in a full run until he stood in front of the service entrance. The gate there was also locked. Chris was so upset he kicked the gate with all his might, causing the propped-up padlock to pop open. Chris kicked the gate once more and the lock fell to the ground. As furious as he was, he didn't even see the lock fall. April grabbed his arm.

"Chris, stop! The lock is off! We can get in!"

He brought his foot down and examined the chain that now hung loosely on the gate. He unraveled the chain and opened the gate, allowing them to enter. For some reason, he reached down on the ground and wrapped the chain around the gate once more. He propped the padlock as he found it and walked toward the stadium with the others following. They made their way quickly through the stadium to the elevators, stopping before the doors.

Each member of the company looked at the doors, wondering what lay in store for them behind those doors. They all suffered so much at the hands of untold mysteries and they all hoped they weren't walking into another trap. As the doors of the elevator opened, they all looked at one another and nodded. One at a time, they walked into the elevator with steely eyes. Their experience during this entire ordeal hardened them and they'd no longer be intimidated by anyone. The members of the group put their game faces on as the elevator made its way downward.

The group discussed with each other back at the field office that they needed to return to the stadium and straighten things out. They all felt that the stadium was the key for putting things back to normal. April made the great point that her father wouldn't destroy anything without a solution. She told them that there was more to her father's plan even though she didn't have any idea what the plan was. Everyone agreed with April and listened to her as she went on to describe scenarios in which her father would quiz her about things when they worked together. She never even thought about any of it until she found out he was her father.

It frightened her how alike she was to her father and she thought much like him as well. This made the group's decision to follow her lead very easy. She explained to them that she didn't doubt the doctor hid a solution in the stadium. They all followed her down into the bowels of the stadium. When they stopped at the elevator below that would take them to the secret portions of the facility, each person was lost in his own thoughts.

April marched up to the door and swiped her golden card that Steve gave her, waiting for the door to answer. The members of the group stood skeptical that the door would open. When the door clicked, they breathed a sigh of relief and moved forward into the elevator car. Once inside, April once again swiped her card and the elevator moved downward quickly. They each took up stations along the wall of the elevator, keeping an eye out for anything irregular. The journey took a few moments and they were anxious as the door opened, revealing another hallway. With no further delay, they walked out into the hallway and noticed more lights down the end of the hallway.

Cautiously, they moved forward as Chris protectively moved to the front and stood with April. When they came to the source of the light and peered inside, everyone's heart stopped. For a moment, no one said a word and then Christopher laughed.

"We came all this way and went through all this so we can come face to face with our friends? What next?"

They all looked at one another with questions in their eyes, but strode into the room anyway. The surprised look on the two unsuspecting girls was priceless, as they certainly weren't expecting to have anyone join them. Both girls nearly jumped out of their skin as the group poured into their room. The reunion was a joyous occasion and many hugs and kisses were exchanged. The entire group felt much relief at seeing the young ladies and asked many questions.

Gus broke up the festivities. "Listen, everyone, I'm just as happy to see these young ladies as anyone else, but will someone tell me what's going on? Why are they here? Why are the lights on and what's our next move?" The old reporter looked seriously at Chris.

Chris and April looked at one another and then back at Gus. Usually Gus was the even keel one but it was plain to see that this encounter frazzled him as much as the rest of them. Chris came up to Gus.

"Of course, Gus. You're right. We just were caught off guard by the ladies being here. All great questions that require immediate answers."

He peered over his shoulder and shouted back, "Girls, what's going on? How in the world did you get in the stadium number one and how on earth did you turn the lights back on? Don't get me wrong. It's wonderful to see you both, but you will excuse my skepticism. We have it seems been betrayed at every turn and now we find you in the dragon's lair. It does not look good, girls. Now talk!"

April stepped protectively in front of the girls. "Chris, what's the matter with you? You know as well as I do these two were stuck in the middle of everything just as we were. Now I think you owe them an apology. This is ridiculous; they're with us. Chris, now!" She stared her man down until she could tell he wasn't going to relent. Then she turned to the girls. "All right, ladies, explain to us what happened."

Lillian began the tale of them making their way to their Memere's house and all that transpired while there. All this Chris and company were aware of and Chris' face relaxed slightly. She went on to explain how Malina thought she could turn the lights on and possibly reboot the system. Lillian elaborated on how Malina deducted that the doctor would have a plan in place to allow the system to be rebooted. Everyone nodded their heads as Lillian spoke as many thought the same of the doctor.

April took both girls in her arms and told them they did a great job. Chris, with his face reddened with embarrassment, apologized to the girls. Malina reached out and gave him a huge hug. Chris smiled back and messed her hair up a bit. Everyone was impressed with how the girls figured out the electricity and could see the computer on. Malina explained how they could get the computer on, but without the server, they could do nothing else.

Everyone sat down and tried to figure out their next move. Not one of those assembled knew anything about the inner workings of computers. Sure, they were used to the computer and how to use it, but fixing them was another matter altogether. They all sat quietly for many minutes, contemplating what to do next when Christopher spoke, "April, take us to Dr. Chase's private lab. The one where he held you. I guarantee we'll find answers there."

April's face went white and she started to shake. Chris noticed this. "Christopher, we can't ask that of her. That would put her over the edge. Just look at her and all you did was mention that place. We must figure out something else. Does anyone else have a better idea? There has to be other options." He looked at his friends and could tell they were all out of answers. His friends were beat up, tired, hungry, and frustrated. If they didn't find answers soon, things would go from bad to worse. After everything this group suffered at the hands of the doctor, they all knew in their hearts that he still pulled the strings.

The shaken woman straightened herself up and turned to address her friends. "It's true that place gives me nightmares. My father of all people put me into one of those tubes made for an artificial human. He froze me like a popsicle and I don't want to describe anymore. My father did that to me. However, I know that you're all right that my father has a plan in place and we're still a part of that plan. He knew we would figure things out and put things right. I know he's watching us right now, still having the last laugh as we scramble once more to figure out one of his foolish puzzles. If he weren't already dead, I'd kill him." She teared up during her last statement and walked across the room to be with her own thoughts.

Chris chose not to follow as he knew she needed a moment to collect her thoughts. He sat with the rest of his friends and discussed with each other what they thought the doctor still had in mind for them. They agreed that the doctor would once again leave a trail of bread crumbs for them to find. As they used each other as a sounding board, it was quite apparent the young girls figuring out the electricity was part of the plan. Gus even made a joke about the girls being a plant by the doctor to have everything in place once he was gone. The only thing was no one laughed as they all knew that could very well be the case. Even the girls looked at each other, realizing that could be a possibility.

In a few minutes, April stood before her company. "We have to find out what the doctor has in store for us. You're all right; we should go to the doctor's lab and find out if he left us any clues. My father wouldn't do this without having a way out. I know in my heart that he only wanted us to have our lives back. He found himself in an impossible situation and did what he could. During this whole ordeal, we did many similar things to get our own life back. I'll take you there but I will not go back in that room."

The entire group surrounded her, letting her know they understood. Without another word, April took the lead and walked out of the lab with her friends following. She confidently guided them through the maze of hallways and rooms until they saw the destroyed doorway. April would go no further and stayed back as they moved forward toward what was left of the door.

Chris and Christopher flew out the door after losing April to the tube in the floor and didn't get a look at their handiwork. Looking at the destruction before him, Chris was shocked at the amount of damage he caused. He then took a moment to look down at his still swollen and cut hands. This painful reminder of almost losing the love of his life made the anger swell up inside him once more. With all his might, he pushed the anger back down and walked into the doctor's lab. Then he was struck with the sight of his blood smeared all over the polished white surface of the lab's floor.

The sight of blood everywhere even made Jessica take notice. As an attorney, she always dealt with crime scenes, but this one being so personal bothered her. She moved over to one side and looked through the bookshelf on the right side of the lab. Each of the other members of the group fanned out and took turns trying to find anything that would help them unlock the doctor's latest mystery. For over an hour, they tore the lab apart, hoping to find anything that might resemble a clue. When totally frustrated by their lack of any clues, they met once more out in the hallway with April. She could see by the looks on their faces that things didn't go well.

"So now what?"

Chapter 45

A wave of guilt and frustration took over April in that moment. The weight of the entire ordeal made its way through her armor and right to her heart. Chris and Christopher losing their football life. Her father and Steve losing their actual lives. Jessica losing the love of her life. Joseph losing his brother. Gus losing his job. The sheer amount of loss by her friends during this time caused her to break down and just let her emotions out. The final straw thinking about her father still pulling strings.

She couldn't help but think about what the doctor still had in store for them. Up to this point, everything the doctor planned worked but any outside observer would just think the doctor was an evil genius. April thought this might be an apt description of her father at this point. Still, she wrestled mightily with the thought of her father being a villain or a hero. No matter what the outcome here today, the amount of loss suffered by this group was too much for her to bear.

Chris joined her on the floor. "April, I'm so sorry about all of this. I knew we should not have brought you here. I knew it would be too much. Lean on me and we'll get out of here. There has got to be another way. We will figure it out. First, let's get you out of here and regroup." He began to get up when April pulled him back down.

April immediately wiped her eyes and looked at him fiercely. "Chris, we're figuring this out now! We haven't come this far for us to fail. Failure isn't an option. Yes, everything hit me at once but I'll get beyond it. You say there is nothing in there but there must be. My father wouldn't have such a secret important lab without having more to it. You know my dad; he loved hidden things. I'm telling you, Chris, the key to everything is in that room!"

At that statement, she shot up and bolted for the door with Chris in tow. Everyone with confused looks followed them back into the room. April, with her golden card in hand, looked at each of the walls for a card reader. She told them all to look for a reader and everyone fanned out across the room, looking for signs of a reader. After minutes of searching, they still were no closer to solving the mystery. They decided to look one more time and still had no luck.

Malina sat down at the computer terminal and stared at the blank screen, hoping it would talk to her. She kept asking herself where the server was but kept coming up empty. After a few minutes, she slammed her hand down on the table, dislodging a small metal plate from the table next to the computer. Using her finger nail, she pried the plate up and lifted it away from the table. To her great surprise, she looked at a slot about the size of a magnetic card. She shouted over her shoulder, "The key, give me the key!"

Everyone ran over to the excited young lady and April handed her the card. Malina placed the card carefully in the slot and waited. While all eyes were on the computer screen, behind them silently the floor moved upward. When nothing happened on the screen, the entire disappointed group turned to leave only to walk straight into a huge computer server now sticking up through the floor. Malina jumped for joy.

"I knew it! I knew it was here! Look at that thing! It's huge!"

They all took turns looking at the large server and noticed the lights were on so they knew it might work. Not one of them knew what to do with the server now that they found it but it was a start. Malina sat back down at the computer terminal and tried every code she knew to log into the server with no success. Lillian tried to offer some solutions based on codes they had used in the past but again nothing worked. All the members of the group saluted the girls for their knowledge, saying they never could have gotten that far.

Malina leaned back in the chair with her arms in the air, stretching. The remaining members of the group just stood staring at the server. They were so close yet so far away. One by one, they sat around the room, trying to figure out what to do next. April paced around the room. She knew her dad wouldn't make it this hard for them. He would have found some way to let them know the key to opening the server.

She got excited once more about the word key. It was one of the last words her father shared with her. She recalled her father telling her Christopher was the key. April called everyone over and told them to come close. When everyone assembled close, she began, "I think I have it! One of the last things my dad told me was that Christopher was the key to this whole thing. Until now, I didn't have a clue what that meant but I knew my father wouldn't make it this difficult on us. No, not after everything we went through. All we have to do now is figure out what he meant by that statement."

April looked into the eyes of her friends and for the first time in a long time, she saw hope. The hope of a renewed life staring back at her. April smiled. "We've been through so much, I'm glad we're here to put things back together. Christopher, did the doctor tell you anything about any of this?"

Every eye fell upon Christopher, whose face by this time was a shade of crimson red. "Guys, I've no idea what you're talking about. Trust me, if I knew anything, you would all be first to now. I've felt helpless this entire time and would love nothing more than to contribute to this solution. The only thing the doctor ever talked about was how I should live a good life and always use my brain. He would always talk about that, using my brain. I get it. I'm new at everything, but that doesn't mean I'm stupid."

April stopped him. "Christopher, he was always talking about your brain, right?"

Christopher nodded. "Yes, it was kind of weird. It was like he thought I might forget."

April smiled. "That's right, he didn't want you to forget!" She turned to her friends. "Christopher is the key! Do you remember how the doctor used those small devices just under the skin of all the clones? Well, we thought we took out everyone's device, right? Christopher, who took yours out?"

Christopher smiled a sly smile. "Dr. Chase took mine out. Do you mean he replaced it with something else? I know he was devious but would he go to all that trouble. Never mind, of course he would. Okay, what do you need me to do? You guys aren't going to do surgery on me, are you?" He looked nervously at his friends.

Chris came up to him and hugged him. "Dude, you did it! You're the key! You will help us make everything right. The weird part is it was right under our noses the whole time and we didn't realize it. I don't know about you, but I just want to go out and tackle someone right now. I need to crush someone, if you get my meaning. Thinking of all this makes me think of the strategy in our game. I love all the counter moves that the coaches and players make on the field. One part of me thinks Dr. Chase would have made a great coach."

April looked at Christopher with a wide smile. "Don't worry, I took quite a few of those things out of the clones when we were told to get rid of them. It's a simple procedure and you will have a little tiny scar that no one will notice. Trust me, I won't hurt you. You're like my brother. I'll take good care of you."

The procedure was very minor and just required a scalpel and a needle for a few stitches. April carefully cut just behind Christopher's ear and felt for the small metallic device. In a few seconds, she located the device and took it out, putting it on a sterile napkin. She sewed Christopher up and cleaned him in a matter of minutes. He rested comfortably with the group as April carefully cleaned the device. When she was finished, she placed it on another napkin and put it on the center of the table for everyone to view.

Looking at the device itself answered no questions. To those looking at the device, it looked more like a flattened coin than an electronic device. They all looked at the small device with puzzlement. The fact that they figured out this part was great, but now that this piece of equipment was in front of them, what were they supposed to do? Each of them saw the devices that were taken out of the clones and this looked nothing like any of those.

Lillian was first to move and she picked up the device. April looked apprehensively at the young lady, but didn't say anything. Lillian held the device between her fingers and gently rubbed them over the smooth material. She let her fingers feel each bump and crevice. She raised an eyebrow.

"There is something in this. This smooth covering is just that; it's covering something underneath. We must find a way to get this open without ruining what's inside. It's almost like some kind of pouch."

Gus came from behind and gently took the device from Lillian. He also examined the device, feeling for edges. "You're right, there is something inside. If I'm not mistaken, this covering is a lead shield. Whatever is in there, the doctor wanted to protect it, that's for sure. The covering is very soft. I can scrape small pieces off with my fingernail. Make sure you're careful though; whatever it is will be fragile."

Malina then took it from Gus. "Don't worry. I deal with this small stuff all the time. Having small hands is useful sometimes. I'll have that thing out of there in no time." She placed the device back down on the napkin and took a scalpel to the lead lining. The lining peeled away quickly and without difficulty, revealed what looked to them to be a fancy microchip. Once the lead lining was removed, they marveled at the gold inlay all over the microchip.

With the chip revealed once again, they knew little about microchips and what to do with one. Malina made her way over to the server once more, looking the large machine up and down. She walked around the server, hoping it would talk to her and help her find an answer. The machine looked very much like any other series of computers with one small difference. On the front of the server, there was a small door that looked like a place for a DVD. Malina reached forward, pressing the small button on the face of the little door. The door slid open, revealing a small tray. Inside the tray, Malina could see a tiny square space in the middle of the tray.

She put her hand out and asked for the microchip. April complied and handed her the chip. Malina then placed the microchip into the tray and closed the door. She once again returned to the computer terminal and tried to log on to the server. To everyone's surprise, the computer responded and booted up before their eyes. Malina's eyes lit up like Christmas trees and she punched keys on the keyboard. As her friends looked on, she kept working the computer and before long, she stopped and looked up at them.

Malina smiled widely. "I think, ladies and gentlemen, I've found what we're looking for. The doctor did indeed leave us all what we need to put everything back to normal, but it's going to take a little longer than a few minutes. I can begin to put some systems back online, but I'm going to need a lot of help from other people. The server is just a backup system for the stadium, but the blueprints to put everything right are here on the chip as well."

She worked the keyboard and read line after line of code. The amount of information at her disposal was enormous. It would take a lot longer than she had right now to make sense of everything. She then looked at the files on the chip. Most of the files she saw had to do with putting the infrastructure back together. One file caught her eye however it didn't have a title, just a small picture of a heart to signify the file. Out of sheer curiosity, she clicked on the file. Her eyes lit up and she turned to April.

"You had better come look at this!"

April moved over to the screen so she could get a good look at the file. It took a few moments for the information on the screen to sink in. April lost control of her body and her knees buckled. Chris caught her and propped her up.

"Honey, what is it? What's wrong?" He held her up but she wouldn't answer. Chris moved her slowly over to the chair and let her sit down. He didn't leave her side but he looked to Malina. "What did she see? What's on that file?"

Malina spoke, "It's hard to describe. I must show you. This is going to be hard to see and take, but here we go! I hope I do this right. He left instructions but they're intricate. I'm going to follow them as closely as possible, so everyone be quiet for a few minutes. I need to concentrate to do this. Seriously, one wrong keystroke and things won't turn out so well."

Without another word, Malina sat back down and went to work. Over the next hour, she said little and the entire group waited for any sign of what she might be working on. April remained in her silent vigil and just stared off into space. Chris tried to speak to her, but even he didn't get through. A full anxious hour went by before Malina announced, "I think I have it. Yes, I did everything right. Watch this!"

Everyone rose and came closer to the pretty young lady at the computer. She waved them to turn and look. Once again, something came up out of the floor and this time it wasn't a server. There was a collective gasp from the group as they saw what was before them in the tube. As the wispy steam from the frost lifted from the front of the tube, Christopher came forward with Agent Bradley and wiped the tube. The two men cleared away the frost and to their surprise, a human man lay before their eyes. Malina told them the whole process would take a few minutes and to be patient.

The more the frost melted the more of the person inside they could see. Initially, they couldn't tell who was in

316

the tube, but within a few minutes, the face became clearer. They stared back at the face of the man in the tube.

Agent Bradley spoke first, "No way, that can't be!" The rest of the group crowded around the tube and questioned what was happening. Chris just stood with a menacing look on his face at the frozen man inside the tube. He was brought back to his struggle to save April from the very same fate. Here was another man who was frozen as she was to protect her life.

Within twenty minutes, the figure inside was fully visible and almost thawed. The computer then came to life and Malina told everyone it wasn't her. The server hummed and the computer screen went crazy. Lines of code and other information flew across the screen. Suddenly, the eyes of the man inside moved underneath still closed eyelids. His face moved and his eyes opened slightly. Soon, the eyes stayed open and then blinked furiously, trying to focus. The computer continued to download code and the man inside the tube shook as if being shocked. His eyes threatened to roll back in his head.

Chris and company, now intrigued by this creature being brought to life, could only stare. When the computer finished its run of code, the figure in the tube relaxed. They could see his eyes focus more. Then they could see recognition in the figure's eyes. The man inside the tube grew frightened as if he didn't see what he was looking for. Then all at once, he smiled and relaxed some more. The server stopped humming and the tube now stood before them with no frost or vapor, but a clear view of the figure inside. The man inside was clearly relieved to be unfrozen and looked ready to be released.

Malina told them that it would just take another minute to do a diagnostic check and make sure the man's vital signs were okay before releasing him into this environment. She rose from her seat and walked over to April. "I can stop this at any time. You just say the word and I will put him back on ice. It's completely up to you and I'll do as you ask. I just need to know soon because the tube will automatically open in a few minutes and we need to make a decision now."

April walked to the front of the tube and stood within a few feet of it. Looking at the person inside, her face twisted with rage. Here before her was the man responsible for all the heartache in this room. The one responsible for the loss of so many. If she allowed this man to return, how could she live with herself if he was allowed to go free? She also knew that they all stood on the brink of leading a normal life once more. If released, would this man be part of the solution or would he be the cause of constant pain and suffering?

She touched the glass and then backed away, walking over to Malina. "Finish it! I want to hear what he has to say. If I don't like one word of what he says, I want your oath that we'll put him back and freeze him forever!" April made that last statement with such conviction that everyone just nodded. They thought the very same and were curious as to what this individual had to say.

Malina finished the sequence and the tube released air with a rush brushing past their faces. The tube opened and for a moment, it looked as though the man was uncertain whether he should step out or stay put. April made the decision for him and stood waiting, glaring at the man. The man slowly stepped onto the brilliant white floor, trying to steady himself. When they saw he couldn't hold himself up,

Chris and Agent Bradley grabbed him and escorted him across the room to a chair.

He sat for a moment and tried to get his bearings. The man took in each of the remaining group and then sadness took him. He looked once more and saw what he was looking for. April approached and a newfound smile came across his face. To this point, the man hadn't spoken a word, but he looked up into April's eyes and croaked, "Well, it took you long enough!"

April's hand shot out uncontrolled and flew across his face, smacking him hard across the cheek. The man's head shot back and it looked as though he would pass out. Chris intervened.

"Honey, you said you wanted to hear what he had to say! If you kill him, we'll get nothing."

She looked at Chris and put her hand down. April towered over the feeble man before her in the chair. "Well, Dad, start talking!"

Chapter 47

It was a rare January day when people shed their winter coats for sweatshirts. The kind of weather that sometimes teased the New England states. On this gorgeous Sunday afternoon, the stars aligned for today's football game. During warmups, the coach went by to talk to each member of his team to get the pulse of how prepared they were for today's game. Each of Coach Ridel's players seemed loose but ready to go. They looked at the coach and nodded as he came by to check on them. The coach knew in that moment, today would be a good day on the field. They were prepared well, having a terrific week of practice, which made the coach very confident.

When the players returned to the locker room for final preparations, the fire in their eyes was evident. Every player knew the magnitude of this game and prepared themselves not to fail. This season was exceptionally trying on the entire team. Due to circumstances beyond their control, the season was delayed and then shortened. Injuries and player movement also made for a difficult season. With the playoffs here, things gelled for the team and they seemed poised for another run at the title.

Coach Ridel felt nervous about this game as they were playing a team whose two-quarterback system gave the whole league fits. This Virginia team carved up the league and they ran up scores along the way. Coach knew if he wanted to win this game, he would have to match scores. His team was capable of big numbers and high scores but his defense needed to play big today. He already took Chris aside and briefed him on the game plan several times.

Chris assured the coach he knew the game plan backwards and forwards, along with the hours of film study he put in. He told the coach the team was ready. The coach always quizzed him on game situations, but this morning, it was overload and his second-year captain told him they were ready. Chris couldn't ever remember the coach this anxious about a game. Sure, the coach would be amped up like his players, but when it came game time, he had the ultimate poker face. Today, Chris could see this game meant more to the coach and he relayed that to the guys in the locker room.

He sat in front of his team, firing them up to take the field and Christopher, as always, was right by his side. The two behemoths faced so much together over the last year that they were inseparable. After a fiery speech, Chris led the team onto the field for the game. Once on the field, all jitters and nervousness made way for the crashing of bodies. Both teams were ready for battle and it would be an epic game.

Usually during January, it would be a terrific home field advantage for the Marauders but today Mother Nature would have other plans. Both teams shared equally in the beautiful weather. No, today's game would be decided by the best team on the field. The beginning of the game was a feeling-out process as both teams played the game close to the vest, hoping not to make a mistake.

Once the second half began, though, it was all bets off and the teams let their offenses loose. It became a scoring fest and both teams continued to match scores. A boring game now became a nail biter. In the closing minutes, the teams were tied and Virginia had the ball. It looked as though they'd work the clock to kick a field goal to win the game and advance to the Championship Game. As the series began,

Virginia ran back the kick and started with great field position near their own thirty-yard line.

On the first set of downs, the Virginia quarterbacks set up for play action, but ran the ball for six yards. On third and four yards to go for a first down, they called a roll-out play and passed for a first down to their own forty-yard line. The clock read one minute thirty seconds and counting. Coach Ridel took a timeout and called for his middle linebacker. Chris came right over to the coach, who grabbed his shoulder pad, pulling him closer.

The coach spoke directly, "Chris, this is it! This moment! This is everything you've ever trained for in football and life. We talk about a single play making a game, well this is the play. We need that ball, Chris, and I, no we're counting on you to get that ball for us. Do you understand what I'm telling you? Go out and win this game for us. Now, get it done!"

Coach always preached situations on the field and he always tested them. Now was his chance to make the play that would turn the tide. He grew up always trying to be the best teammate possible and play within the team concept. That was why the coach loved him. He would always do what the team needed to win. Chris recalled something his high school coach said to him once, "Chris, it is great to be a terrific teammate, but every now and again, you need to know when to take over a game!"

Chris looked at his coach and said just that, "Coach, it's time to take over the game!" The coach nodded and pushed him back onto the field. He went running into the huddle and called the play. A million things ran through his head, but then he saw the formation. He spent so much time studying this team he knew exactly the play they were going to call from this formation. As a matter of fact, his team used a similar play a few weeks back to win a game on the road. This team too pulled out all the stops on the road. It was a trick play where the quarterback would throw to the running back behind the line of scrimmage and then pass to the open receiver down the field. Most teams bit on the stretch run play and would crowd the line of scrimmage.

He barked a few commands to change his coverage and the defensive linemen adjusted their stances to compensate. At the snap of the ball, Chris was off and headed straight for the running back. He got off the ball at the snap so quickly that he was there to catch the ball before the running back had a chance to make a play. Chris caught the ball cleanly and streaked down the sidelines toward the goal line. As he ran, he looked up toward the clock to see under a minute in the game. He slowed down slightly to see how close the defenders were to him. He noticed he still had quite a few yards between him and the nearest defender. Chris then cut across the field at an angle to waste more time. When he was at the goal line, he looked once again and saw the defenders bearing down on him and knew they'd try to strip the ball. He grabbed the ball with both hands and turned to run across the field, just off the actual goal line. Anyone who hit him would push him into the end zone. The first defender was smart enough not to hit him, but tried to chop the ball from his grasp. Another would-be tackler wasn't so smart and barreled into Chris with all his might, hoping to dislodge the ball from his grasp.

Chris could feel himself going to the turf and the only thing he cared about was whether he held onto the ball. He gripped the pigskin with every ounce of strength he had as he bounced off the turf. That was when he felt player upon player jumping on him and into the pile, trying to cause a fumble. He felt fingers jamming him in the eye and other places that hurt quite a bit, but he held tight to that ball. When the referee finally cleared everyone off him, he stood up and held the ball high and slammed it down as hard as he could in the end zone.

He went over and grabbed the ball and brought it over to the equipment manager and asked him to take care of it for him.

He came over to his coach. "Job done, Coach!" The coach, in typical coach fashion, pointed to the clock that read twenty seconds. "Not yet, young man! Not until that clock reads zero! Now, get in there and finish!"

Chris went out for the next series of downs. With Virginia desperate because they needed to score a touchdown, they'd surely pass. He called his best cover defense and shut them down for the first three plays. With a fourth and long play coming with only seconds on the clock, all they needed to do was keep the ball in front of them and knock it down. Once again, Chris noticed the formation he spent a lot of time studying and noticed the tight end shading closer to the line of scrimmage. When the ball was snapped, he planted his foot in the ground and blasted in toward the quarterback. In this formation, they didn't expect a blitzer and were unprepared for Chris. He bared down on the quarterback and caught him from his unprotected side, bringing him down, easily ending the game.

His teammates mobbed him and there was a huge pig pile on the field. Chris lay on the field, looking up into the heavens, thankful for this opportunity. After the events of the last year, he never expected to be here again. He felt just how tired he was as he rose from the field and just knelt with one leg ready to get up. He just leaned forward slightly and let his emotions go. A wave of emotion hit him so hard, it threatened to drown him. Through teary eyes, he saw another figure kneeling with him in the grass. Coach Ridel placed his hand on Chris' shoulder pad.

"Now that, son, is how you play football!"

Chapter 48

April greeted the conquering hero with a huge hug and kisses all over his face. Chris just barely made it to the family section after the hordes of media, led of course by Gus. Gus just asked a typical question about the game, but the two shared an untold answer. The crowd of people in the building at this point was near dangerous, but everyone wanted to be there to be a part of this epic win on their home field.

Christopher was right behind him and Jessica ran up to him to give him a huge hug. Chris looked at his twin and just punched him in the shoulder.

"We did it, man! We did it! Championship, here we come! That Texas team doesn't stand a chance. We're going to cream them!"

Christopher returned the punch. "Sure. Well, next time, save some balls for us, will you? Dude, you were hogging the ball." He laughed so hard he almost fell over. Regaining his composure, he grabbed his twin and bear hugged him. Then he released him and went back over to sit with Jessica.

The celebrating continued as the rest of the team made their way into this section of the stadium. Tales of the terrific struggle to win the game played repeatedly. Chris and company huddled around one another, just so happy to be celebrating life for the moment. They all looked at one another, hoping to stay this way for a long time to come. As the festivities continued around them, they enjoyed their time together. For the first time in a long time, no one chased them and they weren't chasing anyone. Being able to sit and have a great time seemed alien to them.

As they were about to take their leave and go home for the night, the door opened. In walked the coach, along with a few of the other coaches and two other men. Coach Ridel walked straight toward them.

"Gentlemen, have fun tonight! Enjoy the win but we're not done yet! We have work to do tomorrow! A championship doesn't win itself!" He patted Chris on the shoulder. "Until tomorrow then! I leave you in good hands!"

Chris looked at April and smiled. "Look who I found! Your father here was just telling me a little about him being a frozen pop. I can't believe he let himself be frozen like that just to protect you and his research. Honestly, I think he's a little crazy. I do have to say his little plan worked though, with all the clone research destroyed as well as the Artificial Intelligence research. Boy, the government doesn't know what to do with him, considering they think this version is a clone. Brilliant, just brilliant! Listen, I hope you all have a terrific evening and I'll see you all soon."

The coach walked away and turned. "Oh, Dr. Chase, try to stay out of trouble, will you? I'm going to need you for this next game!"

The doctor looked up at the coach with a sly smile. "Well, you know me!"

With that statement, his brother Joseph came alongside the doctor. "Don't worry, Coach. I'll never take my eyes off him again!"

Acknowledgements

As more readers continue to enjoy the Gridiron Conspiracy Trilogy, the more I feel blessed. A project that started out as an inspiration by my students has become a labor of love. Each word written in these pages has special meaning to each member of my family. It is with great love and humility that I thank my family once more for instilling me with the gifts to see this project to its conclusion.

My family and students are a great source of inspiration and drive for me as a teacher, as well as a writer. I continue to learn and thrive on the challenge this journey has provided me. My immediate family is my wellspring. I can only hope to continue to provide pages that they and many others will want to read. As an author, I will continue to give the reader reasons to want to turn the page.

As part of this continuing journey, I have been humbled by the readers of my words. They have been gracious and helpful in my growth process. As a lifelong learner, I am always looking for ways to improve and my readers have allowed me to grow. Independently publishing my works is a daunting task and I continue to fine tune my craft each day.

An independent author finds many friends along the way and I would be remiss if I did not acknowledge my friends at ARIA. The Association of Rhode Island Authors is a magnificent resource for myself as well as hundreds of other authors. My family is my rock for writing my stories but ARIA is my outlet to get my books to the world. With ARIA's help, I now have the support to turn my passion into a profession.

Thank you to all for believing in me. I will strive to create stories that inspire, mystify, and amaze. I hope you will continue to join me on my journey of discovery. The road may be long and winding, but begins with that first step. Though my journey has just begun, I am in awe of what the future looks like. Look for me over the horizon as you never know when I will arrive on your doorstep.

Made in the USA
Middletown, DE
29 July 2017